DEATH AT
WENTWATER COURT

A Daisy Dalrymple Mystery

**Center Point
Large Print**

**This Large Print Book carries the
Seal of Approval of N.A.V.H.**

DEATH AT WENTWATER COURT

A Daisy Dalrymple Mystery

CAROLA DUNN

CENTER POINT PUBLISHING
THORNDIKE, MAINE

This Center Point Large Print edition
is published in the year 2007 by arrangement with
St. Martin's Press.

The text of this Large Print edition is unabridged. In other
aspects, this book may vary from the original edition. Printed in
Thailand. Set in 16-point Times New Roman type.

ISBN-10: 1-60285-035-6
ISBN-13: 978-1-60285-035-4

Library of Congress Cataloging-in-Publication Data

Dunn, Carola.
    Death at Wentwater Court: a Daisy Dalrymple mystery / Carola Dunn. --Center Point large print ed.
    p. cm.
    ISBN-13: 978-1-60285-035-4 (lib. bdg. : alk. paper)
    1. Dalrymple, Daisy (Fictitious character)--Fiction. 2. Country homes--Fiction.
3. Women journalists--Fiction. 4. England--Fiction. 5. Large type books. I. Title.

PR6054.U537D4 2007
823'.914--dc22

2007009772

To Mum,
who remembers Liberty bodices and woolly combies

PROLOGUE

Midnight at Ciro's. The strains of the Charleston died away amid applause for the coloured band. As a babble of talk and laughter arose, the young man led his partner from the dance floor. The older man watching him noted that his well-cut evening togs were slightly rumpled, his face too red even for the aftermath of the vigorous dance. The youthful tart hanging on his arm didn't seem to care, though an excess of face-paint made it difficult to be sure.

Her spangled, low waisted frock was short, in defiance of fashion, which this season had sunk hems back to near the ankle. With her shingled hair and the dangling bead necklace, she might be either a chorus-girl or a "bright young thing."

With a contemptuous sneer, the watcher approached and accosted her partner. "A word with you, old chap."

The young man regarded him with sullen dislike. "Hang it all, can't it wait?" His words were slurred.

"I have just learned that you are going down to Hampshire tomorrow."

"Yes. The gov'nor insists on all the family turning up for Christmas, but I'll be back in town in a fortnight. What's the hurry?"

"I've taken a fancy to see your ancestral acres. Invite me."

"Dash it, I can't do that! Here, Gloria, you go on back to our table." He gave the girl a light swat on her rear end, clad in pink artificial silk—a chorus-girl, then. Carmine lips pouting, she obeyed, but glanced back as she went and gave the older man the come-hither look of a would-be vamp.

"I suppose my sister put you up to this," her escort continued sulkily.

"You may suppose what you please. I want an invitation."

"The pater'll think it deuced odd."

" 'The pater' will think it something more than deuced odd if he should happen to get wind of a certain transaction." The note of menace in his smooth voice made the other's face pale. "I've no ambition to join your family's Christmas celebrations. Boxing Day or the day after will do, and I'll stay to see in 1923—a year of great promise, I feel sure."

"Oh, very well." Now the young man sounded merely petulant. "Consider yourself invited."

He turned away, pushed through the noisy crowd to his table, and ordered cocktails. Five minutes later, as the band struck up again, he took his giggling chorus-girl back to the dance floor to shimmy away his troubles.

By then, the source of his discomfiture had already left the nightclub. He gave the chauffeur his orders and leaned back in the Lanchester, a cold smile of anticipation curving his thin lips.

8

CHAPTER 1

He'll come to a bad end, mark my words, and she won't lift a finger to stop him. It's the little ones I'm worried about." The stout lady heaved a sigh, her old-fashioned mantle, a hideous yellowish green, billowing about her. "Four already and another due any day now."

Daisy Dalrymple was constantly amazed at the way total strangers insisted on regaling her with their life stories, their marital misfortunes, or their children's misdeeds. Not that she objected. One day she was going to write a novel, and then every hint of human experience might come in handy.

All the same, she wondered why people revealed to her their innermost secrets.

When the plump lady with the drunkard for a son-in-law left the train at Alton, Daisy had the 2nd Class Ladies Only compartment to herself. She knelt on the seat and peered at her face in the little mirror kindly provided by the L&SW Railway Company. It was a roundish, ordinary sort of face, pink-cheeked, not one calculated to inspire people to pour out their souls. A confidante, Daisy felt, ought to have dark, soulful eyes, not the cheerful blue that looked back at her.

Near one corner of a mouth of the generous, rather than rosebud, persuasion dwelt the small brown mole that was the bane of her existence. No quantity of face-powder ever hid it completely.

The scattering of freckles on her nose could be

smothered, however. Taking her vanity case from her handbag, Daisy vigorously wielded her powder-puff. She touched up her lipstick and smiled at herself. On her way to her first big writing assignment for *Town and Country*, blasé as she'd like to appear, she had to admit to herself she was excited—and a little nervous.

At twenty-five she ought to be sophisticated and self-confident, but the butterflies refused to be banished from her stomach. She had to succeed. The alternatives were altogether too blighting to contemplate.

Was the emerald green cloche hat from Selfridges Bargain Basement a trifle too gaudy for a professional woman? No, she decided, it brightened up her old dark green tweed coat just as intended. She straightened the grey fur tippet she had borrowed from Lucy. It was more elegant than a woollen muffler, if less practical on this icy January morning.

Sitting down again, she picked up the newspaper the woman had left. Daisy was no devotee of the latest news, and on this second day of January, 1923, the headlines she scanned looked very much like those of a week ago, or a fortnight: troubles in the Ruhr and in Ireland, Mussolini making speeches in Italy, German inflation raging out of control.

Opening the paper, she read a short piece describing the latest wonders unearthed from Tutankhamen's tomb, and then a headline caught her eye:

FLATFORD BURGLARY
Scotland Yard Called In

Daisy had been at school with Lord Flatford's daughter, though not in the same form. Shocking how the merest mention of an acquaintance was more interesting than the most serious news from abroad.

In the early hours of the New Year, thieves had walked off with the Flatfords' house guests most valuable jewellery, not yet returned to his lordship's safe after a New Year's ball.

She had no time to read more, for the clickety-clack of the train over the rails began to slow again and the next station was Wentwater. Wrestling with the leather strap, Daisy lowered the breath-misted window. She shivered in the blast of frosty air, heavy with the distinctive smell of a coal-fired steam engine, and wondered whether a cold neck was not too high a price to pay for elegance.

At least the knot of honey brown hair low on her neck, out of the way of the hat, provided a spot of warmth. For once she was glad she had indulged her mother by not having her hair bobbed.

The train rattled and shuddered to a halt. Leaning out, Daisy waved and called, "Porter!"

The man who answered her summons appeared to have a wooden leg, doubtless having lost the original in the Great War. Nonetheless, he made good time along the platform, swept clear of snow. He touched his peaked cap to her as she stepped down, clutching Lucy's precious camera.

"Luggage, madam?"

"Yes, I'm afraid there's rather a lot," she said doubt-fully.

"Not to worry, madam." He hopped nimbly up into the compartment and gathered from the rack her port-manteau, tripod, Gladstone bag, and the portable type-writer the editor had lent her. Laden, he somehow descended again. Setting everything down, he slammed the door and raised his arm. "Right away!" he shouted to the guard, who blew his whistle and waved his green flag.

As the train chugged into motion, Daisy crossed the footbridge to the opposite platform. She surveyed the scene. The station was no more than a halt, and she was the only person to have descended from the down-train. Signs over the two doors of the tiny building on the up-platform indicated that one end was for Left Luggage, the other serving as both Waiting-Room and Ticket Office.

The Hampshire countryside surrounding the station was hidden by a blanket of snow, sparkling in the sun. Frost glittered on skeletal trees and hedges. The only signs of life were the train, now gathering speed, the uniformed man carrying her stuff across the line behind it, and a crow huddled on the station picket fence.

"Your ticket, please, madam."

She gave it to him to clip. "I'm staying at Wentwater Court," she said. "Is it far?"

"A mile or three."

"Oh, Lord!" Daisy looked in dismay at her luggage, and then down at her smart leather boots, high-heeled

12

and laced up the front to the knee. They were definitely not intended for tramping along snowy country lanes, and the station was obviously too small to support a taxi service or even a fly.

"I shouldn't worry, madam. His lordship always sends the motor for his guests, but likely it's hard to start in this weather."

"The trouble is," Daisy confided, "I'm not exactly a guest. I'm going to write about Wentwater Court for a magazine."

The porter, cum station master, cum ticket collector looked properly impressed. "A writer, are you, madam? Very nice, too. Well, now, if you was to walk, I can get a boy from the village to bring your traps after on a handcart. Or I can telephone the garridge in Alton for a hired car to come pick you up."

Daisy contemplated these alternatives, one uncomfortable, the other expensive. Her expenses would be paid by the magazine, eventually, but she hadn't much cash in hand.

At that moment she heard the throb of a powerful motor engine. A dark green Rolls-Royce Silver Ghost pulled up in the station yard, the brass fittings on its long bonnet gleaming. A uniformed chauffeur jumped out.

"I reckon his lordship's counting you as a guest, madam," said the porter with vicarious satisfaction, picking up her baggage.

"Miss Dalrymple?" asked the chauffeur, approaching. "I'm Jones, from the Court. Sorry I'm late, miss. She were a tad slow starting this morning, which she ain't usually be it never so cold, or I'd've got going earlier."

"That's quite all right, Jones," said Daisy, giving him a sunny smile. God was in His Heaven after all, and all was right with the world.

He opened the car door for her, then went to help the porter stow her bags in the boot. Daisy leaned back on the soft leather seat. There were definite advantages to being the daughter of a viscount.

Of course, she'd never have got the assignment to write about stately homes were it not for her social connections. Though she didn't know the Earl of Wentwater, she was acquainted with his eldest son, James, Lord Beddowe; his daughter, Lady Marjorie; and his sister, Lady Josephine. Her editor had rightly expected that doors forever closed to any plebeian writer would swing wide to welcome the Honourable Daisy Dalrymple.

The Rolls purred out of the station yard, down the hill, round a bend, and through the village of Lower Wentwater. The duck pond on the village green was frozen. Shrieking with laughter, several small children in woollen leggings were sliding on the ice, nothing but bright eyes showing between striped mufflers and Balaclava helmets.

Beyond the little stone church, the lane wound up and down hills, past fields and farms and scattered copses. Here the snow on the roadway lay undisturbed except for two eight-inch-deep wheel ruts made by the earl's motor on its way to the station. Daisy was increasingly glad she had not had to hoof it.

14

In the middle of a wood, they came to a brick lodge guarding tall wrought-iron gates that stood open. As they drove through, Jones sounded the Rolls's horn. Daisy glanced back and saw the lodge-keeper come out to close the gates behind them. A moment later, they drove out of the trees.

Wentwater Court spread before them. On the opposite slope of a shallow valley stood the mansion. The crenellated and turreted central Tudor block, red brick dressed with stone, was flanked by wings added in Queen Anne's time. Virginia creeper, though now leafless, masked the transition from one style to another, and a pair of huge cedars softened the rectangularity of the wings. Closer, at the bottom of the valley, the gravel drive crossed an elaborate stonework bridge over an ornamental lake. The ice had been swept clear of snow, and skaters in red and green and blue skimmed its length or twirled in fanciful curlicues.

"Jones, stop, please," Daisy cried. "I must take some photographs.

The chauffeur retrieved the tripod from the boot for her. "Do you want me to wait, miss?"

"No, go ahead, I'll walk up." She set up her equipment on the edge of the drive and adjusted the camera. A frown creased her forehead.

Most of her photographic experience had been in Lucy's studio. Peering through the viewfinder, she tried to picture the scene before her shrunk to half a magazine page. The skaters on the lake would be mere dots, she decided.

Nonetheless, she took a couple of shots of the entire scene before directing the camera at the mansion alone to take several more. Then she picked up the whole apparatus and trudged down to the lakeside to get close-ups of the skaters and the pretty arched bridge.

The skaters had already seen her, and one or two had waved. As she approached, all five gathered at the nearer foot of the bridge.

"Hullo, Daisy," called Marjorie. "We thought it must be you." Her fashionably boyish figure was emphasized by a tailored cherry red sports coat and matching skirt. Daisy knew that the white woollen hat concealed bobbed hair set in Marcel waves. Her Cupid's-bow lipstick matched her coat, her eyebrows were plucked and darkened, and her eyelashes were heavily blacked. At twenty-one, Lady Marjorie Beddowe was a quintessential flapper.

"Welcome to Wentwater, Miss Dalrymple." Her brother James, a stocky young man some three years older than his sister, wore plus-fours and a Fair Isle pullover patterned in yellow and blue. His face, heavy jaw at odds with an aristocratically narrow nose, was pink from exercise; he had discarded coat, cap, and muffler on the heap piled on a bench on the far side of the lake. "You know Fenella, don't you?"

"Yes, very well. We're from the same part of Worcestershire." Daisy smiled at the shy girl whose engagement to James had recently been announced in the *Morning Post*. "And Phillip is an old friend, too, of course."

"What ho, old thing, haven't seen you in an age."
Fenella's brother, a tall, fair, loose-limbed young man,
grinned at her. Good-looking in a bland sort of way,
Phillip Petrie had been Daisy's brother's best chum
until Gervaise was killed in the trenches. "Taken up
photography, have you?" he asked.

"In a way."

He seemed to be ignorant of the reason for her arrival.
She would have explained further, but Marjorie broke
in eagerly to introduce the fifth skater.

"Daisy, this is Lord Stephen Astwick." She gazed
with patent adoration at the older man. "You haven't
met, have you?"

"I've not had that pleasure," he said suavely. "How
do you do, Miss Dalrymple." At about forty, Lord
Stephen was an elegant figure in a leather Norfolk-style
jacket, his black hair pomaded back from his handsome
face.

"Lord Stephen." Daisy inclined her head in acknowledgement. She didn't care for the way his cold grey
eyes appraised her. "Don't let me interrupt your sport. I
want to take some pictures from a bit farther along the
bank."

"Let me carry that apparatus for you," Phillip offered,
stepping forward. "It looks dashed heavy."

"No, do go on skating, Phil. The more people in the
photographs, the merrier."

A flagged path around the lake had been cleared and
sanded. As she started along it, Daisy noticed Marjorie
taking Lord Stephen's arm in a proprietorial grip.

"Show me that figure again," she said to him with an artificial titter. "I *will* get it right this time, I swear it."

"If you insist, Lady Marjorie," he acquiesced, with a slight grimace of distaste. Daisy's instant dislike of the man was confirmed. Marjorie might be a bit of a blister, but Lord Stephen had no call to show his contempt so plainly.

Finding the perfect position on a short jetty beside a wooden boathouse, Daisy set up her camera. She took several shots of the skaters, with the bridge in the background. Obligingly, they all stayed at the near end of the lake, though she had seen them whizzing under the bridge earlier. It was a pity that colour photography was so complicated and unsatisfactory a process, for the bright colours of their clothes were part of the charm of the scene.

Daisy finished the roll of film. The other rolls were in her Gladstone bag, so she packed up, detaching the camera from the tripod and carefully closing its accordion nose. As soon as she stopped concentrating on her work, she became aware of the biting chill nibbling at her toes and cheeks.

The folded tripod tucked awkwardly under one arm, the camera case slung by its strap over her shoulder, she trudged on around the lake. A path of sanded, well-trodden snow led up from the bench towards the house. Before she reached it, Phillip skated over to her.

"Finished? I'll give you a hand up to the house if you'll hold on half a tick while I take off my skates."

"Thanks, that would be a help."

He skated along to the bench to change his footwear. As she strolled to join him, Daisy wondered if he was about to take up his inconstant pursuit of her. Ever since she had emerged from her bottle green school uniform like a butterfly from its chrysalis, the Honourable Phillip Petrie, third son of Baron Petrie, had intermittently courted her. More for Gervaise's sake than her own, she sometimes thought.

She smiled at him as he relieved her of her burdens. Though she steadfastly refused his periodic proposals, she was fond of her childhood friend and erstwhile pigtail-puller.

"Did you bring skates?" he asked, shortening his long strides to match hers up the hill, slippery despite the sand.

"No, I didn't think to."

"I expect you can borrow some. We could come straight down again. It's a pity to waste such a topping day."

"Yes, but I'm not here as a guest, or at least, not for pleasure. I'm going to be busy."

He looked startled. "What on earth do you mean?"

"I have a commission to write about Wentwater Court for *Town and Country*," she told him with pride.

"You and your bally writing," he groaned. "Dash it, Daisy, it shouldn't take more than an hour or so to put together a bit of tomfoolery for the gossip column. You can scribble it off later."

"Not a paragraph or two, a long article. With photos. This is serious, Phillip. They are paying me pots of money to write a monthly series about some of the more interesting of the lesser known country seats."

"Money!" He frowned. "Hang it all, my dear old girl, you surely don't need to earn your own living. Gervaise would be fearfully pipped."

"Gervaise never tried to tell me what to do," she said with considerable asperity, "and he'd have understood that I simply can't live with Mother, let alone with Cousin Edgar. He couldn't stand Edgar and Geraldine any more than I can."

"Maybe, but all the same he must be turning in his grave. His sister working for her living!"

"At least writing is a whole lot better than that ghastly secretarial work I was doing. I did enjoy helping Lucy in her studio, but she doesn't really have enough work to justify paying me."

"It was Lucy Fotheringay put you up to this independence tommyrot in the first place. Are you still sharing that Bayswater flat with her?"

"Not the flat." Daisy seized the opportunity to avoid the subject of her employment, though she knew she'd not escape his ragging forever. "We have a perfectly sweet little house in Chelsea, quite near the river."

She went on to describe it in excruciating detail, which Phillip was too well brought up to interrupt. Before her narrative reached the attics, they reached the front door. Phillip being laden with skates, tripod, and camera, Daisy rang the bell.

A footman in plum-coloured livery opened one half of the massive, iron-bound, oak double doors. Stepping in, Daisy handed him her card and glanced around.

"Oh, I can't wait to photograph it!" The early Tudor Great Hall was everything she had heard. Linenfold wainscoting rose to a carved frieze of Tudor roses, bulrushes, and stylized rippling water. Above, the walls were white-washed and hung with tapestries of hunting and jousting scenes, alternating with crossed pikes, halberds, and banners. The vaulted hammerbeam ceiling was high overhead.

Daisy despaired of ever doing the vast room justice with her camera.

She shivered. A blazing fire in the huge fireplace opposite her did little to disperse the winter chill rising from the flagged floor. A cold draught blew from the arched stone staircase at one end of the hall. The footman hurriedly closed the front door behind Phillip.

"You'll be the writing lady, miss?"

"Yes, that's right." She had ordered new cards with her profession proudly emblazoned beneath her name, but she hadn't yet received them.

Obviously unsure what to do with her, the footman turned with relief to the stately, black-clad butler who now appeared through a green baize door at the back of the hall. "It's Miss Dalrymple, Mr. Drew." He handed over the card.

"If you'll please to come this way, miss, his lordship will receive you in his study."

"Thank you." She put out her hand as Phillip made to go with her. The last thing she needed was his censorious presence hovering at her elbow when she discussed her work with Lord Wentwater. "Don't wait

21

about, Phil. Go back to your skating in case there's a thaw tonight. I'll see you later."

Quickly powdering her red nose as she followed the butler, she realized that her nerves had vanished. She had never found it difficult to charm elderly gentlemen, and she had no reason to suppose that the earl would be an exception. Half the battle was already won, since he had given her permission to write the article and invited her to Wentwater. Having seen the magnificent Great Hall, she had no doubt that she'd find plenty to write about.

The butler led the way from the Tudor part of the house into the east wing. Here he tapped on a door, opened it, and announced her. As Daisy entered with a friendly smile, Lord Wentwater rose and came round his leather-topped desk to meet her.

A tall, lean gentleman of some fifty years, he did not return her smile but shook the hand she offered, greeting her with a grave courtesy. He had James's straight, narrow, aristocratic nose, and the greying hair and moustache gave him an air of distinction. Daisy thought him most attractive despite his age and the rather Victorian formality of his manners.

The Victorian impression was heightened by the heavy mahogany furniture in the study and the dark red Turkey carpet. A Landseer painting of two black retrievers, one with a dead mallard in its mouth, hung above a superb Adam fireplace.

Still chilled, Daisy gravitated automatically towards the fireplace, pulling off her gloves and holding out her hands to the flames.

"Won't you sit down, Miss Dalrymple?" The earl indicated a maroon-leather wing chair by the fire. Taking the similar chair opposite her, he said, "I knew your father, of course. A sad loss to the House of Lords. That wretched influenza decimated our ranks, and so soon after the War slaughtered the next generation. Your brother, I believe?"

"Yes, Gervaise died in Flanders."

"Allow me to offer my condolences, somewhat belated, I fear." To her relief, he dropped the unhappy subject and went on in a dry, slightly interrogative tone. "I am flattered that you have chosen my home to write about."

"I'd heard how splendid the interior is, Lord Wentwater, and for my January article I couldn't count on being able to photograph outdoors."

"Ah, yes, your editor's letter mentioned that you would be bringing a photographer with you."

Daisy willed herself not to blush. "Unfortunately, Mr. Carswell has come down with 'flu, so I'll be taking my own pictures." She hurried on before he could express his sympathy for the nonexistent Carswell. "It would be most frightfully helpful if you have a small windowless space I could use as a darkroom. A boxroom, or store-room, or scullery, perhaps? As I'm no expert, I'd like to be able to see how well my photos have come out before I leave, in case I need to take more."

That brought a faint smile to his lips. "We can do better than that. My brother Sydney—he's in the Colonial Service—was a bit of a photography enthusiast in his youth, and had a darkroom set up."

"Oh, topping!"

"The equipment has never been cleared out, though you may find it rather old-fashioned. Is there anything else I can do to facilitate your work?"

"I've read a bit about the history of the house, but if there are any interesting anecdotes not generally known . . . ?"

"My sister's the one you need to talk to. She knows all there is to be known about Wentwater and the Beddowes."

"Lady Josephine is here? Spiffing!"

Again the fugitive smile crossed the earl's face. Lady Josephine Menton was as loquacious as she was sociable, a noted hostess and a noted gossip. No one could have better suited Daisy's purpose.

"I'm sure I can trust your discretion, and your editor's," said Lord Wentworth, standing up. "Come, I'll take you to her and introduce you to my wife. They are usually to be found in the morning-room at this hour."

They crossed the passage and he ushered her into a sunny sitting-room furnished, with an eye to comfort rather than style, in sage green, cream, and peach. As they entered, a grey-muzzled black spaniel on the hearthrug raised his head in brief curiosity, twitched his stumpy tail, then went back to sleep. One of the two women sitting by the fire looked up, startled, a hint of alarm in her expression.

"Annabel, my dear, here is Miss Dalrymple. I know you will see that she is comfortable."

"Of course, Henry." Lady Wentwater's musical voice was quiet, almost subdued. She rose gracefully and came towards them. "How do you do, Miss Dalrymple."

Daisy was stunned. She had read in the *Post* that the earl had recently remarried, but she'd had no idea his second wife was so young. Annabel, Countess of Wentwater, was no more than a year or two older than James, her eldest stepson. And she was beautiful.

A warm, heather-mixture tweed skirt and bulky thigh-length cardigan did nothing to disguise a tall, slender figure, somewhat more rounded than was strictly fashionable. Her pale face was a perfect oval with high cheekbones and delicate features, her coiled hair dark and lustrous. Dark, wide-set eyes smiled tentatively at Daisy.

"I leave you in good hands, Miss Dalrymple," said the earl, and turned to depart.

His wife's gaze followed him. In it, Daisy read desperate unhappiness.

CHAPTER 2

So, Daisy, you have taken up a career?" The stout, good-natured Lady Josephine sounded more interested than disapproving. "I'm sure your mother must be having forty fits."

"Mother's not frightfully keen," Daisy admitted. "She'd much rather I went to live with her at the Dower House."

"A stifling life for a young girl. She should thank her lucky stars you are writing for a respectable magazine, not one of the scandalous Sunday rags. Why, I myself have a subscription to *Town and Country*. I look forward to reading your articles, my dear."

"Thank you, Lady Josephine." She turned to the countess. "It's jolly decent of you and Lord Wentwater to let me come. I felt a bit cheeky even suggesting it."

"Not at all, Miss Dalrymple." Lady Wentwater's response was calm and gracious. Her eyes were shadowed now by long, thick lashes, and Daisy wondered if she had imagined the wretchedness. "Henry is proud of Wentwater," she went on. "He's glad of the opportunity to boast of it vicariously."

"True," observed her sister-in-law, "but I'm the one who knows the place inside out. I'll show you around later if you like, Daisy. I expect you'd like to go to your room for a wash and brush-up now. One always feels shockingly grimy after a train journey, doesn't one?"

Lady Wentwater, slightly flustered at this gentle reminder of her duty, rang the bell.

The housekeeper led Daisy back to the Great Hall, up the stone stairs, along a gallery, and into the east wing. As they went, Daisy enquired about the darkroom Lord Wentwater had mentioned.

"Yes, miss, all Mr. Sydney's machines and such are still there," the woman assured her, "and kept dusted, you may be sure. Down in the sculleries it is. The kitchens are a regular rabbit warren. Just ask anyone the way."

"Is there electric light?"

"Oh yes, miss, his lordship had the electric light put in throughout, being safer than gas, though I will say the generator has its ups and downs. If there's aught else you need in the photography line, just ask me or Drew. Here we are, now. That there's the lavatory, miss, and here's your room."

The square, high-ceilinged bedroom was light and airy, with flowered wallpaper and matching bedspread and curtains. The furnishings were old-fashioned but comfortable, and a cheery fire burned in the grate. A small writing desk stood by the window, which faced south, towards the lake. Daisy was relieved to see her camera and tripod on the chest-of-drawers.

An apple-cheeked young maid, in a grey woollen frock and white cap and apron, was unpacking her suitcase. She turned to bob a curtsy. Daisy smiled at her.

"Mabel will take care of you, miss," said the housekeeper with a swift glance around the room to make sure all was in order. "Anything she can't manage, send her for Barstow, her ladyship's maid. Our girls go off duty at eight, except for one who brings round the hot-water bottles and is on call until midnight. The bathroom's through that door there. You'll be sharing with Miss Petrie—her room's on the other side. Coffee will be served in the morning-room at eleven, and luncheon's at one. Will that be all, miss?"

"Yes, thank you."

Beginning to thaw at last, Daisy took off her hat and coat. She changed boots for shoes, smoothed her pale blue jersey jumper suit, tidied her hair, and powdered her nose.

"Please, miss, I can't open your bag."

"No, it's locked, Mabel. There's nothing in it you need deal with, only photographic equipment."

"You're the writing lady, aren't you, miss?" the maid asked, wide-eyed. "I think that's wizard, reely I do. You must be ever so clever."

Amused, but nonetheless flattered, Daisy admitted to herself that Phillip's disapproval had piqued her, so that even the chambermaid's admiration, added to Lady Josephine's acceptance, bucked her up no end. In a cheerful frame of mind, she went back down to the morning-room.

As she entered, the butler was depositing a tray with a Georgian silver coffee set on a table beside Lady Wentwater.

"Has a flask been taken down to the skaters, Drew?" she asked in her soft voice.

Daisy missed his answer as Lady Josephine greeted her. "Just in time for coffee, Daisy. You know Hugh, of course."

Sir Hugh Menton, a gentleman of unimpressive stature eclipsed by his wife's bulk, had risen as Daisy came in. "How do you do, Miss Dalrymple," he said, a twinkle in his eye. "I understand you are now an author."

She shook his hand. "Not quite, Sir Hugh, merely a novice journalist, though I have high hopes."

"Ah, Josephine likes to anticipate the splendid

accomplishments of her friends," he said fondly, with an indulgent smile at his wife.

"Better than anticipating failure!" she said tartly.

"Much better," Daisy agreed. "I remember last time I saw you in London, Lady Josephine, Sir Hugh was in Brazil and we decided his very presence ensured excellent harvests of both coffee and rubber. I hope your trip was successful, Sir Hugh?"

"Perfectly, thank you, though I can't claim all the credit for the harvests. I put good men in charge of my plantations and leave them to get on with it, with occasional visits to keep them up to the mark. There's a fine line between interference and inattention."

That Sir Hugh knew how to tread that fine line Daisy did not doubt for a moment. Besides his extensive rubber and coffee plantations in Brazil, he was reputed to have made a vast fortune in the City. Yet despite his shrewd decisiveness in business matters, he was as courteous and gentlemanly as Lord Wentwater, though in a more modern, worldly, and approachable way. Daisy liked him.

He asked how she preferred her coffee and went to fetch it for her and his wife.

"Will you have some cake, Miss Dalrymple?" Lady Wentwater enquired. She had provided a large slice of Dundee cake for Lady Josephine without asking, Daisy noted with amusement.

Breakfast seemed an age ago. "Yes, please," she said.

At that moment two young men came in. Lady Josephine took charge of the introductions. "My nephews, Wilfred and Geoffrey, Daisy. Miss Dalrymple is to write about Wentwater Court for *Town and Country* magazine."

"Jolly good show." Wilfred, a year or so older than his sister Marjorie, was as much a typical young man-about-town as she was a flapper. From sleek, brilliantined hair, faintly redolent of Parma violets, to patent leather shoes, he was impeccably turned out. Daisy could imagine him languidly knocking a croquet ball through a hoop, but skating was too energetic a pastime for him. A hint of puffiness about his eyes suggested that he probably saved his energy for living it up in nightclubs. His mouth had a sulky twist.

His younger brother, a large, muscular youth, muttered, "How do you do," and stood there looking vaguely uneasy, as if he didn't quite know what to do with his hands. He headed for the coffee table as soon as Wilfred began to speak again.

"I bet you wish you'd gone to write about Flatford's place, Miss Dalrymple," Wilfred drawled. "What a scoop that would have been! You've heard about the robbery?"

"Just that it happened. Something about a house-party and a ball?"

"That's right. It seems to have been one of a series of burglaries, but of course it's the more interesting for being close to home. In fact, some of us went to the ball on New Year's Eve, you know, but the pater insisted on us leaving early so we missed all the excitement."

"You were lucky to go at all," Lady Josephine told

him. "Only a rackety set like Lord Flatford's would hold a ball on a Sunday, New Year or no New Year. I was surprised Henry let you attend. In any case, leaving at midnight made no difference. The robbery wasn't discovered until the morning."

He sighed. "You're right, of course, Aunt Jo. Excuse me while I get some coffee." He drifted off.

"Wilfred is a pip-squeak," said his aunt. "Geoffrey may yet amount to something. He's up at Cambridge, and already he's a boxing Blue though he's only nineteen."

The youngest Beddowe had taken a seat by the coffee table and was silently consuming a huge wedge of cake. The last crumb disappeared as Daisy watched. She found she had picked the almonds off the top of her slice and eaten them first, a bad habit from nursery days.

"More cake, Geoffrey?" Lady Wentwater asked with a smile.

"Yes, please."

"The bottomless pit," said Wilfred, grinning. Unoffended, Geoffrey ate on.

By the time Daisy finished her coffee and went over to beg a second cup, Geoffrey was on his third slice. He had uttered no more than another "Yes, please." Daisy put his reticence down to shyness.

Lady Wentwater was quiet, too. Wilfred held forth about the *Music Box Revue* with the rather desperate air of one who considers it his duty to keep the conversation going under difficult circumstances. Daisy, who had seen the show, threw in occasional comments, and Lady Josephine asked about the sets.

"If the sets are good enough," she said, "one can amuse oneself admiring them during the dull bits. Do you like revues, Annabel, or do you prefer musical comedies, as I do?" she added in a good-natured attempt to draw her young sister-in-law into the discussion.

"I've never been to a revue, and only one musical comedy, but I've enjoyed the few plays I've seen."

"Of course, you've had little opportunity to go to the theatre," said Lady Josephine and turned back to Wilfred. The critical note in her voice surprised Daisy.

The countess looked so discouraged Daisy tried to cheer her. "Shall we do a matinee together next time you come up to town, Lady Wentwater?" she suggested.

"Oh, thank you . . . I'd love to . . . but I'm not sure . . . Won't you please call me Annabel, Miss Dalrymple?"

"Yes, of course, but you must call me Daisy."

She had noted that Wilfred and Geoffrey both avoided addressing their stepmother by her Christian name. No doubt Lord Wentwater would frown on such familiarity, yet to call her "Mother" was equally difficult. It was altogether an awkward situation, her being so much nearer in age to her stepchildren than to her husband. Sympathizing, Daisy wondered whether that was enough to account for her obvious low spirits.

Lady Josephine finished her coffee and heaved herself out of her chair. "Well, Daisy, shall I give you a tour of the house before luncheon? Why don't you come along, Annabel? I'm sure there are stories you haven't heard yet."

"I'd like to, but I simply must write a few letters," Annabel excused herself.

"Though who she has to write to," Lady Josephine muttered as she and Daisy left the morning-room, "I can't for the life of me imagine. When Henry married her she was utterly friendless. They met in Italy last winter, you know," she explained. "Henry had had rather a nasty bout of bronchitis and was sent there for his health, and she was newly widowed."

Her tone told Daisy a great deal about her opinion of young, beautiful, friendless widows who married wealthy noblemen old enough to know better.

The tour started in the Great Hall, which was still used occasionally for large dinner-parties. "I shan't tell you all the stuff you can get from books," said Lady Josephine frankly. "There's quite a good book in the library about the house and the polite history of the Beddowes—you know the sort of thing, who married whom, and who was minister in whose cabinet—but you won't get the family stories."

"I'm relying on you for those."

"Well, the first Baron Beddowe built the place in Henry VII's reign, a clever chap who ended on the right side in the Wars of the Roses—after several changes of allegiance. His grandson was one of the few noblemen to entertain Queen Elizabeth without being bank-rupted."

"How did he manage that?" Daisy asked, scribbling in her notebook in her own version of Pitman's shorthand.

"Rather disgracefully, I'm afraid. She descended on Wentwater with her usual swarm of retainers. The second night, at a lavish banquet in this hall, my ancestor picked a quarrel with one of the courtiers. The Queen had been trying to rid herself of the fellow, without success as he was the son of an influential nobleman. Supposedly in his cups, Wilfred Beddowe stabbed the fellow to the heart with that poniard up there between the halberds." She gestured at a gem-encrusted dagger hanging on the wall, in pride of place over the cavernous fireplace.

"And Elizabeth was so grateful she departed the next day?"

"Yes, expressing shock and censure, of course. However, the Earldom of Wentwater was created not a year later."

Daisy laughed. "That's just the sort of story to make my article interesting. Lord Wentwater won't mind my using it?"

"Good Lord, no. Just don't put the scandals of the last century or so into print." Lady Josephine went on to tell a scurrilous tale of her great-uncle's involvement with Lillie Langtry and Bertie, Prince of Wales. "Henry has rather reacted against that sort of thing," she said. "In some ways he's more Victorian than the Victorians. I do sometimes worry that he won't be happy with Annabel."

"She seems quite a sedate sort of person," Daisy said tactfully.

"But so much younger. If only my chump of a nephew had not invited Lord Stephen!"

Daisy made a token effort to avoid the confidences she was dying to hear. "I haven't been able to place Lord Stephen, though the name Astwick is familiar. Who exactly is he?"

"The younger brother of the Marquis of Brinbury. Always a bit of a black sheep, I'm afraid. In fact rumour has it his father disinherited him, but he made good in the City, though Hugh doesn't trust him an inch."

"Sir Hugh jolly well ought to know."

"Hugh is the knowingest man in the City," agreed his proud wife. "He'd have put paid to Wilfred inviting Lord Stephen if he'd been consulted."

"Wilfred invited him? How odd! I wouldn't think they'd have anything in common."

"High living," said Lady Josephine wisely, "but if you ask me, Marjorie put him up to it. She's potty about the fellow, got it into her silly head she's madly in love with him. Thank heaven he don't show a particle of interest in the girl. If only I could say the same of Annabel! But that's beside the point. Let's go up to Queen Elizabeth's chamber. It hasn't been changed since she spent her two nights at Wentwater."

Her curiosity frustrated, Daisy concentrated on matters historical. The notebook filled with mysterious curlicues she hoped she'd be able to decipher later. As they moved up through the house, she learned about the shocking split in the family when an eldest son fought for Parliament against the Royalists; the daughters who had ended up as old maids because their father had spent their dowries on building the new wings; and the Regency bride who had eloped with a highwayman.

Lady Josephine frowned. "On second thought, perhaps you'd better leave that one out, Daisy. It hits a bit close to home. Not that I mean to suggest there's the slightest chance of Annabel's succumbing," she hastened to add. "But one can't deny that Stephen Astwick is a handsome man, with an insinuating sort of charm— and not a scruple in the world. His name is constantly in the scandal sheets, linked with those of ladies who ought to know better."

"Annabel eloping with Lord Stephen?" Daisy asked in astonishment, turning from the turret window where she had been watching a rider on a bay horse canter across the park.

"They were acquaintances some years ago, I gather, and now he is really pursuing her in the most determined and ungentlemanly way, quite blatant. I'm afraid poor Henry is at a loss what to do. He can't throw Brinbury's brother out of the house as if he were some plebeian bounder. They belong to the same clubs!"

"Gosh, what a ghastly mess."

"Mind you, Henry is far too gallant to mistrust his wife. In fact, I'm not at all sure he's aware of what's going on under his nose. My brother has always been the impassive, stoical sort, you know, impossible to guess what he's thinking. I feel I ought to open his eyes, but Hugh has absolutely forbidden it."

Tears had sprung to the plump matron's eyes and her second chin quivered. Daisy patted her arm and said soothingly, if meaninglessly, "I'm sure Lord Wentwater has everything under control, Lady Josephine."

"Oh, my dear, I should not burden you with our troubles, but it is such a relief to get it all off my chest and simply nothing shocks you modern young things. There, now let us forget all about it. Where were we? Oh yes, this is the very room where Charles II was caught *in flagrante* with the then Lady Wentwater's young cousin. He was not invited again."

She prattled on. As Daisy took down her words, she resolved to keep a close eye on the inhabitants of Wentwater Court. To a would-be novelist, the intrigues of the past were not half so intriguing as those of the present.

Some time later, from yet another turret window, Daisy saw the skaters straggling up the hill towards the house. Lady Josephine glanced out and consulted her wristwatch. "Heavens, how time passes. We must go down if you'd like to see the ballroom before lunch."

"Yes, please. Oh, that's odd. Surely Lord Stephen isn't going off somewhere just before lunch?" A grey Lanchester on its way down the drive had stopped. As Daisy watched, Astwick crossed to it and spoke to the driver.

"I expect he's sending his manservant off on some errand again," said Lady Josephine, irritated. "My maid tells me the fellow is gone more than he's here. I only wish he'd take his master with him!"

Dismissing the unpleasant subject, she took Daisy down to the ballroom, chattering about the splendid formal dances of her youth. The vast ballroom was shrouded in dust covers. Daisy decided not to request that it be exhumed for her to photograph. There was enough of interest in the older part of the house.

Lady Josephine sighed. "Of course, you young things prefer nightclubs these days. Well, my dear, I've shown you the best. Do feel free to wander about by yourself, and I'll try to answer any questions you may have."

"You've been perfectly sweet, Lady Josephine." She riffled through her notebook as they started down the stairs. "I've got loads of material here to start with, and some topping ideas for photographs. I'd like to try a shot of the family in front of the fireplace in the Great Hall, if you think Lord Wentwater will agree."

"I'll speak to him," her ladyship promised.

In the drawing-room, a long, beautifully proportioned room furnished in Regency style, they found several members of the household already gathered. James, with Fenella at his side, was dispensing drinks. He mixed a gin-and-tonic for his aunt, and Daisy requested a small medium-dry sherry.

"I can't drink a cocktail before lunch or I might as well chuck in the towel as far as getting any work done this afternoon is concerned," she said.

"There's no focussing a camera when you can't focus your eyes," James agreed with a grin.

"And it's difficult enough to read my shorthand at the

best of times. Thank you." Taking the glass, she looked around the room.

Nearby Wilfred, his voice a fashionable drawl, was recounting to his stepmother the plot, such as it was, of Al Jolson's musical comedy, *Bombo*. As Daisy watched, he wet his whistle with a gulp from his nearly full cocktail glass. She doubted it was his first. Annabel's sherry glass was also nearly full. She seemed to have forgotten it, standing with bowed head, either listening to Wilfred with more interest than his tale warranted or lost in her own thoughts.

By the fireplace, Sir Hugh and Phillip chatted together—politics, Daisy guessed, hearing mention of Bonar Law and Lloyd George. Marjorie stood by looking bored. She was smoking a cigarette in a long tortoise-shell holder and her cocktail glass held the remains of a pink gin. Daisy guessed that Phillip's glass contained dry sherry. She knew he preferred sweet, but he considered it unmasculine and always asked for dry in company. His nose wrinkled just a trifle as he sipped, confirming her guess.

Lady Josephine went to join her husband, and after a moment Marjorie drifted away from that group. Coming over to the drinks cabinet, she handed her brother her glass.

"Fill it up, Jimmy, old bean."

"It had better be a small one," James warned. "Father will be here any minute."

"Don't be such a wet blanket." She drew ostenta-

39

tiously on her cigarette and blew a stream of smoke over her shoulder.

Daisy hastily retreated from the prospect of a family squabble. She went over to Annabel and Wilfred. Annabel looked up and smiled absently.

"Have you seen the new show at the Apollo, Miss Dalrymple?" Wilfred asked.

"Daisy, please. No, not yet. Is it good?"

"Oh, pretty tolerable, don't you know. The finale was rather a"—his voice died away as Lord Stephen entered the drawing room—"rather a nifty do," he finished with an effort, a gaze burning with resentment fixed on the older man.

Making some casual response to Wilfred's words, Daisy watched Lord Stephen. He went up to the drinks table, where Marjorie greeted him with a languishing look.

"Lord Stephen always has a dry martini," she instructed her brother.

"Make it a gin-and-twist, if you don't mind, old chap," Lord Stephen promptly requested.

"Right-oh." James gave his pouting sister a malicious glance and handed over the drink. He sounded malicious, too, as he continued, "I say, Astwick, would you mind asking my stepmama if she'd like a refill?"

"My pleasure." The bland tone was belied by the predatory curl of his thin lips, the gleam in his hard eyes.

As he approached, Wilfred blanched. "Must have a word with Aunt Jo," he muttered, and sheered off. Why on earth had he invited the man if he detested him? Daisy wondered.

"Miss Dalrymple." Lord Stephen nodded to her but his attention was already on the countess. "Annabel, my dear, Beddowe sent me to find out if your drink needs refreshing, but I see his solicitude was in vain." He ran his fingertips across the back of her hand, holding the still-full glass.

The amber liquid shimmered as her hand trembled. "Yes, thank you. I have all I want."

"All? Few can claim to be so lucky as to possess *all* that they desire," he said with a meaningful smile. "I know I do not."

"But I do, Lord Stephen." She flashed him a glance under her long lashes. Daisy couldn't tell whether she was just flirting, trying to rebuff him, or deliberately leading him on by playing hard to get.

"Come, now, didn't you promise to call me Stephen? Miss Dalrymple will think you don't count me your friend. I assure you, Miss Dalrymple, Annabel and I are very good friends from long ago, aren't we, my dear?" He laid his hand on her arm.

"Yes, Stephen." Her voice quivered with suppressed emotion. She neither shook off his hand nor moved away.

CHAPTER 3

To Daisy's relief, Geoffrey came up and broke the charged tension between Annabel and Lord Stephen. His large, solid, unambiguous presence made Lord Stephen's elegant figure appear slight and rather effete. He brought with him a wholesome breath of fresh air.

"Have you been riding?" Daisy asked. "I thought I saw you from one of the turret windows."

"Yes, I had a first-rate gallop," he said with enthusiasm, his face brightening.

"Isn't it dangerous to gallop when the snow lies so deep?" asked Annabel. Lord Stephen's hand slipped from her arm as she turned towards her youngest stepson.

Geoffrey blushed. "Not when you know the country." His tongue once loosened, he continued, "If you know where the hidden obstacles are, ditches and such, it's absolutely topping. The air's so clear you can see for miles. No mud to make for heavy going, and you don't have to worry about crushing crops. Of course, it's not every horse can cope with snow, but my Galahad's a splendid beast."

Half-listening to a recital of Galahad's finer points, Daisy saw Lord Wentwater come in. At once Marjorie furtively put down her drink and stubbed out her cigarette. Wilfred also disposed hurriedly of his glass. Their father didn't appear to notice.

Good manners demanded that Daisy report to him on

her tour of the house. She slipped away and crossed to his side. Head bent, he listened with civil interest, then gave his permission to use the stories Lady Josephine had told her.

"No doubt every family has skeletons in its cupboards," he said with a wry smile.

The butler came in just then to announce that luncheon was served. Lord Wentwater escorted Daisy into the dining-room and seated her beside him. Since he was so cordial and approachable, she decided not to wait for Lady Josephine to mention her request to him.

"Would you mind if I took a photograph of you and your family in the Great Hall?" she asked as the soup was ladled out. "I think my readers would like to see who lives in the house now, don't you?"

"Probably," he said dryly and paused for a considering moment. Daisy held her breath, afraid he judged her request mere pandering to vulgar curiosity. "I don't see why not. We'll confine it to those of us who are descended from my disreputable ancestors, thus avoiding the thorny question of whether Miss Petrie ought to appear."

And excluding his wife, Daisy noted. Did he fear that by the time the article was printed, Annabel might have run off with Lord Stephen? If so, he gave no sign of it, asking with unaltered calm, "Will it suit you to take your photograph shortly before dinner? I'll ask everyone to come down early."

"That will be perfect," she said gratefully.

A hush had fallen over the table in tribute to a superb

cream of leek soup. Lord Wentwater announced that he expected his children, and invited his sister, to be present in the Great Hall at half-past seven that evening to have their photographs taken. Amid the nods and murmurs, Daisy thought she saw a hurt expression pass across Annabel's face, at the far end of the table. She couldn't be sure, for Lord Stephen said something to the countess and she turned her head to respond.

The two continued to talk as the soup was followed by Dover sole with lemon-butter. Marjorie, on Lord Stephen's other side, attempted several times to interrupt the tête-a-tête. Rebuffed, she lapsed into sulky silence. Geoffrey, too, had relapsed into taciturnity, devoting his attention to his food.

It was worthy of devotion, and Daisy enjoyed every bite. Soon enough she'd be back in Chelsea subsisting largely on omelettes and bread and cheese.

As she ate, she answered the earl's questions about what he politely termed her writing career. She told him of the bits and pieces published in gossip columns, the two short articles bought by *The Queen*, the daring proposal to *Town and Country* that led to her presence at Wentwater.

"I find your ambition and your industry admirable, Miss Dalrymple," he said, to her surprise. "Too many young people in comfortable circumstances fritter away their time in the pursuit of pleasure." His gaze moved from Wilfred, chattering nonsense rather too loudly to a giggling Fenella, to Marjorie, who had by now set up an unconvincing flirtation with Phillip.

Daisy came to the conclusion that Lord Wentwater was not half so oblivious of what was going on around him as he chose to appear. His children's behaviour disturbed him, but to Daisy the interesting question was what, if anything, did he mean to do about Annabel and Lord Stephen?

After lunch, Daisy spent the short remaining hours of daylight taking interior photographs, a slow business with long exposures. As the early winter dusk fell, she carried her equipment across the gallery above the Great Hall towards her bedroom. By that time, she'd have been jolly glad of Phillip's help to lug it all about.

She heard footsteps below, and then James's voice. "Looking for my stepmama?" he asked, a definite sly malice in his tone.

Moving to the balustrade, Daisy glanced down.

Lord Stephen was regarding James with a saturnine air. "Lady Wentwater is not presiding over the tea table this afternoon."

"You might find her in the conservatory."

"Ah, yes, I expect it reminds her of Italy."

"You knew her in Italy, didn't you?" James's eagerness was obvious. "Won't you tell me what . . . ?"

"That would hardly suit my purpose," Lord Stephen said dryly. He sauntered off.

His mouth tight with annoyance, James strode away in the opposite direction.

Daisy pondered the brief scene as she continued on her way. Their innocuous words had been freighted with meaning, unpleasant meaning. James must bitterly resent his beautiful stepmother to keep throwing Lord Stephen at her, regardless of his father's feelings. Stephen Astwick was amused by James's ploys, but quite content to take advantage of them. He had some end of his own in view, doubtless nefarious.

What had happened in Italy? Daisy regretted that she'd probably never find out.

Skipping afternoon tea downstairs, she settled in her room to transcribe her shorthand notes on the type-writer, before she forgot what they said. Mabel brought her a cup of tea, and Daisy asked the girl to draw her a bath in time for taking photos before dinner. Not that she was not perfectly capable of running her own bath, but it was pleasant to have a maid at her service, like the old days before her father's death. Besides, Mabel would coordinate matters if Fenella also wanted a bath.

Fenella, she mused—what did Fenella think of her fiancé's stepmother? One day shy little Fenella would be Lady Wentwater, having to cope with a dowager countess not much older than herself.

Turning back to her work, Daisy forced herself to concentrate. When she finished her notes, she wearily began to collect the picture-taking gear together again. She was certainly earning the imaginary Carswell's fee.

Someone knocked on the door.

"Hullo, old sport," Phillip called plaintively. "Have you shut yourself up in there for good?"

"No, you're just in time." She opened the door and

loaded him with tripod and camera. "I want to set everything up in the hall in advance."

Always obliging, he went down with her and, with the aid of a footman, moved a heavy oak refectory table aside to set up the tripod. Patiently he shifted it from place to place as she chose the best spot for it.

"Those will have to go." She waved at the half-dozen solid, studded-leather seventeenth-century chairs grouped around the fire.

Phillip obliged.

Marjorie wandered into the hall, looking disconsolate. "Have you seen Lord Stephen?" she asked.

"Not for hours," Daisy said. "Would you mind standing over there by the fireplace for a minute while I set the focus?"

Marjorie drifted over and stood drooping, her scarlet mouth turned down. "I can't find him anywhere. I suppose he's chasing my dear stepmother as usual. I can't imagine what he sees in her."

"She's beautiful," said Phillip, surprised.

Marjorie threw him a glance full of scorn. "But he's a sophisticated man of the world and she's so frightfully old-fashioned. Do you know, Daisy, she doesn't smoke, hardly drinks, and doesn't even dance the tango, or fox-trot, or *anything!* Do you think he's trying to make me jealous?"

Phillip snorted and Daisy said hurriedly, "If so, I shouldn't let him see he's succeeding, if I were you. Three inches to the left, please, Phil. That's it, just right. Thanks, Marjorie."

"Sometimes I almost hate him," she moaned. "Maybe he's in the library. I haven't looked there yet."

As she sped off towards the west wing, Phillip said, "Poor little beast, but I'd run for cover if she hunted me the way she does him. A fellow likes to make the pace."

"I hardly think he's running for cover," Daisy contradicted, taking a last look through the viewfinder. "What do you think of him?"

"Of Astwick? He's a good egg, put me onto something very nice in the way of South American silver."

"Oh dear!"

"What d'you mean, oh dear? Confound it, Daisy, you can't pretend you know the first thing about the stock market."

"No." She was too fond of him not to warn him. "It's just that Lady Josephine happened to mention that Sir Hugh doesn't trust Lord Stephen."

"Oh, Menton! The old bird made his pile years ago. He can afford to be conservative, but believe me, one don't rake in the shekels without taking risks," Phillip assured her, but she was glad to see he seemed a trifle uneasy despite his vehemence.

Daisy went upstairs to bathe and change for dinner. The bathroom was immense, at least compared to the cupboard that went by the name in the little house she shared with Lucy. It was dominated by a massive Victorian bathtub, from which rose fragrant steam. Raised several inches above the linoleum floor on feet clawed like the talons of a bird of prey, the bath had brass taps in the shape of eagles' heads.

"They's all different, miss," said Mabel, giggling. "One bathroom has lions, one has dolphins, and there's even one with dragons' heads! I put in the verbena bath-salts, I hope that's all right. The water's that hard we have to use summat."

"I love verbena."

"Me too, miss. Here's your towel, warming on the rail. Will you need help dressing, miss?"

"No, thank you, but I may need help climbing out of the bath!"

"There's a little step stool, see. India-rubber feet it's got, and rubber on top, so's you won't slip. I'll put it right here by the bath mat. But just call out if you needs me, miss. I'll be just through there in Miss Petrie's room soon as I've hung up your frock." Indicating a door opposite the one to Daisy's room, she departed.

Daisy checked the corridor door. It was locked, with a big, old-fashioned key left in the keyhole—probably it was used when there were more guests in the house and not enough bathrooms to go round. She slipped out of her flannel dressing-gown, dropped it on the cork-seated chair in the corner, and plunged into the luxuriously scented hot water.

Getting out was difficult less because of the depth of the bath than because she was enjoying it so much. The water cooled very slowly. At last, hearing Fenella's voice next door, she dragged herself from the heavenly warmth, dried quickly, shivering, and returned to the bedroom. At her request, Mabel had laid out her old grey silk evening frock. She'd be handling magnesium

49

powder this evening and didn't want to risk stray sparks holing her best dress.

Wearing the grey silk depressed Daisy. Bought after Gervaise was killed in the trenches, it had seen service when her darling Michael's ambulance drove over a land mine, and again when her father succumbed to the 'flu epidemic.

She caught sight of her gloomy expression in the mirror and pulled a face at herself. There was enough despondency at Wentwater Court without her adding to it. Her amber necklace, the colour of her hair, both brightened and smartened the dress. She powdered and lipsticked and went down to the hall.

The Beddowe brothers were already there, all in blackand-white evening togs, yet quite distinct from each other. James, heir to the earldom, though impeccably turned out, appeared very much the stalwart country gentleman in comparison with the elegantly languid Wilfred. Geoffrey, taller and broader than his brothers, seemed constrained by his clothes, as if he'd be more comfortable in safari kit, striding about some outpost of Empire. He asked Daisy about her equipment, and she was explaining the magnesium flashlight when Marjorie joined them.

Marjorie's décolleté dress, violently patterned in black and white, could have been designed—and had certainly been chosen—to stand out in a group photograph. Daisy sighed. She had hoped to portray the dignity of the Beddowe family in their ancestral hall, but the eye of any reader of *Town and Country* would be instantly drawn to that jazzy dress.

It was too late to ask her to change. The grandfather clock by the stairs struck the half hour and the earl arrived.

He looked around, his gaze pausing on his daughter's frock, then moving on. "Annabel's not here yet?" he said. "Nor my sister? We'll wait a minute or two if you don't mind, Miss Dalrymple."

Daisy agreed, surprised. She thought he had deliberately excluded Annabel, and she was sure Annabel had the same impression. But perhaps he merely meant that his wife had come down before him and he had expected her to be present. At any rate, when Lady Josephine arrived with Sir Hugh, he called to his sister to join the group by the fireplace without further mention of Annabel.

Arranging her subjects, whose height bore no relation to their importance, was no easy matter, but Daisy had worked it out beforehand and soon had them posed. She opened the shutter and detonated the percussive cap in the trough of flashlight powder.

A blinding glare lit the hall to the rafters.

"My hat!" exclaimed Wilfred.

"Drat!" Blinking against an after image of six startled white faces, Daisy hastily closed the shutter. Clouds of magnesium smoke drifted through the hall. "I'm rather afraid that was too much light. The film will be frightfully overexposed."

"The professional touch." Phillip, grinning, strolled in with Fenella. "Try again, old thing, but mind you don't blow up the house."

Daisy gave him a cross glance and set up for a second shot. This time the magnesium powder fizzled damply. Where was Carswell when she needed him?

Her third effort was perfect. "But I'd like to take a couple more, to make sure," she said hastily as everyone began to move.

They settled back into their places. Marjorie looked furious, Lady Josephine distressed, Wilfred nervous, and James smug. Such a range of emotions could hardly be explained by a request to stand still, Daisy thought. She turned her head and saw that Annabel had entered the room, with Lord Stephen.

When she turned back, her subjects' faces had smoothed into the vacuous expressions worn by the vast majority of people having their portraits taken. She shot another picture, wound on the film, and prepared the flash for the final exposure.

Lord Stephen's insinuating voice came from behind her. "You're shivering, Annabel. You are cold."

"No, I'm quite all right."

"Nonsense! There's a beastly gale of a draught in here. Come into the drawing-room."

A pause, then Annabel said in a colourless tone, "Yes, Stephen."

Daisy heard their departing footsteps as she pressed the button.

"Better take one more," James suggested. "My eyebrow twitched just as the flash went off."

"It might be a good idea, if no one objects," said

Daisy, though she knew he was just trying to make mischief, to leave Annabel and Lord Stephen alone together for a few more minutes. She was a bit anxious about her photos, and not at all sure the extra money was worth the trouble.

Dinner was as delicious and as uncomfortable a meal as lunch had been. After coffee, Sir Hugh repaired to the smoking-room for a cigar, and Lord Wentwater to his study to write letters.

In the drawing-room, Wilfred said to Phillip, "What do you say to shoving the balls about a bit, Petrie? But you play a dashed sight better than I do. You'll have to give me a hundred."

"All right, old chap," said Phillip with his usual good nature. "Though billiards ain't exactly my game, you know. I rather prefer more active sports."

"Wilfred would look less wishy-washy," said his aunt, dispassionately censorious, "if he took up an outdoor pursuit other than attending the races."

"Oh, I say, Aunt Jo!"

"In my view, keeping fit is of the utmost importance," Lord Stephen put in, running a preening hand over his black hair. "Besides a regular regimen of Swedish gymnastics, I rise every day at dawn, take a cold bath followed by outdoor exercise—skating at present—and then a hot bath before breakfast."

"Dawn's not that early at this time of year," Wilfred muttered in Daisy's ear.

Marjorie gazed up at Lord Stephen with fluttering

eyelashes. "You must be frightfully strong," she breathed.

"A cold bath and skating at dawn, eh?" Phillip visibly suppressed a shudder. "Sounds like one's jolly old school-days and I must say one felt pretty good then, up to anything. I'll give it a try."

Daisy considered it highly unlikely he'd do anything so uncomfortable. He and Wilfred went off to the billiard-room.

Fenella was at the piano, James turning the pages for her. "Why don't you play some dance music?" Marjorie suggested brightly. "Do you know that new fox-trot, 'Count the Days,' Fenella? Or we could see what's on the wireless, or put a record on the gramophone. We can roll back the carpet. Wouldn't you like to dance, Lord Stephen?"

"Certainly, if Annabel will grant me a waltz."

"Oh, no, Stephen, I . . . I must not neglect my other guests. I have scarcely had a chance to talk to Daisy all day."

She shot a glance of desperate appeal at Daisy, who promptly moved to a love seat and patted the place beside her. "Do come and sit here, Annabel. I want to ask you about . . . about the gardens," she improvised. She was beginning to believe Annabel accepted Lord Stephen's attentions because she was afraid of him.

Marjorie managed to corner Lord Stephen. "The waltz is frightfully old-fashioned," she said, and prattled on about the latest dances from America, the camel-walk, the toboggan, the Chicago. Geoffrey was

54

talking to Lady Josephine. Daisy overheard snippets of both conversations as she chatted with Annabel. It turned out she had picked a good subject, for Annabel had missed English flowers while in Italy and took a great interest in Wentwater's gardens. Gradually she relaxed and even grew enthusiastic.

The quiet background of piano music changed as Fenella and James sang a sentimental song together, a tentative soprano and a robust baritone.

"Charming," Lady Josephine applauded.

"It's called 'Lovely Lucerne,' Aunt Jo, a new hit that's not from America for a change."

"Do give us another song," she requested.

James set a sheet of music on the stand and they launched into "The Raggle-Taggle Gypsies." Paling, Annabel lost the thread of what she was saying. Lord Stephen stared at her, his gaze at once avid and cold. With a smirk, James began the second verse:

It was late last night when my lord came home
Enquiring for his lady-o.
The servants said on every hand,
She's gone—

"Enough!" commanded Lady Josephine.

The innocent Fenella stopped with her mouth open, bewildered.

Annabel jumped up. "Excuse me," she said in a stifled voice. "I . . . It's been a tiring day. I'm going up now." She fled.

"James, I wish to play bridge," Lady Josephine declared. "You may partner me. Has Drew set out the cards?"

"Yes, Aunt Jo, as always."

Fenella and Geoffrey did not play. Marjorie was roped in, but Lord Stephen begged off. Daisy was afraid she'd be asked to take a hand, but Sir Hugh came in just in time to save her.

As the foursome moved to the card table, Lord Stephen said, "I believe I'll be off to bed, too. Dawn rising, don't you know." He sauntered out, unhurried yet purposeful.

Dismayed, Daisy felt she ought to do something but couldn't think what. Then Fenella turned to her with a plaintive, "I don't understand, Daisy. Why . . . ?"

"I suppose Lady Josephine doesn't like that song," Daisy said quickly, and asked for news of her family at home in Worcestershire.

Phillip and Wilfred returned from the billiard-room shortly thereafter, Phillip having won even with the agreed handicap. He proposed a game of rummy. Geoffrey had disappeared, but the four of them played until it was time for the late weather forecast on the wireless. The bridge game broke up at the same time and they all listened to a promise of another day of freezing temperatures before retiring for the night.

On her way to bed, Daisy went to the library to borrow the book about Wentwater Court recommended by Lady Josephine. Though the evening had ended peacefully, it had been fraught with overwrought emotions, and she hoped a little of the duller kind of history would send her straight to sleep. Through the open connecting door to Lord Wentwater's study she saw the earl sitting in a wing chair by the fire, his face set in stern, melancholy lines. In his hands he warmed a brandy glass and a half-full decanter stood at his elbow.

So perhaps Lord Wentwater was not indifferent to Stephen Astwick's pursuit of his young wife. Daisy wished he would hurry up and decide how to put an end to it.

In the morning, Daisy rose with the sun, which, as Wilfred had pointed out, was not particularly early at the beginning of January. Skipping the cold bath and postponing the outdoor exercise, she dressed warmly and went down to the breakfast parlour, a pleasantly sunny east facing room. James, Fenella, and Sir Hugh were there before her. Sir Hugh lowered his *Financial Times* momentarily to wish her a good morning before retreating once more behind that bastion.

She helped herself to kedgeree from the buffet on the sideboard and joined them at the table.

"Will you skate with us this morning, Daisy?" Fenella asked. "I know you're frightfully busy but this weather may not last and we don't get such spiffing freezes very often."

"Yes, I'd like to, if I can borrow skates?"

"We have a cupboardful," James assured her. "There's bound to be something to fit you."

"Jolly good. I'll finish off the roll of film in the

camera down at the lake, and spend the rest of the morning developing my pictures."

Sir Hugh, emerging from his newspaper, told her he owned shares in the Eastman Kodak company and asked about the developing and printing process. Daisy explained as she ate. James and Fenella lingered over their coffee until she had finished her breakfast, then took her to look for a pair of skates.

Outside, the air was crisp and still. Daisy couldn't resist leaving a footprint or two in the glistening untrodden snow beside the path. It crunched underfoot.

James carried the skating boots down the hill for her as she was laden with camera and tripod. While she set them up, he and Fenella sat on the bench and put on their skates. They circled slowly at the near end of the lake, waiting for her.

"Go ahead," she called, already chilled fingers fumbling at the stiff catch that attached the camera to the tripod. "I'll be with you in half a mo."

Waving to her, they joined hands and whizzed off towards the bridge. As they reached it, James yelled, "Stop!"

They swerved to a halt beneath the arch. James moved cautiously forward into the black shadow cast by the low sun. And then Fenella screamed.

CHAPTER 4

As scream after scream shredded the peaceful morning, Daisy raced along the lakeside path towards the bridge. Stepping down cautiously from the bank onto the ice, she was under the stone arch before she saw what had stopped James and Fenella in their tracks.

In the shadow of the bridge, the ice was shattered, and in the inky water floated a man, facedown.

With a gasp of shock, Daisy turned to Fenella. "Be quiet," she ordered sharply. "Don't look."

The ear-piercing screams ended in a sob, half buried in James's chest as he pulled his fiancée into his arms. He glared at Daisy over her shoulder.

"She's upset!"

"So am I, but hysterics won't help. Send her away."

He nodded sober understanding. "Fenella, I want you to go up to the house and tell Father, or Sir Hugh if you can't find him. Come and take your skates off. I suppose I'd better get a boathook," he added to Daisy.

"Yes, though I'm sure it's too late."

Finding the camera in her hands, Daisy tried to regard the gruesome scene as a problem in photography. The shadow was less deep now that her eyes were accustomed to it, and on the far side the jagged edge of the hole was in sunlight. Her shaking hands steadied as she moved around taking shots from different angles, venturing as close to the dark water as she dared. The ice,

59

roughened by skate blades, felt solid beneath her feet, but of course the man must be much heavier than she was.

The man. Though she kept calling him that to herself, she knew who he was. The tight waisted, tight-cuffed leather jacket, ballooned with air, supported his torso and arms on the surface. His legs dangled invisible below. His head was just submerged, the slick black hair a darker patch, the nape of his neck white and strangely defenceless in death.

Lord Stephen.

She began to feel sick, picturing him scrabbling desperately at the ice for nonexistent handholds. Though he had been one of the least likeable people she had ever met, she wouldn't wish such a horror on her worst enemy.

James returned from the boathouse. He spread some coconut matting on the ice to give a footing, then, in grim silence, he caught the back of the collar with a gaff, the waistband with a boathook. Awkwardly, one pole in each hand, he hauled the body to the edge of the hole.

"Sorry, I can't manage it by myself."

Daisy hung the camera around her neck, took the gaff pole, shut her eyes, and pulled.

"Lift a bit."

She obeyed. As the body came free, she staggered backwards, slipped, and sat down.

"Oof!"

"Are you all right? I say, Daisy, you're a jolly good

sport." James stooped to unhook the gaff and the boathook, and turned the body over. "Astwick, poor brighter. Dead as mutton. I'll get him onto the bank."

Recovering her breath, she gathered herself together and followed. As James dragged him across the ice, Lord Stephen's limp feet in their skating boots flopped pathetically sideways. With a shudder, Daisy averted her eyes.

"Hullo, there's a great gash on his forehead. Look, here on the temple. It's hard to see because his face is all blotchy. He must have knocked himself out on the ice when he fell through. I wondered why the poor devil hadn't pulled himself out."

"He wouldn't have known he was drowning then," she said, saved from her ghastly imaginings. The sound of voices drew her attention up the hill. "Here comes your father."

Lord Wentwater, Sir Hugh, and Phillip joined them. In a solemn circle they stood staring down at the mortal remains of Lord Stephen Astwick, all except Daisy, who watched the men.

The earl must surely feel relief at the very least. His face showed nothing but the natural grave concern of a man whose guest has met with a fatal accident on his premises. Sir Hugh frowned, possibly foreseeing the unpleasantness of enquiries into the victim's City dealings. Had he been more involved in Astwick's business affairs than he was ready to admit?

Phillip regarded the body with the mingled curiosity and distaste of one to whom corpses are nothing new.

Of all the young men Daisy knew who had gone through the War in France, he had emerged least affected, perhaps saved by a lack of imagination.

And James, who had done his brief military service safe in a ministry in London, was morose. His plot against his stepmother was now missing an essential part.

Sir Hugh was the first to stir, the first to speak. "We must send for the police."

Lord Wentwater's head jerked up. "No!"

"I'm afraid so, Henry."

"Dr. Fennis will write out a death certificate . . ."

"Precisely: death by drowning. No chance of even you persuading him Astwick died in bed of heart failure. Any unexpected death requires an inquest, especially a violent death, however obviously accidental, and the coroner will require a police report."

"Ye gods, I can't let Wetherby pry into my affairs!"

"Wetherby?" asked Sir Hugh.

"The Chief Constable," James explained. "He and Father have a running feud on every subject under the sun. Colonel Wetherby would revel in a chance to tear us to pieces."

"Surely it needn't go beyond your local johnny," said Phillip. "Your local constable, I mean. One look ought to be enough to get him to swear to an accident at the inquest."

"Job Ruddle?" James laughed. "You've got something there, Petrie. The Ruddles have been family retainers for centuries."

His father shook his head. "He'd have to write a report, and one way or another it would reach Wetherby's ears."

"It's not the kind of thing that can be hushed up," Sir Hugh reaffirmed. "What I could do is telephone the Commissioner of the Metropolitan Police. He's an old friend, and maybe he can send down some discreet C.I.D. officer from Scotland Yard. I don't know what the protocol is, but it might be possible to keep it from the local police."

"Try it." Lord Wentwater's shoulders slumped as he accepted the necessity of calling in the authorities. "Thank you, Hugh. James, see to having . . . this removed to the boathouse. We don't want anyone coming across it unexpectedly."

"Yes, sir."

Sir Hugh looked down at the dead man, sprawled on his back at their feet. "I believe we ought to have some photographs, before he's moved again. Miss Dalrymple, do you feel up to it?"

"Good Lord, no!" said Phillip, belatedly protective. "Hang it all you can't ask a young lady to do anything so bally beastly. Daisy, you shouldn't be here at all."

His protest erased her qualms. "Don't be a silly ass, Phillip. Of course I can do it. I helped James pull him out."

He stood guard over her like an anxious mother hen until she sent him to fetch the tripod from the other side of the lake. As she finished the roll of film, James returned with a couple of under-gardeners, one all agog, the other timorous. They laid out a tarpaulin like a shroud on the snow beside the path.

The body was a person again, not just a pattern in the viewfinder. Daisy turned away. "I'm going up to develop these now," she said.

"I'll come with you, old thing, unless you need a hand, Beddowe?"

"No, go ahead."

Leaving James and the gardeners to their grisly task, they set off up the path.

"Jolly rotten luck," Phillip observed, "having a guest drown in one's ornamental water. One can't blame Wentwater for being sick as a dog over it. I dare say Lady Wentwater won't be any too bobbish, either. Astwick was an old friend of hers, one gathers."

"So he told me." Daisy marvelled at the way the currents of emotion swirling through Wentwater Court had apparently washed right past Phillip's oblivious head.

"Rather bad form, having the busies in the house," he went on. "I wonder if the mater'd want me to take Fenella home?"

"Don't leave, Phil." She felt a need for his familiar, comforting presence, even if he was a bit of a chump. "I expect the police will want to talk to Fenella, as she was one of those who found the body. She might even have to attend the inquest."

"Lord, wouldn't that just put the cat among the pigeons! The gov'nor will have my head on a platter if I let her appear in court."

"I'm sure they could call her as a witness even if you

64

did take her home. But she didn't see anything that James and I didn't see too. They won't need her evidence."

"Right-ho." He sighed with relief. "I'll ring the parents up on the telephone, but unless they insist or Fenella gets the wind up, we won't leg it."

On reaching the house, Daisy retired to Sydney Beddowe's scullery-darkroom. A narrow, windowless room with whitewashed walls and a stone flagged floor, it was lit by a shadeless lightbulb dangling by its flex from the ceiling. At the far end was a zinc sink with a cold-water tap and slate draining boards. One long wall was taken up by a stained wooden counter where the equipment, old-fashioned but in good condition, was ranged, including an electric lamp with a red bulb. Empty shelves on the opposite wall had doubtless held supplies.

Absorbed in her work, Daisy managed to forget for a couple of hours the unpleasant end of the unpleasant Lord Stephen Astwick.

Sydney's enlarger was still in perfect working order. Daisy decided to make prints of the pictures the police might want to see. As she set them out to dry, some of the horror returned. Nonetheless, she was rather pleased with the way they had come out. She had succeeded in shading the lens from the glare of sun on snow and ice. Most of both close-up and more distant shots were clear, with jolly good contrast. Lucy would be proud of her.

With a puzzled frown, she took a closer look at one of

the pictures. Those marks on the broken edge of the ice, almost as if . . .

A knock on the door interrupted her train of thought. "Miss?"

"It's all right, you can come in."

The door opened two inches and an eye appeared. "I don't want to spoil your pitchers, miss."

"Thank you, but really, it's all right now."

Gingerly, a footman stepped into the scullery. "Luncheon will be served in quarter of an hour, miss, and the detective's asking to see you."

"A Scotland Yard man?" Daisy asked, flipping electrical switches to Off. "Here already? Or is it the local police?"

"From Scotland Yard, miss, a Chief Inspector. Seems he was in Hampshire on business anyway. He's already seen Miss Petrie and Master James—Lord Beddowe, that is." He stepped back to let her precede him through the door and along the dimly lit corridor.

"Well, I don't want to keep him waiting, but I'm starved. Is he lunching with the family?"

"Crikey, miss, I shouldn't think so! I mean, a p'leeceman's not a real gentleman, is he? But you better ask Mr. Drew." He dodged past her to hold open the baize door from the servants' quarters.

The butler was in the dining-room, casting a last glance over the table before announcing lunch. "His lordship has not intimated to me that he wishes the detective to join the family," he said austerely.

"A Chief Inspector won't be frightfully happy to be

expected to eat in the servants' hall! I suppose you'll give him a tray in . . . wherever he is?"

"The Blue Salon, miss. The detective has not requested refreshment."

"The poor chap's bound to be glad of a bite to eat. I'm sure Lord Wentwater won't mind if you take him some soup and sandwiches. Tell him I'll be with him right after lunch." She would willingly have shared the policeman's sandwiches, but she wanted to see how Lord Stephen's demise affected the company.

Fenella appeared to have recovered from the shock of finding the body. James and Phillip sat on either side of her, treating her like a piece of priceless porcelain. She basked in their solicitude.

Marjorie was absent. "The poor prune came unstrung," Wilfred told Daisy, seated beside him. "Dr. Fennis doped her up. Doesn't know when she's well off," he added in an undertone. "Astwick was a rotten swine."

"I can't say I cared for him myself, but he's dead now."

"*De mortuis,* et cetera." He pulled a face. "Hypocritical bunkum."

Since Wilfred was distinctly cheerful, the smell of gin on his breath was presumably not from drowning his sorrows but from celebrating. Lady Josephine was also in sunny spirits which, whenever she glanced at her thoughtful husband, she tried guiltily to hide behind a more appropriate cloud of solemnity.

Annabel, on the other hand, was even paler and quieter than usual, and seemed to have lost her appetite. The removal of her persecutor ought to have bucked her up no end. Daisy wondered whether she was mistaken in believing that the young countess had feared Lord Stephen. Was she now mourning her lover?

The earl certainly had every reason to rejoice, yet he was as soberly formal, as unreadable, as ever.

After lunch, Daisy declared her intention of skipping coffee and going to see the C.I.D. man. At once Phillip, James, Lord Wentwater, and even Sir Hugh offered to accompany her.

"Heavens, no, thank you," she said, laughing. "I don't imagine he'll use the 'third degree' on me." Leaving Wilfred to explain that American term to his father, she went off to the Blue Salon.

She was eager to meet the detective. The only contact she'd ever had with policemen was to enquire after the family of the local bobby at home in Worcestershire, and occasionally to ask the way of a London constable. A Chief Inspector was a different kettle of fish, not a "real gentleman," in the footman's words, but a man of a certain power and influence.

Despite her refusal of support, she was a trifle nervous when she entered the small sitting-room. Facing north, decorated in pale blue and white, the room had a chilly atmosphere that the small fire in the grate battled in vain. No doubt that explained why it was little used by the family in winter and could be spared for the police. Daisy shivered.

The man who looked up from the papers on an elegant eighteenth-century writing table was much younger than she had expected, in his mid-thirties, she thought. He rose to his feet. Gentleman or not, he was well dressed in a charcoal suit, with the tie of the Royal Flying Corps. Of middle height, broad shouldered, he impressed Daisy as vigorous and resolute, an impression reinforced by rather intimidating dark, heavy eyebrows over piercing grey eyes.

Daisy was not about to let herself be intimidated. She advanced across the blue Wilton carpet, held out her hand, and announced, "I'm Daisy Dalrymple."

"How do you do." His handshake was cool and firm, his voice educated—though not at Eton or Harrow. "Detective Chief Inspector Fletcher, C.I.D. I understand I have you to thank for my lunch, Miss Dalrymple."

"The servants seemed to think that a policeman is above such mortal needs as food, Mr. Fletcher."

He grinned, his eyes warming, and she noticed that his dark, crisp hair sprang from his temples in the most delicious way. Altogether he was rather gorgeous, she decided.

"This policeman was hungry. Thank you." He became businesslike. "I hope you don't mind describing to me the events of this morning."

"Not at all." Remembering, she changed her mind. "Well, not much. But I shouldn't think I can add anything to what James—Lord Beddowe—and Fenella Petrie have told you." She sat down on the nearest chair, and he resumed his seat.

"You can hardly tell me less." He grimaced. "I'm glad you didn't bring any guardians with you."

"I suppose Phillip—Mr. Petrie—and James insisted on protecting Fenella from you."

"They hardly let her say yes or no."

"And James would have been standing on his dignity, no doubt. I'll see what I can do."

"I'm sorry to put you through this, Miss Dalrymple. Just tell me what happened in your own way."

He picked up a fountain pen and took notes, without interrupting as she spoke until she reached the point where she returned to the house to develop the photographs.

"Thank you, that's very clear," he said then. "You succeeded in developing the pictures?"

"Yes, and printed them. The darkroom has all the necessary equipment."

"I'll want to see them later, but first a question or two. You say you and Miss Petrie and Lord Beddowe went down to the lake right after breakfast."

"After finding skates and collecting my camera and stuff."

"Right, but it was still quite early." He glanced over his notes. "Nine thirty, or thereabouts. Weren't you surprised to find Lord Stephen there before you?"

"No, not at all. I was pretty sure it was him even before I recognized the jacket. You see, he went on and on last night about keeping fit and going out at dawn to exercise."

"Ah, that makes all the difference. I couldn't understand what he was doing there in the first place." Capping his pen, the detective straightened his papers with an air of finality. "Obviously it was just an unfortunate but straight-forward accident."

"Well, I'm not sure." Daisy persevered in spite of his sceptically raised eyebrows. "You'll probably think I'm a complete fathead, Mr. Fletcher, but I wish you'd come and look at the photos."

"I'll have to look at them before the inquest, but I'm down here on another case and I can't really spare the time . . ."

"Please."

"Right-ho," he said indulgently. "I do appreciate your taking the trouble to photograph the body."

"Trouble! It was perfectly beastly." Bursting with indignation, Daisy led the way through the kitchens to the darkroom.

Following her, Alec Fletcher recognized her annoyance and was amused. He smiled at her stiff back.

Even the tailored tweed skirt and blue woolly jumper failed to conceal her shape as she marched ahead of him. Not plump, but not the straight up and down boardlike figure young women strove for these days. Cuddlesome was the word that had sprung to his mind the moment she walked into the Blue Salon. Cuddlesome from gold-brown hair and round face with that delectable mole—"the Kissing," it would have been called as an eighteenth-century face-patch—all the way down to the neat ankles in fashionable beige stockings.

She had been friendly, too, in contrast to young Beddowe, who appeared to consider Alec's presence an impertinent intrusion. He found it difficult to think of her as an Honourable, or even simply as a witness to be questioned.

Sternly, he recalled himself to duty. In gratitude for her cooperation he'd give her photos the praise she evidently craved, then get back to the business that had brought him to Hampshire. He'd have to attend the inquest, but luckily Astwick's death was clearly pure mischance.

The local G.P., Dr. Fennis, had assured him that the cause of death was drowning. Astwick must have hit his head on a jagged edge of ice as he fell. The laceration on the temple had probably been caused by a blow sufficient to make him dizzy and weak, perhaps even unconscious, obviously unable to pull himself out of the frigid water. Fennis could not confirm the time of death, since icy conditions retarded *rigor mortis,* always unpredictable in any case. However, since Astwick would hardly have gone skating in the middle of the night, the time was not in question. No autopsy was needed. He had died in an unfortunate accident, thank heaven.

Alec had no desire to tangle with Beddowe's father, Lord Wentwater. Even in this modern day and age an earl had to be handled with kid gloves, as the Commissioner had made quite plain over the wire.

Miss Dalrymple opened a door into a small, stone-floored room with whitewashed brick walls and a sink. The air had a chemical tang. "Don't touch the pictures; they're still damp," she warned. "There's something

". . . odd. I won't point it out. See if you notice it."

He studied the photographs. No wonder a well-brought-up young lady had considered taking them perfectly beastly, but the only odd thing he could see was their excellence. He'd expected amateur shots taken from a safe distance, but these could almost have been produced by a police photographer.

"These are very good," he complimented her. "Quite professional."

"You needn't sound so surprised! I worked for a friend in her studio for nearly a year. As a matter of fact, I'm here as a professional photographer."

He stared. "I thought you were a guest."

"Well, not quite. You see, I'm writing an article about Wentwater for *Town and Country*, and Carswell, the photographer who was supposed to take pictures to go with it, is ill." She blushed to the roots of her hair, and went on defiantly, "That is—I suppose I ought to tell the police the truth—he doesn't really exist. My editor doesn't believe women can take good photographs, so I invented Carswell so that I could earn the money."

Alec gave a shout of laughter. "Ingenious. So you are a working woman as well as a scion of the nobility?"

"Yes. Promise you won't tell about Carswell?"

"I promise, unless for some unlikely reason he comes into this investigation." He still hoped an investigation would prove unnecessary, but while he could easily dismiss the fancy of a bored society girl, the doubts of a practical woman deserved serious scrutiny. "Will you show me what has aroused your suspicion?"

"Here, and here." She pointed at a couple of photos of the hole in the ice.

"Those marks?" He took the magnifying lens she handed him.

"When I was down on the lake, I didn't really notice them. I just assumed they were made by skate blades. But you see how short and deep they are? Nicks all along the edge? The sun throws them into relief. I'm fearfully afraid they might be . . . they might be the marks of an axe."

"They might." He frowned. "Are you suggesting that someone deliberately weakened the ice?"

She shuddered. "I don't want to suggest anything."

"I'd better go down to the lake and have another look," Alec said with a sigh. "Will you come with me? Bring your camera and take some more shots of that particular spot."

Donning coats, hats, gloves, and mufflers, they walked together down the path. The dark waters that had taken a man's life gleamed in the sun. Gingerly Alec approached, noting how the ice was roughened by skating. Miss Dalrymple followed him.

"Keep back," he said. "Let me test the ice."

"It seemed to me very solid. That's another reason . . . And wouldn't you expect cracks radiating from the hole?"

"Hmm." He was chary of committing himself, but the ice did in fact feel perfectly safe beneath his feet. Taking out a tape-measure, he went down on hands and knees.

74

Quite different from the skate-marks, the notches appeared at curiously regular intervals on the very edge of the hole, all the way around. Grimly he confirmed her guess. "They look like the work of an axe to me. But it looks more as if someone cut a hole, rather than simply weakening the ice. There are not nearly enough pieces of floating ice to fill the hole, as if a large central piece was removed or shoved under the edge."

"To save time, rather than chopping it into bits as if it broke? Yes, there is far too little ice floating."

"Surely Astwick would have seen a hole in time to stop. He didn't come down before daybreak, did he?"

"Not as far as I know. This bit of the lake would have been in the shadow of the bridge, though. You remember, in the photos you could only see one side of the hole properly? He was here earlier and the shadow would have been longer. After the dazzle of the sun on ice and snow, he wouldn't have seen anything. I was really close before I made out what James and Fenella were looking at, though the one side was in sunlight and I already knew something was wrong."

"Will you take a few more shots, please?"

"If you like," she said doubtfully, "but the sun is too high now to provide the contrasting shadows. I shouldn't think you'll see much."

"I can get them blown up. They may be useful."

As she moved about with her camera, Alec searched for cracks in the ice around the hole, and for signs that it might have been thinner in that spot. He wanted it to be an accident. He had plenty on his hands with the big jewel robbery at Lord Flatford's place. One disgruntled peer was enough. To affront the Earl of Wentwater with the news that further investigation was warranted would be to risk blighting his career.

Miss Dalrymple finished and returned to his side. "Well?"

"I'm not convinced that it wasn't an accident, but nor am I convinced that it was, I'm afraid. It'd be a dashed peculiar way to commit suicide, so it seems to be a deliberate effort to harm someone, probably the actual victim in view of his known habit of skating at dawn. There will have to be an autopsy—it's involuntary manslaughter at least. But who would have it in for Lord Stephen Astwick?"

"Half the residents of Wentwater Court," Miss Dalrymple informed him unhappily.

CHAPTER 5

Chief Inspector Fletcher looked no happier than Daisy felt. "You'd better tell me," he said resignedly. "You are to some degree an outsider here, so you may not know the inside story but I'm hoping you can be reasonably impartial."

Her heart sank still further. She felt she was betraying the Wentwaters' hospitality, yet it was her duty to help the police. One couldn't let people get away with deliberately drowning other people, however despicable.

"All right. Let's go back to the house. I'm cold."

"So am I, and my knees are wet. Besides, I must telephone my sergeant and the mortuary and the coroner."

"Will I have to give evidence?"

"What I want from you is your impressions, even guesses and hearsay, to give me some idea of where to start. If you have to give evidence it will be of facts only, of what you have actually observed," he reassured her as they trudged up the path.

She nodded, grateful for his understanding. If she had to assist the police in their enquiries, at least she had a sympathetic policeman to deal with. "I don't know where to begin."

"Astwick must have a friend here, I imagine, or he wouldn't be a guest. Who invited him?"

"Wilfred. Lord Wentwater's second son. But I'm sure they're not friends. Quite apart from Wilfred being twenty years younger, he seems . . . seemed to be afraid of Lord Stephen. He was almost indecently cheerful at lunch today. Come to think of it, he actually told me Lord Stephen was a rotten swine and that Marjorie was well out of it. Admittedly he was rather sozzled."

"Marjorie?"

"His sister. She was madly in love with Lord Stephen and pretty cut up over his death. The doctor put her to bed with a sedative. Of course, she was madly jealous, too. Do you think she might have done it to give him a nasty fright, then been shocked when he actually drowned?"

"Possibly. It would take considerable strength to hack through that ice."

"She's a sporty type, skating, tennis, golf, riding, and

so on. As strong as Wilfred, I reckon. He's a stage-door-johnny, not good for much more than lifting a glass or a croquet mallet."

"A graphic description! What about Lord Beddowe?"

"James is pretty strong. Huntin', shootin', fishin', you know. Only he had nothing against Lord Stephen, no motive, rather the reverse. Geoffrey, the youngest, is even stronger, but he's just a boy and never paid any heed to Lord Stephen, neither liking nor disliking."

They reached the house. Mr. Fletcher, ignoring Drew's disapproval, went off to make his telephone calls. Daisy repaired to the Blue Salon, where she rang for a footman to build up the fire to dry out the detective's damp knees.

What a ghastly business it was! She couldn't help recalling Annabel's wan face at lunch. Could she have aimed to scare off Lord Stephen with an icy wetting, underestimating the risk of his hitting his head and knocking himself unconscious? No, with the threat of revealing her past to hold over her, he'd only have bullied her even worse afterwards.

Which meant that if Annabel had done it, she had intended his death.

In spite of the roaring fire, Daisy shivered. She wouldn't point out that bit of deduction to the Chief Inspector.

He returned. Standing in front of the fire, steaming at the knees, he said, "Sergeant Tring will be on his way as soon as the locals can get my message to him. The coroner has agreed to adjourn the inquest after evidence of death and identity, which means we need not say yet *where* Astwick died. And the body's off to the Yard's pathologist for postmortem examination. The Commissioner himself told me to keep the locals out of it as much and as long as possible."

"The less the local people find out, the happier Lord Wentwater will be."

"So I gather. Well, he has to live with them. I'll do what I can. Now, Miss Dalrymple, you said Lord Beddowe had no apparent motive. What about his fiancée's brother, Mr. Petrie?"

"Phillip! Heavens no. At least, he called him a good egg. There was some sort of transaction between them, but he was surprised when I told him Sir Hugh distrusted Lord Stephen. That was last night, so he couldn't have heard in the interim that he'd been cheated, could he? I've known Phillip all my life. He's a bit of a juggins but he'd never do anything underhanded like that."

"I see." Mr. Fletcher sounded rather sceptical. "Who is Sir Hugh?"

"Lord Wentwater's brother-in-law, Lady Josephine's husband. It was he who insisted on calling the police and arranged to have someone discreet sent by Scotland Yard."

"Someone discreet, eh?" He grinned. "I thought it was just because I was already down here."

Daisy smiled at him. "Oh no, your superiors must have a high opinion of your discretion. Sir Hugh is a friend of your Commissioner. He's a big noise in the

City, which is how he knew Lord Stephen was not to be trusted. I'm sure he's much too knowing to have let him cheat him. Besides, if he wanted to retaliate, he'd do it financially, don't you think?"

"I certainly hope so. I'd hate a friend of the Commissioner to be my chief suspect." He felt the knees of his trousers and sat down in the chair opposite her. "Lady Josephine?"

"Good Lord, no! She was worried, but she's too goodnatured—and far too stout—to take an axe to the ice."

"We can count out Miss Fenella Petrie, can't we?"

"I should think so. Yes, of course. She's just a child and he never showed any interest in her." Daisy was flattered by the inclusive "we," by the Chief Inspector's apparent trust in her judgement. Nonetheless, she dreaded the next few minutes. "That leaves only Lord and Lady Wentwater." And she liked them both.

"Before we tackle them, let me go back a little. You said, or implied, that Lord Beddowe liked Lord Stephen, that Lady Marjorie had cause for jealousy, and that Lady Josephine was worried."

She tried to postpone the inevitable. "You have a very good memory."

"It's part of the job." He paused. His grey eyes were sharp again beneath the heavy brows, as if he had guessed her reluctance. "Would you mind explaining?"

Daisy took in a deep breath and let it out in a sigh. "James didn't *like* Lord Stephen. He *used* him, to further his feud against his stepmother. Not that it was necessary, if you ask me. Lord Stephen was in determined pursuit without any need of encouragement from James."

"You mean Lord Stephen was aiming to seduce Lady Wentwater? It scarcely seems possible!"

"That's certainly what it looked like. She's about my age and quite stunning, you know."

"So naturally Lady Marjorie was jealous. Was Lady Josephine worried that her sister-in-law might . . . er . . . succumb to his blandishments?"

"Yes."

"Did it appear likely to you?"

She hesitated. If she said yes, Lord Wentwater's motive for doing away with Lord Stephen was strengthened and Annabel appeared in a disgraceful light. If she said no, she'd have to explain, which would give Annabel an otherwise absent motive, as well as hinting at something shameful in her past.

The detective's steady gaze was upon her. She sighed again. The truth was the only way. "She hated him and feared him. If she had succumbed, it would have been through fear."

He nodded thoughtfully. "It sounds like blackmail, as does Wilfred Beddowe's invitation. A thoroughly unsavoury character, Lord Stephen Astwick."

"Wilfred was right, he was an absolutely rotten swine."

"Lady Wentwater had a motive, then, as did her husband." He groaned. "So instead of Sir Hugh, my chief suspect is the earl! And now I have to go and tell him I want to interrogate not only his household but himself."

There went any chance of ever making it to Superintendent, Alec thought. In comparison, the indiscreet way he was confiding in Miss Daisy Dalrymple was insignificant. Something about her guileless blue eyes invited confidences, and after two nearly sleepless nights he lacked the energy to resist. Besides, he had reason for trust if she hadn't drawn his attention to the marks on the ice, Astwick's death would have passed as pure accident.

All the same . . . "I shouldn't be talking to you like this, especially when I'm posing as a model of discretion. I'll be well and truly in the soup if you repeat what I've said."

"As though I would!" she said indignantly. "I haven't told anyone about the photos. I know police business is confidential." Unexpectedly she giggled. "Though I couldn't have guessed it from the way you've been blathering on to me. People do, you know," she consoled him. "It's very odd."

Alec came to a decision. "I'm going to ask a further favour of you. Do you by any chance take shorthand?"

"Yes, sort of. That is, I learned it and I worked for a while as a stenographer, but being in an office all day was simply frightful."

"You've forgotten it?" he asked, disappointed.

"Not exactly. I use it when I'm making notes for my writing, but it's not quite Pitman's any longer. I don't think anyone else could read it. I can, as long as I transcribe it before I forget what it says."

He laughed. "I'll risk it. It'll be better than nothing. I want to interview people while they think I believe the drowning was accidental, but my officers won't be here to take notes for some time."

"You want me to do it?" She sounded astonished and not a little excited, her eyes sparkling.

"A highly irregular proceeding," Alec admitted. "Expecting a simple accident, I've come ill prepared for a serious investigation. The other case I'm working on, the one that brought me to Hampshire, also involves a number of influential people. We're short-handed and I can't just abandon it."

"I'll help, as long as no one objects."

"Thank you, Miss Dalrymple. I count on you not to repeat anything you hear. I'll see that you're paid for your work, including the photography." Even if he had to pay her himself.

"Spiffing! I'll send for . . . no, I'll go and fetch my notebook. I don't want Mabel messing about with my papers."

She went off, a spring in her step. Alec rang the bell and asked the footman who appeared to inform Lord Wentwater that he desired a private interview.

"His lordship is occupied in the estate office with his agent," the man told him loftily.

Alec turned on the hapless menial the look that made his subordinates jump to attention and crooks shake in their shoes. "Then you know where to find him," he said.

"Yes, sir. At once, sir."

While he waited, Alec planned his approach to the earl. Had he enough evidence to insist on questioning the household if a polite request was refused?

He read over the notes he had made on the thickness and solidity of the ice, the missing piece or pieces, the lack of cracks radiating from the hole, the curious marks on the edge. Glancing at the photographs, he admired again not only Miss Dalrymple's competence, but her perspicacity in noticing something amiss.

His thoughts wandered. From what she said, it sounded as if she was working for living, however cheerfully. At first he'd assumed she was merely amusing herself, like Lady Angela Forbes with her florist's shop off Portman Square, before the War, when he did his years on the beat after University. Surely an Honourable Miss, the daughter of a baron or viscount, could not be so devoid of family as to make employment necessary. Yet she didn't seem the rebellious, or quarrelsome, or shameless sort of girl who might have cast off or been cast off by her family.

He shook his head, rubbing tired eyes. It was none of his business. What he wouldn't give for a pipe!

The footman returned. "His lordship will see you in the estate office, sir, if you'll please to come this way."

The estate office was a small room cluttered with ledgers, monographs on raising beef cattle, silver cups won by prize sows, and the general paraphernalia of running a busy estate. Lord Wentwater, seated at the desk, dismissed his land agent with a nod.

"I trust your investigation is completed, Chief

Inspector." He spoke with courtesy but did not invite Alec to sit down.

Alec put him down as an aristocrat of the old school, mindful of his responsibilities and taking his privileges for granted. His son and heir was like him in many respects, but in a changing world Lord Beddowe was less certain of his privileges and therefore more insistent on them. Perhaps that uncertainty had bred the undercurrent of resentment Alec had sensed in James Beddowe. The young man would have to work hard to earn the respect his father received as his due.

"I'm afraid not, sir," Alec said. "I find I must pursue further enquiries. I'd like your permission to ask a few questions of your household, your guests, and yourself."

"What!" The earl gave him a cold stare. "I shall give no such permission."

"I fear I must insist, sir. If you wish, I can report to the Commissioner at Scotland Yard by telephone and ask him to explain the necessity to you."

"I suppose you consider you have sufficient reason for this extraordinary demand?"

"Of course, sir." As though he'd risk his career for a whim! He was not prepared to state his reasons, however, and he prayed Lord Wentwater would not ask. "I need not say that I shall do my utmost not to give offence with my questions, and all answers will remain confidential, with the usual provisos." Unless needed as evidence in a court of law, but he wasn't going to point that out. He hurried on. "I'd be very grateful for your cooperation, sir."

There, with any luck polite but firm should do the trick.

"But you will go your way with or without it," said Lord Wentwater with an ironical look. "Very well, you may tell my family and my servants that I expect them to cooperate with you. For my guests I cannot speak. I am busy at present, but I shall submit to interrogation later this afternoon."

"Thank you, sir." Though he'd rather have interrogated the earl first, he felt he had got off lightly. No use pressing his luck.

He found his way down endless corridors back to the Blue Salon. As he approached the open door, he heard a worried voice he recognized as that of the brother who had so persistently protected Miss Petrie from him.

"But hang it all, Daisy, you've been in here for hours. What's going on?"

The Honourable Phillip Petrie was standing by a window seat where Miss Dalrymple had ensconced herself. Alec remembered that she had known the fellow all her life. Though she called him a bit of a fool, she had spoken of him with affection. He was her elder by two or three years, her equal in rank, and handsome in a rather weak way. They were obviously on the easiest of terms.

"For heaven's sake, don't get all hot under the collar, Phillip," Miss Dalrymple advised him. "Those photos Sir Hugh had me take turned out to be useful, that's all. And now Mr. Fletcher is employing me as a stenographer since his sergeant isn't here yet."

"Employing you? The bounder! What unmitigated cheek."

"Bosh! It's jolly decent of him to offer to pay me when I would have done it for nothing. I'm thinking of writing a detective story some day, instead of any old novel. They're madly popular."

"You and your confounded scribbling," Petrie groaned. "It's beyond me why you won't go back to . . ."

"Here's the Chief Inspector," Miss Dalrymple interrupted, spotting him and greeting him with a cheerful smile.

Alec had the feeling he came as a welcome respite. "Thank you for coming so quickly, Mr. Petrie," he said smoothly. "I only have a few questions to ask you. Shall we sit down?" His courteous gesture invited the young man to take a seat on a small sofa with his back to Daisy. His face would be adequately illuminated by the next window along, and it wouldn't hurt if he forgot that every word he spoke was being recorded.

Petrie sat down, slightly flushed and looking sheepish. He must be wondering if he'd been overheard describing as a bounder the police officer who was about to question him. "I came to find Miss Dalrymple," he blustered. "I didn't know you wanted to see me."

"A matter of routine."

As usual the soothing formula worked: Petrie visibly relaxed. "Oh, right-ho. Where was I between seven and nine this morning and that kind of rot, eh?"

Alec took the wing chair opposite him. "Between seven and nine?"

"Well, that must be about when the poor fish . . . er . . . chappie fell through the ice, mustn't it? Stands to reason. Too dark before, and he was found not much after nine. I say, you're not going to put Fenella through it again, are you? Deuced upsetting business for a female, don't you know."

"No, I don't expect to have any further questions for Miss Petrie," said Alec dryly. A fat chance he'd have of getting any answers out of her. "Where were you, then, between seven and nine?"

"Swigging down the jolly old early-morning tea, dressing, finding my way to the nose-bag, and so on. You know the routine, old bean . . . er . . . Chief Inspector."

"Finding your way to the nose-bag?"

"The breakfast parlour, I mean to say. Got there about ten minutes before Fenella toddled in with the news."

"You are unfamiliar with the house, Mr. Petrie?"

"By Jove, not that unfamiliar. Just a manner of speaking, don't you know. I've been down here since the day after Boxing Day, came to keep m'sister company. She's engaged to Beddowe."

"So I understand. You've never been here before?"

"Never. I've often met the Beddowes in town, of course, but we're not particularly pally."

"And you knew the deceased in town?"

"Astwick? More in the City. He put me on to a good thing just a few weeks ago."

To Alec's ears, Petrie sounded distinctly uncertain about the good thing. If he were brilliantly acting the part of the upper-class twerp he appeared to be, surely he'd have hidden his doubts. It couldn't be an act, though. Miss Dalrymple had known him all her life.

After a few more questions, Alec let him go and rang the bell. As he instructed the footman, Daisy glanced through her notes, clarifying an odd squiggle here and there.

"Please ask Geoffrey Beddowe to spare me a few minutes."

"I don't b'lieve Mr. Geoffrey's come home yet, sir."

"Come home?"

"Mr. Geoffrey went out riding early and telephoned to say he was going to spend the day with a friend, sir."

"All right, I'll see Lady Josephine next."

The footman left and the detective came over to the window seat.

"Did you manage to get it all down?" he asked.

"I think so. Why Lady Jo? I'm sure she can't possibly have had anything to do with it."

"I expect you're right, but having begun by chance with Mr. Petrie I might as well get the least likely out of the way first."

"Then you don't think Phillip did it?" she said, relieved.

"He doesn't seem to know the place well enough to lay his hands on an axe without poking about or asking the servants a lot of awkward questions, which we'll soon find out if he did."

"So that's what you were after. Frightfully clever."

"Somehow I can't picture him packing an axe in his luggage."

She laughed. "If he did, you may be sure the servants would know all about that, too."

"I must say, it wouldn't suit me to have my every sneeze discussed in the servants' hall. The trouble is, even with servants swarming about, no one's going to have an alibi."

Daisy nodded. "The ice could have been hacked at any time between nightfall and daybreak. I wondered why you wanted to know about seven to nine."

"I didn't, but he wanted to tell me," said Mr. Fletcher. "In fact, it led to the business of his being unfamiliar with the house, so it was worthwhile. What about the married couples? No chance of eliminating them, I suppose."

"I don't know about their sleeping arrangements," Daisy said, blushing, "but Lord Wentwater spent most of the evening in his study, Annabel went to bed early, and Sir Hugh disappeared to the smoking-room after dinner. I don't know if he was gone long enough to do it."

"You were in the same room as Lady Josephine all evening?"

"From about half past seven. It was dark long before that." While she was enjoying her leisurely bath, anyone could have been down at the lake. "Most of the maids go off duty at eight, though there would have been a few servants around until midnight or so. It wasn't till after dinner that Lord Stephen talked about skating early."

"He'd been here a week and the lake's been frozen for

90

three days, I gather; the servants must have known," said the detective with a sardonic look. "Which means anyone could know. Well, we're getting nowhere fast. Are you comfortable there, Miss Dalrymple? It's a good, unobtrusive spot."

"That's why I chose it," she said smugly. "Watching someone write down my words would jolly well shut me up. Phillip had forgotten I was here by the time he left." To herself she admitted to being a bit piqued.

As if he guessed, Mr. Fletcher said consolingly, "After all, that's just what we want." He glanced at his wristwatch. "Where has Lady Josephine got to? You know, it's odd that Geoffrey is out, in the circumstances."

Daisy considered the matter. "I hadn't even noticed that he didn't turn up to lunch. He's big, but so silent he's easily overlooked. He must have left before the body was discovered."

"Surely whoever spoke to him on the 'phone would have told him."

"Not if he just left a message with a servant, and even if he was told, he might not see any reason to return. It was nothing to do with him."

"True. But if he left the house early, he may have seen Astwick skating, or on his way down to the lake. Every little scrap of information helps. If he doesn't put in an appearance soon, I'll have to see if I can get hold of him on the telephone. Incidentally, what about the servants? Might any of them hold a grudge against Astwick?"

"I haven't the foggiest. I only arrived yesterday,

remember. I could have a chat with the chambermaid who waits on me, if you like."

"By all means have a chat about the general feeling in the servants' hall, but I don't want you asking specific questions. We'll leave that to Sergeant Tring."

At that moment Lady Josephine put in an appearance, followed by her husband. Alec sighed, inaudibly he hoped, and went to meet them.

"You won't mind if I sit in on this interview, will you?" Sir Hugh asked, affable but with a determined edge to his voice.

"Of course not, sir. I need to speak to you as well."

He needn't have worried that Sir Hugh's presence would render his wife monosyllabic. A large lady of uncertain years, clad in bulky tweeds and superb pearls, she gushed, "This is all most frightfully exciting, Chief Inspector. A dreadful business, of course," she added hastily. "Why, Daisy dear, I almost didn't see you hidden in that corner."

"I'm acting as Mr. Fletcher's stenographer, Lady Josephine, since he's come without one."

"How clever you young women are nowadays! You want us to sit here, Mr. Fletcher? Do be seated, won't you? It must be quite wearying asking questions all day. That's better." She beamed at him. "Now, how can we help you?"

Alec found himself warming to the earl's sister in a most unprofessional way. He understood why Miss Dalrymple refused to believe her guilty, whether or not she was physically capable of chopping a hole in the ice. "Perhaps you would begin by telling me what you know of Lord Stephen Astwick, ma'am," he said.

"He was an utter cad!" she declared forthrightly. "He was paying the most objectionable attentions to my sister-in-law, which is only what one might expect of a man who is a byword in the most scandalous weeklies. Not that I read them! But I've heard him linked with a dozen names: Lady Purbright, Lady Amelia Gault, Mrs. Bassington-Cove, Gussie Warnecker . . ."

"Just a moment!" Three of those names were familiar to Alec. "Miss Dalrymple, are you taking this down?"

"Names are tough."

"Would you mind repeating them, Lady Josephine, and continuing a little more slowly?"

"I'm not telling you anything you couldn't find out from past issues of *Tittle-Tattle*," she said anxiously.

"Of course not, ma'am. You are simply saving me time and trouble, and everything you say will remain confidential." As hearsay it was not allowable in evidence, however useful he might find it.

She looked to Sir Hugh, who nodded, faintly amused, to Alec's relief. He was very much interested—and puzzled—by the names she reeled off. She recalled another five of Astwick's presumed conquests before her memory ran dry.

"There are more, Mr. Fletcher, but they have slipped my mind."

"You've been extremely helpful, Lady Josephine. If any more occur to you, be so good as to write them down for me. I don't suppose you happen to know—by reputation or through staying in the same house as Lord Stephen on a previous occasion, perhaps—whether he was also in the habit of, er, paying his attentions to, er, females of the lower orders?"

"Did he run after the maids, you mean? I don't believe so. In a sense, you might say that he was fastidious, though that is far too complimentary a word for the rotter. But he did demand a certain breeding in his mistresses."

Alec bit back a smile at her frankness. "I see. Now, one more question, if you please. Did you know, before Lord Stephen spoke of it last night, that he was in the habit of skating before breakfast?"

Her ladyship snorted. "Pure bunkum! As though there were something positively virtuous about exercising at dawn. Yes, I did know. My maid told me it was quite a joke in the servants' hall."

"Thank you, ma'am. I need not trouble you further for the present." Alec rose to his feet.

"No trouble, Chief Inspector. It's our duty to help the police. A most worthy group of men, I'm sure. Hugh, shall I stay?"

"No, no, my love, no need." Her husband patted her hand. "I've a feeling we'll be talking business, and you know how anything to do with the City confuses you."

"Yes, dear. I'll be off then." Halfway to the door, Lady Josephine turned. "Just one thing, Mr. Fletcher," she said earnestly. "My brother didn't realize Lord Stephen was chasing after Annabel. I'm sure he didn't. He can't have. He never showed any sign that he knew."

"I shall take your opinion into consideration, ma'am," Alec assured her. Damn! he thought. People read too many detective novels these days.

"Yes, Chief Inspector," said Sir Hugh with a mocking smile, "even my wife has worked out that you think Astwick's death was no accident."

The keen-eyed baronet was going to be a worthy opponent, if opponent he proved to be. However, he was the one who had called in the Met, Alec reminded himself.

"I'm afraid I can't discuss that, sir," he said. "Will you tell me about Astwick's business dealings?"

"Stephen Astwick was a swindler, Mr. Fletcher. He never did anything straight if he could make a penny more by doing it crooked. I could give you particulars of dud investments, the names of many men he cheated, a few ruined, but I won't, unless you really need them."

"Not at present, thank you, sir, except that I'd like to know if he ever cheated you."

"I cut my eyeteeth long before he arrived in the City. And before you classify that as an evasive answer—no, he never attempted to embroil me in his fraudulent schemes, and I have no investments in any of his companies."

"Anyone else here now?"

"I've wondered about young Petrie. He's been nosing about the latest nonexistent South American silver mine, but if he's been bitten I don't believe he's aware of it yet."

"Hmmm," said Alec noncommittally.

"I ought to tell you, perhaps," Sir Hugh continued, "that in my opinion Astwick's holding company is a hollow sham which will collapse in shards when news of his death breaks. It couldn't have lasted much longer anyway."

"Good Lord!" Alec drew in a long breath and thanked heaven he'd never had the money to invest in stocks and shares.

"That, of course, is a secondary reason why I asked your Commissioner to send down a discreet man, the first being my concern for my wife's family."

"Lady Josephine's description of Astwick as an utter cad seems scarcely adequate."

"Adequate to his social misdeeds, I dare say, which is all that concerns my wife."

"May I ask, do you and Lady Josephine share a bedroom?" Seeing Sir Hugh stiffen, he added, "I should prefer not to have to ask the servants."

"We do."

"I understand you went down early to breakfast."

"I like to read *The Financial Times* in peace, so I am often the first to arrive in the breakfast room. The footman on duty gave me to understand such was the case this morning."

"You saw nothing of Astwick?"

"Nothing."

"Then I think that's all I need ask you for now. Thank you for your patience, Sir Hugh."

He nodded acknowledgement of Alec's thanks and started to leave the room. Like Lady Josephine, he

96

turned halfway to the door. "It's my turn for a parting word. My wife is as at home in society as I am in the City, Chief Inspector. What she has told you may be hearsay, but she'd not have repeated it had she not been convinced of its truth."

"Whew!" Miss Dalrymple exclaimed as the door closed behind him. "I suppose it must have been someone in residence here who chopped that hole? It sounds as if there are countless deceived husbands and swindled businessmen all over the country with excellent reasons to be out for Lord Stephen's blood!"

CHAPTER 6

Alec sent the footman for Lord Beddowe before responding to Miss Dalrymple. "It certainly would appear that Astwick was heading for a sticky end sooner or later. We'll check with the lodge-keeper whether he admitted anyone last night. However, I'm pretty sure someone in this house reached him first."

"Then why were you so interested in the names Lady Jo gave you?"

"You never miss a trick, do you? It's probably just an odd coincidence, but eight out of ten of those names are connected with the other case I'm working on."

She flipped through her notes. "She only remembered nine."

"Seven out of nine, then. A significant proportion, you'll allow."

"Yes, but connected how? What is your other case?"

She stood up and stretched, then moved to the fire and held out her hands to its warmth. "Come on, Mr. Fletcher," she said when he didn't answer, turning her head to look back at him. "I know it's none of my business, but you can't leave me dangling."

Alec shrugged. "A big jewel robbery. I'm sure you must have read about it in the papers."

"I saw a headline in the train yesterday, but I didn't have time to read any further."

"It looks like one of a series of burglaries of country houses, all over the south of England. In each case, the thieves have taken a huge haul of jewellery, chiefly from house-party guests, while ignoring other valuables."

"As if they knew what to look for."

"Exactly. We've recovered a lot of the smaller pieces from fences, but none of the major stones has turned up."

"Those seven women who were involved with Lord Stephen are all guests who were robbed at one time or another? The latest burglary was near here? And Lord Stephen turned up in the neighbourhood, having practically invited himself? It does sound vaguely fishy."

"Only vaguely, I'm afraid. But I would like to know his manservant's whereabouts."

"Isn't he back yet? I saw him drive off yesterday, before lunch. Perhaps he came back last night and chopped that hole in the ice, only you'd think he could come up with an easier and more certain way to dispose of his master if he wanted to."

"He might have wanted merely to inconvenience him."

"There must be a hundred thousand easier ways for a servant to inconvenience his employer!"

"True," he admitted.

"Lord Stephen might have met someone else there, though, by arrangement," Daisy suggested. "Someone who biffed him on the head and happened to have an axe in his motor-car."

"Interesting that he went down to meet this mysterious someone wearing his skates."

She grinned. "Well, perhaps not. No, a rendezvous with an outsider is out, and anyone in the house would have found somewhere inconspicuous to meet him indoors."

"Unless it was a moonlight tryst, a romantic skating party for two."

Daisy didn't care for that line of thinking. "It was far too cold to be romantic, and . . . Wait, he wouldn't have walked down there with skates on in the morning, either. What happened to his ordinary boots?"

"Now that is a very good . . ." Alec paused as the door opened. "Ah, Lord Beddowe."

"What's all this about?" the young man demanded aggressively. "I've told you all I know."

"I find further enquiries are necessary. Lord Wentwater was good enough to assure me of his family's cooperation."

"Oh, very well." Crossing the room towards the sofa Alec indicated, he suddenly stopped. "What the deuce are you doing in here, Daisy?"

She had slipped back to her window seat. With a reproachful glance at Beddowe, she picked up her pad and pencil, leaving Alec to answer.

"Miss Dalrymple is my stenographer."

"You can't expect me to answer your bally questions in the presence of a young lady."

"I admit that it is somewhat irregular. If you strongly object, we can go to the local police station to find an officer able to take down your statement."

"Good Lord, no! I suppose a Chief Inspector considers himself too important to take shorthand," he sneered.

"You need not write that down, Miss Dalrymple," Alec said dispassionately.

Beddowe noticed her shocked stare and had the grace to look a little ashamed of himself. Taunting one's inferiors was not part of the code of a gentleman. He didn't apologize, however, and he showed no sign of shame when he started talking about Astwick and his step-mother.

"It's too obvious for words," he said contemptuously. "Like a cheap, sordid melodrama. They were lovers in Italy, and then my father comes along, a wealthy peer infatuated enough to offer marriage, and she drops Astwick like a hot coal. Here she is, living on velvet, when who turns up but her lover, threatening to reveal all and wreck the cosy nest if she doesn't jump back into bed with him."

"Have you evidence that Astwick and Lady Wentwater were lovers?" Alec regretted that Miss Dalrymple had to hear such an outpouring of venom. Like the others, Beddowe appeared to have forgotten her presence.

"Not exactly evidence, but anyone could tell he had a hold over her, knew some nasty secret from her past. She had every reason to get rid of the bounder."

Alec couldn't resist a dig. "Naturally, for your father's sake, you did all you could to prevent Astwick's persecution of your stepmother."

"Protect that scheming adventuress, after she wheedled her way into my father's confidence! Of course, I'm sorry he's going to be disillusioned, but divorce isn't such a ghastly business nowadays, is it? As the guilty party, she wouldn't get a penny out of him. Oh yes, she hadn't much choice but to dispose of Astwick."

He seemed prepared to carry on endlessly in a similar vein. Alec stopped him with a question about Astwick's boots.

"Boots? I haven't the foggiest. They must have been by the bench at the bottom of the path, where we sit down to change, but I can't say I noticed them. I was carrying my own skating boots, and Miss Petrie's and Miss Dalrymple's."

"Who carried everything back up to the house?"

"I told the under-gardeners who moved the body to the boathouse to clear everything up. I suppose they put away the boathook and gaff and brought the rest back to the house. I wouldn't put it past them to swipe Astwick's boots. After all, he didn't need them any longer."

Much as he disliked Beddowe's attitude towards his

servants, Alec silently agreed that the theft was possible, and if that was the case, the boots might very well remain unaccounted for. Miss Dalrymple hadn't seen them, or she wouldn't have raised the point. Miss Petrie might have, though he'd think twice about believing anything she said with her overbearing guardians beside her. He'd have Tring question the under-gardeners, but it looked like another dead end.

He asked for the names of the gardeners, put a few more questions to Lord Beddowe, then let him go.

"What an absolute beast!" Daisy burst out as Mr. Fletcher rang the bell. "I know James egged Lord Stephen on, but I never would have guessed he had such a foul mind. And so frightfully vulgar! Annabel isn't at all . . ." She broke off as the footman came in.

"Mr. Wilfred, please," the detective requested.

"Mr. Geoffrey's come home, sir."

"Thank you. I'll see him first. By the way, is Lady Marjorie still out of circulation?"

"Yes, sir." Having abandoned disdain in favour of obedience, the footman now became communicative. "Cora, that's Lady Marjorie's maid, said as how Lady Josephine had her take another dose of that stuff the doctor left. Crying and carrying on something awful, she was."

"Mr. Geoffrey, then." He waited until the servant left before saying to Daisy, "You see what I mean about the servants discussing every sneeze! Dash it, I must see Lady Marjorie some time. What was it I wanted to ask Geoffrey?"

"Whether he saw Lord Stephen on his way to or at the lake," she told him, pleased that she remembered. She was glad she had taken on the job. It was fascinating, though she'd just as soon not have heard James's diatribe. "I can understand James resenting his father's second wife," she said with a frown, hunting through a drawer of the writing table for a pencil sharpener. "Annabel has taken his mother's place and diverted his father's attention from him. But why should he loathe her so bitterly?"

"In a word, money." He took the sharpener and her three pencils from her.

"Money? I don't believe she's at all an extravagant sort of person. She cares more for flowers than for fashion."

"Nonetheless," he explained, "she represents a drain on the estate that's liable to continue as long as Lord Beddowe lives. Also, there's always the possibility of children who would, I presume, be provided for out of his inheritance. He has motive enough to wish to break up the marriage."

"Enough to risk someone else's life in order to blame Annabel for it?" Daisy demanded, sceptical yet hopeful. As a villain, James was greatly to be preferred to Annabel.

"It's conceivable. On the other hand, a mere wetting would hardly have suited his purpose. I can't imagine Lord Wentwater divorcing his wife for playing a trick on the man who was trying to seduce her."

"No, but if James made Lord Stephen believe

Annabel was responsible, he might well have been angry enough to tell Lord Wentwater whatever his nasty secret was. Thank you." She took the three perfectly sharpened pencils he held out. "You won't let James influence your view of Annabel, will you?"

"I'll try not to," he promised, adding gently, "but you must be aware that it's difficult to blackmail someone who has led a blameless life."

"I know." Daisy's despondency was quickly overcome by curiosity. "I wonder what Wilfred did to give Lord Stephen a hold over him?"

"I hope to discover very shortly. Nothing, I trust, to shock a young lady."

"Nothing could possibly shock me as much as James's malevolence. I wonder if I ought to warn Phillip that he's not at all a suitable husband for Fenella."

"I shouldn't interfere, if I were you."

"I'll have to think about it. I expect Wilfred's misdeeds are innocent in comparison, gambling debts and borrowed money probably. He's that sort. Here he is," she said as the door opened. "Oh no, I forgot, Geoffrey first."

The large, stolid youth entered, still in riding breeches, his colour high from cold air and exercise. "You wanted to see me, sir?" he enquired, in the apprehensive tone of a schoolboy called to the headmaster's study.

"I shan't keep you a moment. What time did you leave this morning?"

"Eightish. Maybe a bit earlier."

"After breakfasting?"

"No, there's a farmhouse on the way to Freddy's that does a jolly decent spread. That's Freddy Venables. I was at school with him."

"I assume you've been told by now what has happened. Did you see Astwick this morning, either in the house or out-of-doors?"

"No, sir. The stables are at the back of the house and I went off that way, nowhere near the . . . the lake."

Daisy was surprised by the tremor in his voice. She wouldn't have thought he was so sensitive as to be shaken by the drowning he had not witnessed of a man he did not care about. Though possibly he was just disappointed to have missed all the excitement, she thought with sympathy. Finding a body would have been a ripping story with which to regale his pals at Cambridge.

"Chief?" A shining pink dome appeared around the door, its pristine glory set off by the luxuriant grey walrus moustache below. A massive body followed, clad in a regrettable suit of large yellow and tan checks. Stunned by this apparition, Daisy scarcely spared a glance for the wiry young man in modest brown serge who entered after him.

"Sergeant! I was beginning to think you lost in a snow-drift. Thank you, Mr. Beddowe, that will be all for now."

Geoffrey departed, and Mr. Fletcher introduced Detective Sergeant Tring and Detective Constable Piper to Daisy.

"Miss Dalrymple has been helping me," he explained. "I'd intended to have one of you take her place when you arrived, but I've other things for you to do. Piper, you'd better get down to the lake right away before it starts getting dark. Have a hunt around, for anything out of the way but especially for a pair of boots. I didn't see anything, but you never know. Have a word with the lodge-keeper. Ask if he opened the gates to anyone between dusk and dawn. And if not, see if you can find footprints approaching the lake from any direction other than the house."

"Sir!" The constable saluted and went out.

"Tom, let me explain what's going on. Miss Dalrymple, I count on you to interrupt if I leave anything out."

Mr. Fletcher's précis was rapid but comprehensive. Daisy admired his ability to bring all the necessary information together in a clear and concise account.

"Ah," said Sergeant Tring ruminatively when he finished.

"So I want you to tackle the staff. You're good at that."

"Ah." The sergeant winked at Daisy and preened his moustache. She gathered he had a way with female servants. Extraordinary, though no more extraordinary than the slimy Lord Stephen's conquests. "It's a rum thing," Tring elaborated on his monosyllable in a rumbling bass, "that there man of Lord Stephen's being missing. I've a notion he's the one could blow the gaff. You see, Chief, there's been developments." He glanced sideways at Daisy.

"You can speak before Miss Dalrymple, Tom. She knows about that case, too."

"Well, 'tain't much to go on, but we've picked up a fellow driving a motor that's been seen lurking about near the Flatford place on and off the last few days. Rang a bell, it did, and I went through the reports of the other jobs. Seems there's been a grey Lanchester spotted in three out of four."

"A grey Lanchester!" Daisy exclaimed. "Lord Stephen's car was a grey Lanchester."

"Is that so, miss. Don't happen to know the number-plate, do you?"

"I was too far away to read it, and I don't suppose I'd remember if I had. Jones, Lord Wentwater's chauffeur, is certain to know."

"Very true, miss. The one we've got is a London number, Chief. Inspector Gillett wired for identification. Obscured by mud, it was—a right laugh, that, with the paintwork gleaming, the brass bright as gold, and no mud this side of the Channel that's not froze solid. We're holding chummie on that and on not having no driving license on him. The inspector sent his dabs up to the Yard, too."

"Dabs?" Daisy queried.

"His fingerprints, miss. To find out if he's got a record."

"I take it he's not talking?" Mr. Fletcher asked.

"Dumb as the knave of diamonds, Chief." Sergeant Tring's little brown eyes twinkled as Daisy laughed. He was brighter than he looked, she decided.

"Astwick may turn out to have been the king of diamonds," said the Chief Inspector dryly.

"Not to mention king of hearts!" Daisy put in.

"Miss Dalrymple and I already had a vague inkling of some connection. If the number-plates match, well and good, but it wouldn't surprise me if the plates turn out to be faked or recently stolen. Either way, we'll search his room before we go, Tom. Let's get the interviewing done first. On your way to the servants' quarters, you'd better ring up Gillett and tell him on no account to let the chummie go; and tell the footman to send in Mr. Wilfred."

"Right you are, Chief." He removed his bulk from the room with an unexpectedly light, swift tread.

Daisy was bursting with questions. "Why would they bother to cover a stolen number-plate with mud? It just made it conspicuous."

"I'd say that was the servant's idea, not Astwick's, if he is in fact involved. He strikes me as too canny a man to do anything so stupid."

"But a Lanchester is a pretty conspicuous motor-car to use in the first place. I'd use a Morris, or a Ford, something people wouldn't look at twice."

"Astwick would have looked pretty conspicuous rolling up to Wentwater Court in a Morris Oxford," Mr. Fletcher pointed out patiently. "Admittedly his man could have switched vehicles before he approached the burgled house, but that would complicate matters no end. Whereas a Lanchester is not likely to be stopped, short of an outright breach of the law, because it can only belong to a man of wealth and therefore of influence."

"So . . . Oh, botheration!" Daisy scurried to the window seat and took up notebook and pencil as Wilfred breezed in.

"What ho, my dear fellow!" he greeted the detective airily. "What can I do to help the jolly old coppers? Hullo, hullo, playing the scribe, are you, Daisy?"

She nodded and gave him a small smile, but left it to Mr. Fletcher to answer.

To Alec's ears, the slight young man in his natty suit sounded distinctly nervous. Seated, he fidgeted constantly, crossing and uncrossing his legs, straightening his tie, smoothing his sleek, pomaded hair. When Alec took a moment to shuffle a pile of irrelevant papers, Wilfred Beddowe burst into speech again.

"Rotten business, this, what? Gave me a nasty turn when my man brought the news with my tea. I mean to say, a guest here, not just any old passing tramp."

"More particularly your guest, Mr. Beddowe, I understand."

"Yes, I invited him," he agreed with a hint of his elder brother's belligerence. "What of it?"

"May I ask why you invited Lord Stephen Astwick to join a small family party?"

"Happened to run into him in town just before Christmas. I thought he might fancy a glimpse of the old homestead."

"Let me get this straight. You happened to run into Astwick in London—in your club, perhaps, or in the street?"

"At Ciro's."

"Ah, in a nightclub—and you thought he might like to see Wentwater Court, so you invited him down for a few days. You and he must have been very good friends." He gave Wilfred an enquiring look which elicited silence. "Interesting, when he was nearly twice your age. No doubt he was in some sort a mentor?" Silence. "A pity you should choose a rogue to guide you."

"I didn't! He wasn't! We weren't even friends."

"You invited a rogue who was not your friend to stay with your family?" Alec asked with feigned incredulity.

"Yes. No. I didn't want to but he insisted," he said sulkily. "Dash it, I knew Marjie would be pleased at least."

"But you were not pleased."

"Pleased to be stuck in the same house with that infernal fellow!" Wilfred exclaimed, shuddering.

"Then why . . . ?"

"All right, if you must know, I owed him money."

"Gambling debts?"

"How I wish it had been! I'd've gone to the gov'nor sooner than let Astwick blackmail me. He'd have read the riot act, maybe cut my allowance and gated me, but he'd have paid up. He's a bit of a fossil, my father, but not such a bad old stick."

"Then what was it you couldn't tell Lord Wentwater?" Wilfred crimsoned. "Breach of promise," he confessed.

"Whispering sweet nothings to a shopgirl, eh?" Alec

hoped his voice had covered the muffled snort from Miss Dalrymple.

"A chorus-girl."

"Letters?" He shook his head as Wilfred nodded. "Silly young chump. So Astwick lent you money to buy her off and then threatened to tell your father."

"The pater would have blown me sky-high. I'm *glad* Astwick's dead," said Wilfred defiantly. "They're all sitting around trying to pretend nothing's happened, but I want to break out the champagne."

"Yet it gave you a nasty turn when you heard of his demise."

"Gad, yes. I mean to say, not the sort of thing a chap likes to hear first thing in the morning when he's not feeling too bobbish."

"First thing? What time was this, Mr. Beddowe?"

"Oh, half past tennish." His confession over, he was regaining his insouciant air. He took out a chased silver cigarette case and offered it to Alec, who shook his head. Wilfred lit up.

"You had a late night last night?"

"Not at all. Went to bed early as a matter of fact. There's nothing to do in the country. I daresay I was all tucked up cosy by one, but my man has strict instructions never to wake me before ten-thirty."

"You didn't retire immediately after the weather forecast?"

"No, Jimmy—my brother—and Petrie and I went to the smoking room for a nightcap. But Jimmy's a yokel at heart and Petrie had this asinine notion of skating with Astwick at dawn, so we weren't long."

Alec pricked up his ears. "Mr. Petrie told you he intended to go skating at dawn?"

"He told everyone, when Astwick was blathering on about Swedish exercises and fitness, after dinner. Said it sounded like a ripping idea. All rot, if you ask me. I take it he came to his senses, or he'd have been there to pull Astwick out."

Unless he'd been the one to fall in, Alec thought. This put an altogether different complexion on things. Who knew Petrie planned to skate early? Did someone not care if they injured the wrong victim? Or could that amiable ass possibly be the intended victim?

CHAPTER 7

I completely forgot about Phillip's pronouncement," said Daisy, full of remorse. "It changes everything, doesn't it?"

"It does alter matters somewhat," the Chief Inspector agreed tiredly, rubbing his eyes.

"You see, I know him jolly well and I was pretty sure he wouldn't turn out at dawn, so it didn't make much impression on me. No one else knows him so well, though, except Fenella, so everyone else *may* have expected him actually to skate with Lord Stephen."

"Does your memory agree with Wilfred's as to who constitutes everyone?"

"Lord Wentwater and Sir Hugh weren't in the drawing-room. I can't say whether the rest were all listening." She thought hard. "The only others who joined in the conversation were Lady Josephine and Marjorie, and Marjorie was so busy fluttering her eyelashes at Lord Stephen she may not have heard what Phillip said."

"Marjorie! I *must* speak to that young lady but I can't wait about for the sedative to wear off. I suppose tomorrow will have to do. Let's see, that means Lord Wentwater and Sir Hugh were unaware of Mr. Petrie's plans, and Lord Beddowe, Geoffrey, Lady Marjorie, Lady Josephine, and Lady Wentwater may or may not have known."

"It doesn't help much, does it?" Daisy said with a sigh. "I can't believe anyone would have deliberately risked hurting Phillip instead of Lord Stephen—he's such an inoffensive idiot!—but we can't be sure who heard him."

"It shouldn't be difficult to . . . Ah, Piper. Any luck?"

Detective Constable Piper entered the room with the heavy tramp of a policeman on the beat. Daisy saw Mr. Fletcher wince, remembered Tring's catlike tread, and deduced that Piper had only recently joined the plain-clothes branch.

"Nothing, sir. No boots nor nothing out of the way. The bloke at the lodge didn't let anyone in, nor did his missus. And there weren't no footprints, 'cepting on the paths and the drive." The young man appeared bitterly disappointed. "Couldn't someone've come up behind the house, sir, and walked round by where the snow's trampled?"

"A good thought, Constable. Would that be possible, Miss Dalrymple?"

"Possible, certainly, but it's miles to any road other than the lane by the lodge. And from the lane you'd have to walk miles around to come up behind the house without leaving footprints near the drive."

"I suppose someone could have left a vehicle outside the park wall, climbed over, and tramped for miles through the snow in the dark just to play a trick," the Chief Inspector mused, "but it seems highly improbable. Besides, it's not likely any outsider would know Astwick had taken to skating at dawn since the lake froze, let alone that he'd be on his own. No, I think the mysterious someone is out. Any other ideas, Piper?"

"Just that, seeing the hole in the ice is evidence, sir, p'raps I ought to report as the wind's in the south and like as not there'll be a thaw afore morning."

"Thank you, that's certainly worth knowing. Luckily we have excellent photographs, thanks to Miss Dalrymple. Well, there's no sense in your looking for an axe. I'm sure there are several about in the outbuildings, and no one would have gone out without gloves last night just to provide us with fingerprints. You'd better relieve Miss Dalrymple."

"Sir!" Pad and pencil appeared on the instant.

"I don't want to be relieved," Daisy protested.

The daunting stare he turned on her, intensified by dark, baleful eyebrows, made her quail. It vanished in a moment and he grinned. "I'd almost forgotten you're not one of my officers. I appreciate your hard work,

Miss Dalrymple, but at present the best thing you can do to help is to begin transcribing your notes. I promise I'll not leave without letting you know what's going on."

She pulled a face. "Oh, very well. I'll try and get them done before you go. Do you mind spelling mistakes? I type faster if I don't have to worry about spelling."

"Just as long as you think I'll be able to make a guess at what the garbled words are supposed to be."

"I'm not *that* bad! Cheerio for now, then."

As she moved towards the door, Piper hurried forward to open it for her. Before he reached it, it opened and Lord Wentwater appeared. He held the door for her with his usual grave politeness. Turning towards the stairs, Daisy decided she was after all quite glad to be relieved of her note-taking duties. She respected the earl and didn't want to listen while he explained or defended—or incriminated—himself.

Alec would have been happy to avoid that duty. Not for a moment did he believe in the innate superiority of the aristocracy. The malignant James Beddowe would have disabused him of that notion if he had. What concerned him was their perceived superiority, the influence they wielded by virtue of their birth and their belief in their own importance.

Lord Wentwater had never doubted his right to special treatment, Alec was certain. Nonetheless, he had to admire the earl's calm dignity and iron self-control. Impossible to imagine this distinguished gentleman on his knees hacking at the ice with an axe.

Yet Alec knew from experience that a man in the throes of jealousy and hate is capable of actions he'd never dream of otherwise.

Buoyed by that knowledge, he gently steered Lord Wentwater towards the seat where he wanted him. Even more than with his other suspects, it was essential to be able to read every nuance of expression on the earl's face.

Piper slipped inconspicuously into the window seat favoured by Miss Dalrymple, and Alec sat down opposite the earl, not waiting to be invited. Here, he was in charge. "Would you please give me your opinion of Stephen Astwick, sir?" he requested.

"As I am sure you have heard by now, Chief Inspector," Lord Wentwater said in an even voice, "the man was an unmitigated blackguard."

"Yet you entertained him in your home."

His mouth tightened. "No doubt you have discovered that Astwick is the brother of the Marquis of Brinbury. Brinbury and I went to school together, are members of the same clubs, sit in the House of Lords together. Astwick also belonged to some of those clubs. While I would never have invited him to Wentwater, it would have been an intolerable insult to ask him to leave."

"I understand his own family had disowned him. Have they been informed of his demise?" Alec ought to have seen to that long ago. If only there were more hours in a day! Two nights' lack of sleep was suddenly catching up with him at just the wrong moment, and he saw no prospect of a full eight hours tonight.

"I telephoned Brinbury."

"And?"

"He asked me to let him know when his brother was safely underground," Lord Wentwater said dryly. "Perhaps you find it difficult to understand, Chief Inspector, but the views of his family in no way altered my obligation towards Astwick as a member of that family. No doubt you have colleagues at Scotland Yard with whom you are obliged to associate against your wishes."

True, but he didn't take them home, Alec silently protested, and even the most objectionable had never chased his wife, let alone blackmailed her. Was it possible the earl had been as blind to Astwick's conduct as his sister believed?

"The laws of hospitality supersede the natural desire for a faithful wife?" he asked, trying to make the question sound like simple curiosity rather than impertinent prying.

"Astwick was not my wife's lover!" The anger in Lord Wentwater's tone was unconvincing, and for the first time in the course of the interview he did not meet Alec's eyes. A muscle twitched twice at the corner of his mouth.

An outright lie seemed out of character. As Alec murmured an apology for his crassness, he wondered whether the earl might be attempting to convince himself, as much as his interrogator, of Lady Wentwater's faithfulness. A proud man, he'd not easily admit to himself that he had been cuckolded. Possibly he was also a charitable man, eager to give his wife the benefit of the doubt. Possibly he was simply an old man with a young wife who accepted as inevitable that she would take lovers.

No, not an old man. He must be about fifteen years older than Alec, still the erect and vigorous product of an active, healthy country life. He looked quite robust enough to satisfy a young wife—or to hack a hole in the ice.

Alec rubbed his eyes. God, what he'd give for a pipe and a cup of coffee, or even tea, but he couldn't ask Lord Wentwater for it any more than he could ask him whether he shared a bedroom with his lady. Thank heaven Tring would be finding out that most pertinent bit of information from the servants.

No doubt the sergeant would also be wallowing in tea and cakes. He had that effect on cooks for some inscrutable reason, witness his waistline.

Doggedly Alec continued questioning the earl. He felt as if he'd lost the thread of the investigation, or rather, as if he'd never found it. His questions and the answers seemed equally irrelevant, and he wished Miss Dalrymple were there to discuss them with him. With any luck everything would fall into place when he talked to Lady Wentwater, though it was still conceivable that her only connection with Astwick's death was as the object of the gallantries that roused Lady Marjorie's jealousy.

Why had that death so shattered Lady Marjorie that she needed several doses of a sedative? Was she truly broken-hearted over the loss of a man she was deeply in love with? Or was she appalled that her vengeful mischief, intended to discomfort, had killed him?

"I take it this farce is at an end?" said Lord Wentwater impatiently.

Alec realized that he had failed to follow up an answer with another question. "I have nothing more to ask you for the moment, sir," he said. "May I have your permission to search Astwick's bedroom?"

"If you must."

"Also, I still need to speak to Lady Wentwater, and to Lady Marjorie, who, I gather, is not to be seen today. I shall have to return tomorrow. My constable will remain here. I'm afraid I must request that no one leave Wentwater before my return."

"Very well." Lord Wentwater appeared to be resigned to the continuance of the investigation.

Either innocent or very sure of himself, Alec decided as the earl left the room. Right at that moment, he didn't care which. He only hoped he'd make sense when he was talking to Lady Wentwater.

The footman took a confounded time to answer the bell. When he arrived, he preceded a parlourmaid bearing a heavily laden tea tray.

"Miss Dalrymple's orders, sir," he announced.

"Bless the woman!" Alec fell upon the teapot like a fox on a hencoop.

Piper was not far behind. "No lunch, sir," he explained, putting away dainty, triangular, trustless Gentleman's Relish sandwiches by the fistful.

"At least you had more than two hours sleep last

night," Alec grunted, pouring his second cup. The tea was no wishy-washy Earl Grey but a strong Darjeeling brew, which he put down to Tring's presence in the kitchen. It was wonderfully revivifying.

Resuscitated, he felt ready for anything by the time the footman ushered in Lady Wentwater. Nonetheless, her loveliness took away his breath.

Miss Dalrymple had said she was young and beautiful. He had not expected the figure of an Aphrodite, undisguised by her fashionably shapeless crêpe-de-Chine tea-dress, and the exquisite face of a sorrowing Madonna. Her dark, melancholy eyes cried out for sympathy. Alec knew he'd have to fight to maintain a balance between favouring her and reacting too far the other way.

No wonder the earl had married her, Astwick had pursued her, and Lady Marjorie was jealous of her. Lord Beddowe's antipathy might be based more on sheer sexual jealousy than he himself realized. Fenella Petrie was a candle to her sun.

But Lady Wentwater was more moon than sun. Pale from weariness of climbing heaven and shining on the earth . . . Shelley, wasn't it? Daisy Dalrymple was really more to Alec's taste. Pretty rather than beautiful, but cheerful rather than tragic, she reminded him of Joan, who had never let slender means nor the hazards of war dampen her spirits.

Surely Lady Wentwater ought to have perked up a trifle now that her persecutor was gone. Was it possible Miss Dalrymple had misinterpreted the situation, that the young countess had been Astwick's willing lover and now grieved for his death? She didn't look strong enough to chop a hole in the ice, though she was taller than average and desperation could augment a person's strength in the most amazing way.

As Alec greeted her, she looked around the room distractedly. "I thought . . . someone said Daisy was here. Miss Dalrymple." Her voice was low and soft, with a pleading note.

"She was, but my constable has taken over from her. Would you like someone with you? Another lady, or your maid?"

She bit her lip. "Miss Dalrymple, please, may she come back?"

"Of course, Lady Wentwater." He sent the footman to fetch her, and while they waited he asked with considerable curiosity, "You have known Miss Dalrymple long?"

"I met her for the first time yesterday, but she is very . . . *simpatica,* the Italians say. I feel she is already my friend."

If a stranger so quickly became a friend, she must feel herself friendless indeed in her husband's house, and who could blame her? Her husband and his sister suspected her fidelity; her stepson hated her; her stepdaughter regarded her as a rival. Whatever she had done, Alec pitied her.

He had to warn her. "You are aware that Miss Dalrymple has been actively aiding me in this investigation?" Nodding, she managed a hesitant smile. "I believe Daisy would throw herself wholeheartedly into whatever situation she came across. She's not the sort to stand by and let things happen."

A trait that might prove awkward at times, Alec thought.

Daisy hurried in, breathless, a few minutes later. "Mr. Fletcher, you need me? I haven't quite finished the typing."

"Lady Wentwater requested your presence."

"Oh, Annabel, I didn't see you. Of course I'll stay if you want me." Sitting down on the sofa beside the countess, she impulsively took her hand. It was cold, and trembled slightly. Annabel had cause to dread the coming inquisidon, whether she had anything to do with Lord Stephen's death or not.

The detective, at his most formidable, went straight to the point "Was Stephen Astwick blackmailing you, Lady Wentwater?" he asked abruptly.

"Oh, no, he never demanded money."

"Money is not always what a blackmailer seeks to extort."

"I suppose not. Yes, you could call it blackmail. He threatened to . . . betray me if I refused to . . . to . . ." She faltered, clutching Daisy's hand.

"To become his mistress. Did you?"

"No! I put him off and put him off. It was horrible! He didn't even really want me so much as he wanted revenge. He wanted to ruin my life, one way or another."

"Revenge?"

"I had refused him before. Once, when I was a girl, he asked me to marry him, and then later, in Italy, he tried . . . but my . . . my first husband forced him to leave me alone. I think Rupert knew something about Stephen he couldn't afford to have known."

"Birds of a feather," Mr. Fletcher grunted, and Daisy glared at him.

To her surprise, Annabel straightened and flew to her first husband's defence. "Oh no, Rupert would never have blackmailed anyone. He just used his knowledge to defend me."

"I beg your pardon, I spoke out of turn." He passed his hand wearily across his brow. "I plead fatigue. What was it Astwick threatened to reveal to Lord Wentwater?"

"That has not the least relevance to your enquiry," Annabel said with dignity. She had recovered her composure—and Mr. Fletcher had lost the initiative.

"As you will. Let it pass, for the moment. You will not deny that you loathed and feared Astwick?"

"How can I? He was a fiend."

"You hated him enough to kill him?"

A tremor ran through her and her grip on Daisy's hand tightened again. "Perhaps. I don't know. If I had known how. Do you mean you suspect that his death wasn't an accident?"

"It seems probable that the hole in the ice was deliberately cut."

"Why should I do that? He'd be as likely just to take a wetting as to drown. I tell you, he wanted to wreck my life far more than he wanted to . . . seduce me. The first thing he'd do would be to go to Henry. I'd have gained nothing."

Ay, there's the rub. The only bit of *Hamlet* Daisy remembered from school trickled through her thoughts. Whether 'twas nobler in the mind to suffer the slings and arrows of outrageous fortune, or to take arms against a sea of troubles, and by opposing end them . . . but Annabel's troubles would not have ended if Lord Stephen had merely been soaked to the skin. In Daisy's view, she was in the clear.

Mr. Fletcher asked her a few more halfhearted questions, then let her go with thanks for her frankness. "Piper, find out how Sergeant Tring's getting along," he ordered, and slumped back into his chair.

"Not enough sleep?" Daisy queried.

"Just a couple of hours, two nights in a row."

"Well, make sure you have at least eight hours tonight," she said severely, "or you won't be fit for anything tomorrow. How can you solve one case, let alone two, if you can't think straight?"

"I can't," he admitted with a rueful smile. "I feel as if I've run headfirst into a brick wall and I'm not sure whether it's an extraordinarily confusing case or I'm just confused."

"I'm confused too, though after all it is my first case."

"And your last, I sincerely trust!"

"Probably," said Daisy, sighing. "It's very interesting but rather painful. Annabel couldn't have done it, could she? It wouldn't make sense."

"Not much. The weather wasn't exactly suitable for her to lure him to a romantic midnight tryst by the lake, sock him on the head, and drop him in."

"Besides, he wouldn't have been wearing skates."

"Damn those missing boots!" said Mr. Fletcher explosively. "I beg your pardon for the language, Miss Dalrymple, but it's enough to try the patience of a saint. What happened to them?"

"I don't mind the language," she assured him, "but won't you call me Daisy? I rather fancy calling you Chief."

"My name's Alec."

"Alec in private, Chief when your officers are around. Perhaps Sergeant Tring has found the boots."

"Them boots?" The stout sergeant had entered the room unnoticed with his peculiarly silent tread, which Piper, following, appeared to be trying to imitate. "Sorry, Chief, the gardeners don't remember how many pair they carried up. Albert, the bootboy, thinks he cleaned a pair of Astwick's, but it might've been the day before and he hasn't a clue if they was his only boots. And they might've been someone else's. Not too bright, our Albert. The vally can tell us that, if he'll talk, which it's my belief he will when he hears about his master's nasty end."

"If your chummie is in fact Astwick's manservant. Any luck with the number-plate?"

"The number we got on the Lanchester is quite different from what Jones remembers on Astwick's, and Sir Hugh's chauffeur, Hammond, agrees with him. But this vallychauffeur Payne's description matches chummie." He grinned. "I couldn't have put it better meself. 'Ferret-face,' says the cook. 'More like a weasel,' says her ladyship's maid."

"Do the earl and countess share a room?"

"They do, but his lordship's rally hemmed and hawed and allowed as how his lordship's been known to sleep in his dressing-room. I couldn't pin him down as to the last few days, Chief. A cagey laddie and I didn't want to push too hard in case he shut up altogether."

"Quite right. We'll have another go tomorrow if it seems necessary."

"I talked to the chambermaid while I was gone," Daisy put in. "She said none of the staff much liked Astwick, but no one had a specific grievance against him, either. He never said a pleasant word, but nor was he actively unpleasant."

"That's what I heard, too, miss," said Tring. "He was indifferent to them and they was indifferent to him's the impression I got."

"No help there, then," the Chief Inspector sighed. "It looks like one of the family. If only we could pin down the time the hole was made to something less than twelve hours! No one has an alibi for the whole period. At least, did you find out anything else useful, Tom?"

"Nowt vital. I'll give you the rest of the dope on the way back to Winchester, to save time, shall I? Now why don't you let me and Piper search Astwick's room while you have a bit of a kip, Chief?"

"Is it so obvious I'm running out of steam? All right,

Tom, go ahead. I'll put my feet up, if Miss Dalrymple will excuse me."

"There's a footstool by the fireplace," said Daisy. "That will be just the thing."

Piper sped to fetch it, saluting with a blush when Daisy thanked him. He and Tring went off and Alec settled back with a sigh, loosening his necktie, his booted feet on the crewelwork footstool.

"You'd be more comfortable without your boots," Daisy suggested.

"But how embarrassing if someone came in to make a confession and found me shoeless."

"When I leave, I'll tell the footman not to let anyone in without warning you first. And I *will* leave you to sleep, but you did promise to tell me what Lord Wentwater said."

Alec bent down and untied his bootlaces. "He denied that Astwick was his wife's lover."

"You didn't expect him not to, did you?"

"Not really." Slipping off the boots, he wiggled his toes as he leaned back again.

"So what it comes down to is whether you believe he believes she's not." Daisy noticed that the toes of his navy socks were neatly darned. Had he mended them himself, or was there a woman in his life? She quickly looked up.

He was already asleep, his head drooping to one side. Daisy fetched a cushion and gently stuffed it between his ear and the wing of the chair. He didn't stir.

Before going upstairs to finish the typing, Daisy

asked the way to Lord Stephen's bedroom. It was at the far end of the east wing, in a corridor parallel to the one where her room was located. The two corridors were connected by a third, off which were situated the earl and countess's suite on one side, the linen-room and more bedrooms on the other.

As Daisy reached the corner, a housemaid came out of a room carrying a coalscuttle.

"Was that Lord Stephen's room?" Daisy asked her. "No, miss, Mr. Geoffrey's. That one next to the end, t'other side o' t'bathroom, were Lord Stephen's. Them p'leecemen's in there now, miss."

"Thank you."

The maid bobbed a curtsy and disappeared through a swing-door in the opposite wall, presumably to the back stairs. Daisy went on to the door she'd pointed out, knocked, and entered.

Tring looked round, his frown clearing as he saw her. "Ah, it's you, miss. Does the Chief want summat?"

"No, he's fast asleep. I just wondered if you've found anything yet."

"We only just started, miss. I 'spect the Chief'll tell you if we comes across owt of interest. A real help, you've been, and no mistake."

"Oh, well, it was just lucky that I took those photographs and . . ."

"Sergeant!" Piper emerged backwards from the wardrobe, waving a Manila envelope. "Beg pardon, miss. Look here, Sarge, I found it in a sort of a hidden pocket in the lining of his overcoat."

"You'll go far, laddie, you'll go far," said Tring benevolently, taking the envelope and opening it. "Now what have we here. Ah, the Chief'll want to see this. Two passports and . . . well, knock me down with a feather! So Lord Stephen Astwick and his ferret was planning to scarper, was they?"

"Was . . . I mean, were they?" Daisy demanded. "Booked on the S.S. *Orinoco*, sailing from Southampton 3:00 P.M. day after tomorrow, for Rio."

CHAPTER 8

D o you have to wake him?" Daisy gazed down upon the semirecumbent Chief Inspector. His face relaxed in sleep, he looked years younger.

"Bless you, miss, he'll have me hide if I don't, and quite right, too. I'll see he gets a decent kip tonight, but we got to get back to Winchester first."

"He said I'm to stop here, Sarge," said Piper apprehensively. "No one's to leave, but if they try, what'm I s'posed to do?"

"He don't expect the impossible, laddie. You're a reminder, that's what you are, a reminder of the majesty of the law."

The constable's shoulders squared and a determined light shone in his eyes.

Daisy laid her hand on Alec's shoulder and gently shook him. "Chief? *Chief,*" she said softly. "Time to wake up."

Muscles tensed beneath her hand and he sat up

straight as his eyes flickered open. "Wha'?" he mumbled, thick tongued. "Daisy?"

"I finished typing the notes." She had been politely but firmly dismissed from Lord Stephen's room while Tring completed the search. "I put them with your other papers. But the sergeant has something much more exciting for you."

"Tom?" Alec was already alert, kicking away the footstool and fumbling for his boots as Tring waved the Manila envelope at him. "What have you found?"

"Young Piper here found a ticket to Brazil, Chief, and there's this, too." He flourished a dark brown leather despatch case, then set it on the stool. "Locked with a fancy combination lock, it is."

Alec groaned. "I don't suppose Astwick left the number lying about."

"No, Chief, but it just so happens as we found a scrap of paper with a number on it in the pocket of the laddie in the Lanchester. Inspector Gillett kept it, of course, but it just so happens as Detective Constable Piper has a habit of memorizing stray numbers."

"The first part's me auntie's birthday, sir," Piper explained eagerly, "and the last bit's the number of inches in an elf. Forty-five sir," he added as they all looked at him blankly.

Shaking his head in wonderment, Alec gestured at the despatch case. "Give it a try, Ernie."

"Yes, *Chief!*" Beaming, he started rotating the lock.

Alec and Tring exchanged a significant nod. A rite of

130

passage had taken place: Piper had earned his place on Alec's team.

The lock clicked open. Alec leaned down, unfastened the brass catch, and opened the case. On top lay another Manila envelope, larger than the first. He removed it, opened it, and slid a sheaf of papers halfway out.

"Bearer bonds," he said, but the others were staring at the case, which was filled with small drawstring bags of yellowish chamois leather.

Alec reached for the nearest. Loosening the drawstring, he tipped the contents onto the palm of his hand. As he tilted his hand this way and that, the electric light struck blue fire from the huge cabochon-cut star sapphire.

A vast contentment filled him. "Mrs. Bassington-Cove's Star of Ceylon." From a second pouch he spilled out six glittering diamonds, smaller than the sapphire but perfectly matched. "We've got the goods, Tom. Let's get going. I find myself eager to have a little chat with your Lanchester driver."

"Right, Chief. I'll drive so's you can kip, but we'll take your motor, shall we? You won't want to risk young Ernie having to use it in an emergency."

"Hey, what d'you mean!" Piper protested.

Alec grinned. "I'll have to risk it. You're right, Tom, you'd better drive, and you'll never fit behind the wheel of mine. It's an Austin Seven," he explained to Daisy, slipping the sapphire and diamonds back into their chamois bags, depositing them and the envelope with the rest, and relocking the despatch case. "Tom can barely squeeze into the passenger seat. More to the point, this lot will be safer in the official car till we can lock it up in the safe at the station."

"I wish I could come," she said wistfully. "I'm dying to know what the ferret has to say. Don't look so worried, I know I can't."

"You may learn something useful here," he consoled her. "Keep your eyes and ears open, won't you? We'll be back tomorrow. Tom, will you bring the car round, please? I must leave Lord Wentwater a receipt for the loot in case Astwick's family kicks up a fuss about the disappearance from his room of a fortune in gems and bonds."

As Tring left the Blue Salon, the dressing gong sounded through the house. Reluctantly Daisy followed him.

On her way to her room, she stopped to see how Marjorie was doing. Awake, though dopey, she clung to Daisy's hand and wept. Nonetheless, Daisy received the impression that her grief was not profound, in fact that the tears were a mask. If Marjorie was capable of deep feeling, Lord Stephen had not evoked it.

She was growing cynical, Daisy reproached herself as she went on to her own room. Just because she had put him down as a nasty specimen the moment she met him, she refused to believe anyone could fall in love with him.

On the other hand, Marjorie didn't need to be desperately in love for his indifference to make her furious, a matter of hurt pride rather than spurned love. She might

132

have wanted to punish him, or she might have hoped to win him over by lavishing sympathy on him after his wetting. Either way, chopping up the ice made much more sense for Marjorie than for Annabel.

Running late, Daisy hurriedly changed. She put on her old grey dress again, since there had after all been a death just this morning and her best dress was rather on the bright side.

Drew announced dinner two minutes after she reached the drawing-room, so she had no time for the cocktail she felt in need of. A glass of wine with the hors-d'oeuvres and a second with the soup perked her up no end, and she refused a third with the fish. She noticed that wineglasses around the table were being refilled with abnormal regularity. Yet everyone was sombre, speaking in low voices to next-door neighbours or not at all. Having the police in the house was as sobering as if the death had been in the family. Daisy was glad she was seated between the urbane Sir Hugh and the silent Geoffrey, neither of whom was likely to embarrass her with questions about the investigation.

Coffee, brandy, and liqueurs were served in the drawing-room. Everyone was present, perhaps feeling there was safety in numbers.

Lady Josephine, her colour high, said defiantly, "I don't see why we shouldn't have a quiet rubber of bridge." She looked around for players.

"Do you play bridge?" Daisy asked Annabel.

"Badly."

She lowered her voice. "Do you *like* to play?"

"Not at all. It's the sort of thing a hostess can't always escape."

Daisy took her arm. "Then quick, come over here and tell me about the gardens in Italy. Are they all as formal as what we call an Italian garden? Patterns of square box hedges and dreary cypresses like ninepins?"

Annabel smiled. "I take it you play bridge but hate it."

"I wish I'd never learned," said Daisy with a shudder.

They sat down on a sofa at some distance from the fireplace. Sir Hugh, Phillip, and James joined Lady Josephine at the card table; Wilfred chatted brightly with Fenella, the taciturn Geoffrey sitting with them though not taking part in the conversation as far as Daisy could see; Lord Wentwater sat by the fire reading *The Field*.

Daisy kept an eye on them all as Annabel described the garden of the ramshackle villa near Naples where she had lived. A wilderness of pink oleanders, purple bougainvillea, pale blue plumbago, and scarlet hibiscus, it had been anything but formal.

"It was gloriously colourful, and Rupert loved to paint it," she said in a low voice, "but I missed forget-me-nots and daffodils."

"Rupert was an artist?"

"Yes. He wasn't at all like what the detective seemed to think. He was gentle, and vague, and not very enterprising, and he didn't care about money, which was just as well as he hadn't much. My aunt—the aunt who brought me up—deeply disapproved of him and refused to let me marry him."

"So you ran away with him?"

"He had a weak chest and he was advised to go to a warmer climate. I couldn't bear never to see him again, so I went too."

"How often I wish I had taken the bull by the horns," Daisy exclaimed bitterly. "Even if we had only had a few days together . . ." Her throat tightened and she blinked hard.

Annabel laid a comforting hand on her arm. "Your parents disapproved of the man you loved? Or his circumstances?"

"Oh, his income was adequate and his family socially acceptable, but he was a Quaker, a Conscientious Objector. Instead of doing the proper thing and getting blown up in a trench, he joined a Friends' Ambulance Unit and got blown up with his ambulance."

"My dear, I'm so sorry."

Daisy was unused to wholehearted sympathy. "You don't despise him?" she asked.

"Despise him! He laid his life on the line to help others, so his physical courage was as great as any soldier's, and besides that he had the moral courage to stand up for his beliefs. How could anyone despise him?"

"It's obvious you've been living abroad. People still speak sneeringly of conchies and some of them were in prison for years. There were over a thousand in Dartmoor, shut up with the worst felons."

"That makes their courage the greater," Annabel said gently.

"My parents didn't see it that way. We decided to wait until the War was over in the hope that . . ."

"More brandy, anyone?" James had pushed back his chair from the card table, where Phillip was dealing in the methodical way Daisy remembered from childhood games. "Benedictine or Drambuie? Whisky?"

"Benedictine, please, dear boy," said Lady Josephine, handing him her liqueur glass. Daisy asked for the same. Under Phillip's stern eye, Fenella shook her head, and Daisy saw the wheels turning in Phillip's head as he decided he needed to keep it clear for the card game. Sir Hugh requested a brandy and soda. Geoffrey's brandy glass was barely touched, unless he had at some point replenished it himself.

"Father?" James enquired.

"Yes, a drop more brandy, please, neat. Annabel, my dear, what will you have?"

"Nothing, thank you."

"G-and-t for me, old bean," said Wilfred as his brother passed behind his chair on the way to the drinks cabinet. He turned back to Fenella. "No, I'd not do anything so dashed uncomfortable as bashing ice about in the middle of a bitter winter's night," he said, obviously continuing what he had been saying, "if I wanted to do away with someone, which of course I don't."

James stopped beside Fenella. "There's only one person here who had good reason to want to do away with Astwick," he said loudly, with venomous intensity, staring at Annabel. "What better motive than to rid oneself of an importunate lover?"

"Shut up!" Geoffrey rocketed from his seat, his left arm swinging as his solid length unfolded. James stepped back, but Geoffrey's fist caught him on the side of the jaw, staggering him. He tripped and fell on his back, and Geoffrey was upon him, grabbing his shoulders and banging his head on the floor while he, dazed, feebly tried to push his brother off.

"Here, I say!" Wilfred jumped up, seized the back of Geoffrey's collar and hauled ineffectively.

Fenella screamed. Phillip sprang to his feet, sending the card table flying, and rushed to help Wilfred.

"Stop it!" Lord Wentwater's cold, incisive voice cut through the bedlam.

Geoffrey's shoulders slumped. He stood up and brushed vaguely at his clothes. With Wilfred's aid, James sat up, clutching his head.

"Geoffrey, go to your room. James, to my study, and wait for me."

"It's not true!" Geoffrey turned to his father, pleading, hands outstretched. "He's lying. You mustn't believe him. Stop him saying such things!"

"You may leave me to deal with your brother."

"Yes, sir." His head bowed, Geoffrey trudged towards the door, cradling his left fist in his right hand. His face was pale and to Daisy's eyes he looked utterly exhausted.

As he neared her, his steps hesitated. He raised his head and shot a glance of heartrending entreaty at Annabel, before he plodded on out of the drawing-room.

Daisy realized that Annabel was quietly weeping, huddled in the corner of the sofa with her hands over her face. Sitting down, for she too had jumped to her feet, Daisy took Annabel in her arms. She glared at James as he stumbled after his brother, tenderly feeling the puffy red swelling on his chin.

Quietly Lord Wentwater apologized to his guests and thanked Wilfred and Phillip for their intervention.

Wilfred brightened, then visibly braced himself. "It was nothing, sir, but I say, Geoff was right. Jimmy shouldn't keep spouting off like that, not quite the article, don't you know."

"Thank you, Wilfred, I do . . . Annabel!"

Annabel, who had been sobbing on Daisy's shoulder, had broken free and was hurrying from the room. Her husband's appeal failed to slow her pace. He strode after her.

"Oh dear," said Lady Josephine, and turned to Sir Hugh, her plump chin trembling.

With Sir Hugh comforting his wife, Phillip comforting his bewildered sister, and Wilfred righting the card table, Daisy decided she had had enough for one evening. Even her promise to Alec to keep watch was insufficient to detain her in the drawing-room.

"I believe I shall go to bed now," she announced and, receiving no response, did a bunk.

Yet she was too het up to concentrate on her neglected writing, or even to read, let alone to sleep. Instead, she went to the darkroom-scullery. Though it was absolutely freezing, at least concentration on the mechanical process of printing her photos kept her mind off the Beddowes and their problems.

She was astonished when a knock on the door presaged the arrival not, as she half hoped, of a kitchen maid offering hot cocoa, but of Lord Wentwater.

He apologized again for the scene in the drawing-room.

"How is Annabel?" Daisy asked. She refused to enquire after James, and thought it unwise to enquire after Geoffrey.

"She is asleep. I persuaded her to take half of one of the bromide powders Dr. Fennis left for Marjorie." Standing there with unfocussed eyes fixed on her pictures, he said absentmindedly, "You are very diligent, Miss Dalrymple."

"I haven't worked on my article all day."

"No, I suppose not. The policeman didn't believe me, did he?"

"I beg your pardon?" she said, startled.

"Chief Inspector Fletcher." The earl's harrowed gaze met hers. "He thought I was lying when I told him I didn't believe Annabel was Astwick's mistress. It's true. I know her. I trust her. But she's keeping something from me."

Obviously the secret Astwick used to threaten her, Daisy thought. Did he imagine she knew it, or that she'd tell if she did? Did he even know Annabel was being blackmailed? Daisy wasn't going to be the one to tell him. "I'm glad you trust her," she said. "I like her, very much."

"She needs a friend." He hesitated, then went on sombrely, "I expect you feel I've handled everything badly. Besides the sheer impossibility of demanding Astwick's departure, I never realized—I swear I did not realize!—that James was behåving so abominably."

Reflecting on the past two days, Daisy said, "No, as I recall he always did his worst when you weren't there. Geoffrey told you what he's been up to?"

"Yes. It is true, then? I find it so very difficult to credit that my own son could be so cruel."

"I can't honestly blame Geoffrey for attacking him."

"Nor I, though it's past time he learned that fists are rarely an effective solution."

"He's the strong, silent type. He takes after you."

"After me?" Lord Wentwater exclaimed, startled. "Good Lord, is that how you see me?"

"Not resorting to fisticuffs," Daisy hastily assured him.

He shook his head, frowning. "Perhaps I have been too silent, and not strong enough. Since their mother died I've not had much interest in society or entertaining. I have divided my time between estate business and the House, leaving my children very much to their own devices. I suppose I relied on their schools to form their characters, and on Josephine to chaperon Marjorie after she left school."

"Marjorie's no sillier than a hundred other debutantes with nothing to occupy their time or their minds but their amusements and their emotions. I must say I jolly well admired Wilfred when he stood up for Geoffrey this evening."

"Yes, possibly Wilfred is not without redeeming traits."

"If you ask me, they both need an occupation," she said severely, then bit her lip. "But you are not asking me. I beg your pardon, Lord Wentwater."

"There's no need." He smiled ruefully. "I've been rattling on at you about my troubles, so how can I resent your advice? I can't imagine why I've disburdened myself into your patient ears. It's for me to beg your pardon."

"Not at all." Daisy decided it would be untactful to tell him that he was by no means the first to confide in her.

"No doubt you will feel obliged to repeat what I've said to the detective."

"Not unless it's relevant to Lord Stephen's death. If you wish, I'll tell him you really do trust Annabel."

The earl put on his mask of hauteur. "He chose to disbelieve my statement. Reiteration will not make him believe."

"Probably not," she conceded. "I'll have to tell him about Geoffrey, though I'm sure he'd hear about it one way or another even if I didn't."

"And James's filthy accusations?"

"Didn't you know? James himself made Mr. Fletcher a present of those."

Lord Wentwater looked stunned. Then, his jaw set, his mouth a stern line, he strode from the darkroom.

He had had three purposes in coming to her, Daisy realized: to assure her of his trust in Annabel, to find out whether what Geoffrey told him of James's conduct was true, and to persuade her not to repeat James's accusations to the Chief Inspector. But any damage James could do was done.

Suddenly exhausted, Daisy cleared up the darkroom. Heading for bed, she was returning along the servants' wing corridor when a footman came through the green baize door from the Great Hall.

"Oh, miss, I was just coming to find you. There's a telephone call for you, a Miss Fotheringay."

Hurrying to the hall, Daisy picked up the apparatus from the table in the corner and sat down in the nearest chair.

"Lucy? Hello, is that you, Lucy? Darling, how too heavenly of you to ring up. Are you in a call box?"

Lucy's voice came tinnily over the wire. "No, I'm at Binkie's flat and he's treating me to the call so we can blether on forever. Don't worry, it's perfectly proper, Madge and Tommy are here too. We had supper at the Savoy. Daisy, darling, you sound positively desperate. Is Lord Wentwater too frightfully stuffy for words?"

"Good lord, no!"

"Stuffy" was now about the last word she'd think of applying to the earl, but she couldn't possibly tell Lucy all that had been going on. Quite likely a switchboard-girl or two was listening in, but in any case, what she had learned in confidence was not to be betrayed even to her dearest friend. "The earl's been quite friendly," she said lamely.

"And what about that mysterious new wife of his?

Who is she?" Though living independent of her family, Lucy was inclined to dwell on family trees.

As far as Daisy knew, Annabel had no noble connections. "Annabel's a dear," she said. "Guess who's staying here. Phillip Petrie."

"Oh yes, his sister's marrying James Beddowe, isn't she? Has Phillip taken up the pursuit again?"

"In a desultory way. He's fearfully disapproving of my writing. But Lucy, I've met a simply scrumptious man."

"Darling, how spiffing! Who is he?"

Too late she realized the trap she had dug for herself. "He's a detective."

"A 'tec? An honest-to-goodness Sherlock Holmes? My dear!"

"No, a Scotland Yard detective."

"A policeman! Surely not a guest at Wentwater?"

"He's investigating Lord Flatford's burglary. You must have read about it. The people here were at the New Year's ball." Daisy congratulated herself on telling the truth without giving away the real reason for Alec's presence at Wentwater.

"Too, too exciting, but there must be something wrong with the line. I thought you said the policeman was scrumptious."

"He is."

"But Daisy darling, isn't he frightfully common? I mean, people one knows simply don't go into the police."

"He's not at all common," she snapped, then sighed.

"But for all I know he has a wife and seven children tucked away in some horrid semi-detached in Golders Green."

"Cheer up, darling." Lucy sounded relieved. "I'll find someone for you yet. Just a moment—yes, Madge, I'm coming. I have to go, Daisy. Madge and Tommy are giving me a lift home. They send their love, and Binkie, too. When will you be back?"

"I'm not sure, I'll send a wire. Thanks for ringing, Lucy, and thank Binkie for me. Toodle-oo."

"Pip-pip, sweet dreams."

Daisy hung up the receiver and put down the set. Talking to Lucy had brought a welcome reminder of the outside world, but had done nothing to dispel the day's tensions.

She went up to bed. Tired as she was, she lay awake for what seemed hours, memories, doubts, and speculations racing through her mind. The drama in the drawing-room that evening played itself out on the screen of her closed eyelids. Why had Geoffrey violently attacked his own brother in defence of his stepmother? Why had he begged his father not to believe James? The anguished look he had cast at Annabel as he left the room suggested an all too reasonable answer.

Geoffrey was in love with his beautiful young stepmother. Nor was it a selfish infatuation such as Marjorie had felt for Astwick. The quiet youth doubtless saw himself as a chivalrous knight, worshipping his lady from afar yet always ready to rush to protect her.

Which added Geoffrey to the list of those with excellent motives for wishing Astwick harm. Moreover, he might well have considered a ducking sufficient punishment and warning, without seeing any need to dispose permanently of his beloved's persecutor. Yes, if Astwick's death was the result of mischief gone wrong, Geoffrey was definitely a suspect. Who else?

Lord Wentwater? Impossible to imagine a haughty gentleman, so bound by convention that he refused to ask an unwelcome guest to leave, doing anything so undignified as wielding an axe on the lake at midnight. The earl had confessed himself stymied, unable to deal with the situation, yet he seemed too dispassionate to resort to such desperate measures.

Phillip? Daisy couldn't believe it. If he knew he'd been defrauded, Phillip would grumble ineffectually and convince himself that the next silver mine he invested in would turn into a gold mine. If he did go so far as to hunt out an axe and cut a hole in the ice, he'd have been there to see no serious accident occurred. Surely not Phillip!

Marjorie? Wrapped up in her emotions, the silly girl would never consider the possible dire consequences. Marjorie had to be considered a likely suspect.

The Mentons? Dismissing Lady Josephine and Sir Hugh out of hand, Daisy plumped up her pillow and turned on her other side. James was really the most satisfactory villain, she thought drowsily. She wouldn't mind at all if James went to prison for manslaughter for a few years.

Sleep still evaded her as the image of Lord Stephen's

drowned body came to haunt her. That frightful gash on his temple—if it hadn't been for that he might have pulled himself out. What was it Alec had said? Something about a romantic tryst by moonlight and Annabel biffing him on the head—the weather kiboshed that—no, it was Daisy herself who had said perhaps the manservant met him and biffed him, but he wouldn't have been wearing skates. Whatever had happened to his blasted boots, he must have drowned when he went down to skate in the morning.

His death was mischance—Annabel couldn't have risked his surviving—Annabel wasn't responsible—so it must be one of—

Daisy slept.

CHAPTER 9

I'm sorry, sir, I can't let you leave." Detective Constable Piper, barring the open front door, sounded nervously determined.

"Bosh, my good fellow, you can't stop us." That was Phillip, at his most pompous. Dressed in his drab motoring coat, he slapped his gauntlets impatiently against his hand. Beside him stood Fenella in a blue travelling costume, the dust veil of her hat thrown back, plucking timidly at his sleeve.

As Daisy reached the bottom of the stairs, she called to him. "Phillip! What's going on?"

He swung round. "This confounded chappie is bally well trying to stop me taking Fenella home. You have a word with him, Daisy. You're in cahoots with the ruddy coppers."

"Do be reasonable, Phil. He's only doing his duty. I heard Chief Inspector Fletcher tell him not to let anyone leave. Will you shut that door, please, Officer? There's a frightful draught through here, though at least it's a bit warmer today, thank heaven."

"Right away, miss!" Piper threw her a look of worshipful gratitude and turned to close the door.

"Mr. Fletcher's coming back this morning," Daisy assured the Petries, "and I expect he'll let you go, but I do think you ought to wait till he arrives."

"The pater said to take Fenella home," Phillip said obstinately. "I didn't catch him on the 'phone till quite late last night, after that nasty mix-up, and he said to bring her home straight away."

"It's fearfully early still. Have you had breakfast? Why on earth do you want to leave so early?"

"It's a deuce of a way."

"The roads will be perfectly ghastly with this thaw. You're sure to get bogged down on the way. Haven't you some relative or other a bit nearer than Worcestershire where Fenella can stay for a few days?"

"There's Aunt Gertrude and Uncle Ned, Phil. Reading isn't far, is it? I'd like to stay with Aunt Gertrude, and I'd like more than a cup of tea before we leave. You rushed me so." Fenella took off her gloves, and Daisy noticed her engagement ring was missing.

"Oh, right ho," Phillip grumbled. "I'll have to ring up Aunt Gertrude and make sure it's all right. Hang it,

Officer, you'd better tell Lord Wentwater's man we'll be leaving later and he's to put the car back in the garage."

"Yes, sir." Piper saluted and opened the door just wide enough to slip out, closing it firmly again behind him.

"Come on, Fenella," said Daisy, "to the breakfast room. I'm starving."

Already on his way to the telephone table in the corner of the hall, Phillip turned, frowning. "You'd better order a tray in your bedroom, Fenella."

Daisy raised her eyebrows quizzically. "I promise I'll not let her be either murdered or corrupted at the breakfast table, and she can stick to me like a leech till Mr. Fletcher comes. You'll join us, won't you, when you've finished telephoning?"

"Yes. As a matter of fact, I only had a cup of coffee and a muffin and I'm still dashed peckish," he admitted with a sheepish grin.

Daisy and Fenella found Sir Hugh in the breakfast room, ensconced behind *The Financial Times*, which he lowered briefly to bid them good morning. His plate and cup were already empty, Daisy was glad to see. By the time the girls had helped themselves from the sideboard, he was folding the paper and standing up.

"Nothing about this business in the papers yet," he said approvingly. "That's a good man they sent down from Scotland Yard."

"Is there any more news of the jewel robbery at Lord Flatford's?" Daisy asked.

"Just a paragraph in my paper, saying the police are

holding a man for questioning and expect an imminent arrest. *The Financial Times* doesn't go in for that sort of news, though. You'll find the *Daily Mail* on the table in the hall."

Daisy thanked him, but she knew she'd find out more from Mr. Fletcher than from the *Mail.* Besides, at present she was itching to discuss Fenella's departure.

The moment Sir Hugh left the room, she said, "So your parents want you to go home?"

"*I* want to go! I simply can't marry James after all."

"Very sensible of you. He is not a nice person."

"Phillip called him a deuced rum fish," Fenella revealed, glancing over her shoulder at the door. "What shall I do if he comes in?"

"You'll say good morning and then preserve a dignified silence," Daisy advised, spearing a piece of sausage. "Did you love him very much?"

"I don't really know. I think not, because I am more shocked than upset. He was always perfectly polite and kind, and when Mummy told me he wanted to marry me I thought I should like to be a countess one day. Only, he was quite horrid to Lady Wentwater, so I could never be sure that one day he might not be horrid to me, too, could I?"

"Quite right. These are jolly good sausages."

"The cook makes her own. James showed me the pigs on the home farm. He's frightfully keen on farming, and I like animals. I did think we might be happy together." She sniffed unhappily. "Suppose no one else ever wants to marry me?"

149

Daisy hastened to support her resolve. "I'm not married and I'm perfectly happy," she pointed out. Seeing Fenella blanch, she quickly added, "But I'm sure you'll easily find a husband. The boys your age weren't in the War, after all. You haven't even spent a season in London yet, have you?"

"No. James and I met at a house-party last summer."

"There, you see? Engaged before you're even out. You don't need a brute like James."

They had nearly finished breakfast before Phillip came in to report that all was well. "Aunt Gertrude will be pleased to see Fenella, and I talked the parents into agreeing. Actually, Daisy old bean, it was a dashed good idea of yours, because I'll be able to get back here this evening to look after you. I was pretty worried about leaving you on your own for the best part of two days."

Daisy did her best not to snap at him. "Thank you for the kind thought, though I assure you I can look after myself."

"Come to think of it, old thing, I expect the inspector chappie would let you go, too. You'd be better off buzzing back to town out of this fishy business."

"I'm not leaving, Phillip," she informed him through gritted teeth, "so you might as well save your breath to cool your porridge. Fenella, I'm going to the darkroom. Do you want to come or will you hang about with Phil?"

Fenella chose to accompany her and fiddled quite happily with magnifying lenses while Daisy printed a few more shots. Some kindly soul had put a paraffin heater in the scullery so they were reasonably comfortable once their noses grew accustomed to that smell on top of the developing chemicals.

Finishing her printing, Daisy studied the prints she had made last night, thoroughly dry by now. They included the shots she had taken by magnesium flash, and she was anxious to see how they had come out.

"I didn't print the two disastrous ones, of course," she explained to Fenella. "The one where your beastly brother accused me of trying to blow up the house, and the one that fizzled. But look, this isn't bad, nor this."

As she had expected, Marjorie's black-and-white dress inevitably drew the eye. Though she couldn't do anything about that, the background of the Great Hall fireplace, carved frieze, tapestries, and ancient weapons had come out surprisingly clearly. Even Queen Elizabeth's dagger was plain to see. Through a magnifying glass, she could make out the details of the frieze and the solemn faces of the family group.

"They're jolly good," said Fenella. "Are they really going to be in a magazine?"

"Yes, though I don't know which ones the editor will choose." She picked up another of the Great Hall shots. Studying it through the lens, she gasped, then threw a quick glance at Fenella.

"James doesn't *look* like a rum fish," Fenella was saying. She hadn't heard Daisy's gasp. "I don't see how I could have guessed."

"You couldn't. Just be thankful you found out in

time." Daisy remembered James's smug expression after she had taken the first flash photograph that worked right. Wilfred had looked apprehensive, Lady Josephine upset, and Marjorie angry, and when Daisy had turned her head she'd seen Annabel and Lord Stephen.

What she hadn't realized at the time was that while those four of her subjects had reacted after the shot, the other two had reacted quicker. Lord Wentwater's and Geoffrey's faces had been impassive by the time she looked up from the camera. Dazzled by the flash, she had not noticed the turbulent emotions of father and son, so quickly hidden, so clearly visible now in the print.

"It's just another of the same," she said as Fenella reached for the photograph in her hand. She shuffled it into the pile Fenella had already examined.

As they returned through the kitchen passages towards the main part of the house, they met a footman.

"Miss Dalrymple, her la'ship says if you'd be so kind as to step up for a word wi' her in her boodwah when you has the time." Well trained, the man was as expressionless as if nothing had ever occurred to disturb the peace of Wentwater Court.

"Lady Wentwater? Of course. Fenella, I'll just see you safely back in Phillip's care first."

"Mr. Petrie's in the billiard-room, miss."

Fenella delivered to her brother, Daisy headed for the stairs.

Annabel's boudoir-dressing-room was beyond the

Wentwaters' bedroom. Daisy heard no response to her knock, but Annabel might be too miserable to call out loudly, she decided. In view of her invitation she went in.

No one was there. From beyond a door on the opposite side of the boudoir from the bedroom came the sound of running water. Daisy hesitated on the threshold, glancing round the room.

The near end held chests-of-drawers, wardrobes, a cheval glass, and a dressing table. At the far end, under the window, stood a small table and two cane-backed chairs, with a roll-top bureau in one corner, a matching glass-fronted bookcase in the other. In the centre of the room, grouped around the fire, were two armchairs and a chaise-longue covered in light brown chintz with tiny butter cup yellow flowers. The walls were hung with a Regency stripe wallpaper in cream and brown, colours picked up by the Axminster carpet. A pretty, cosy room.

Daisy crossed to the fireplace to examine the picture hanging over the mantelpiece. It was an impressionistic oil painting of a dark-haired girl in a yellow dress descending a flight of steps in a garden full of flowering shrubs and vines.

She swung round as a door closed behind her.

"Yes, that's Rupert's work." Annabel's red eyes were conspicuous in her pale face. She wore a simple coat-frock of turquoise jersey, so beautifully cut it must be straight from Paris. "Henry insisted on my keeping some of his paintings. Oh Daisy, he's been so kind, so sympathetic. I can't seem to stop crying."

"Isn't it funny how sympathy does that, much more than someone being beastly? It was Geoffrey's defence that made you cry last night, not James's attack, wasn't it?"

Annabel nodded, joining Daisy by the fire, and they both sat down. "Henry feels terrible about it. He keeps apologizing for not being the one to protect me, for having been blind to James's spite."

"James took pretty good care not to let him see it, until last night. And I imagine Geoffrey was brought up not to tell tales on his brothers."

"Henry says *I* should have told him, but I couldn't, could I? I didn't want to worry him, or to make trouble between him and his son. I hoped in time James would realize I really do love Henry, and then he'd grow accustomed to having a stepmother. But instead I've ruined his life. You know Fenella has broken off the engagement?"

"Yes, I've been hearing about it all morning."

"So I've ruined her life, too."

"What rot, Annabel. It's a good thing she discovered in time what James is like." Daisy looked up as the silvery chime of the Dresden china clock on the bureau began to play. "Quarter to eleven. Are you coming down for coffee?"

"I don't know. Should I? Henry said he'd go down with me, but he doesn't usually join us for morning coffee and I didn't want everyone to think I'm afraid to face them without his support."

"Are you? Are you afraid of meeting James?"

154

"No, he's confined to his room. As soon as the police go, he's to be sent to live in Northumberland. Henry owns a small property there, and James is to run the farms. You see why I say I've ruined his life," Annabel finished despairingly.

"What tommyrot! It's entirely his own fault, and besides, James likes farming. Everyone will think he's buzzed off to the wilds because Fenella jilted him." Unless he ended up on trial for manslaughter. "What about Geoffrey? Will meeting him upset you?"

Hesitating, Annabel studied her hands as she answered. "I ought to thank him, but he's confined to his room too. Henry's grateful to him for standing up for me, but he's also angry about the brawl in the drawing-room."

"It certainly wasn't a display of what my governess used to call drawing-room manners!" Daisy wondered whether Annabel was embarrassed because she knew Geoffrey was in love with her. Yet she hadn't talked of ruining *his* life. Was Lord Wentwater aware that his son was in love with his wife? Another ghastly situation, but fortunately not one Daisy felt called upon to deal with. "Come on, I could do with coffee and a biscuit. I've been working hard this morning."

Annabel managed a smile as she stood up. "I miss my work. In Italy I used to arrange things for English people who came to stay in the area—you know, hiring servants and interpreting and so on. That's how I met Henry." She stopped by the dressing-table and peered at herself in the mirror. "Oh Lord, I can't go down with my eyes like this. The cold water didn't do any good."

"They're not as bad as they were when I came in. It's the contrast with your pale cheeks. Try a bit of rouge."

"I'm not very good at it. I hardly ever bother with anything but powder."

"Nor do I, because I always look frightfully healthy. I've always wanted to be pale and interesting like you. But I've watched Lucy put on rouge and she always looks marvellous. Shall I give it a go?"

"Please do."

Daisy's efforts met with her own and Annabel's approval. "Now lipstick," she said. "There. Your eyes aren't at all noticeable now."

They both powdered their noses and went down to the morning-room. The elderly spaniel, who seemed to live there, ambled over to greet Annabel. Wilfred, nobly entertaining his aunt with the latest gossip from the theatrical world, stood up.

"Good morning, Daisy. Good morning . . . er . . . Mother." He turned pink and gave a self-conscious laugh. "I feel like a dashed idiot . . ."

"Please, call me Annabel." She blinked hard and bit her lip, fondling the dog's head. Afraid she was going to burst into tears again at Wilfred's touching gesture, Daisy squeezed her hand.

"The gov'nor wouldn't like it," Wilfred objected diffidently, smoothing his hair with a nervous hand.

"Never mind that. I'll talk to him. Please?"

"Right-oh, Annabel."

"That's better," said Lady Josephine, her plump face

benevolent. "It's so very awkward when no one knows what to call anyone. You modern young things are delightfully casual about proper forms of address. In my youth it was unthinkable for any gentleman to address a lady other than his sister or wife by her Christian name."

She chattered on as the morning coffee was brought in and Lord Wentwater and Sir Hugh joined them. Phillip and Fenella came too. Coffee was poured, cakes and biscuits passed around, polite small talk exchanged, just as if Lord Stephen had not drowned and James had not disgraced himself. The only reminder of recent events came when Phillip grumbled to Daisy, in a hushed mutter, because the Chief Inspector had not yet returned.

He moved on to a lengthy story about his car, an elderly Swift two-seater which, Daisy gathered, he kept running with spit and string. It was a pity his noble antecedents ruled out employment as a motor mechanic, she was thinking, when Marjorie came in. Soberly dressed, the scarlet lipstick missing, her wan, hollow-eyed presence was a sudden reminder of unpleasant reality. A momentary silence fell.

Wilfred broke it. "Feeling better, old bean? I'll get you some coffee."

"Thanks, Will," she said gratefully as the buzz of conversation resumed.

Lord Wentwater crossed to her and took both her hands. They spoke to each other in low voices, Marjorie nodding once or twice, assuring her father she was recovered, Daisy assumed. Wilfred took her a cup of coffee. The earl put his arm about her shoulders in a brief embrace before he left them, going to Annabel.

Daisy heard him say, "I have work to do, my dear," as he stooped to kiss her cheek. She gazed after him with a look of devoted gratitude mixed with a yearning in which Daisy read something of hope—and something of dread.

Before Daisy had a chance to ponder Annabel's curious expression, Marjorie approached.

"Phillip, if you don't mind, I'd like a word with Daisy."

He sprang to his feet with gentlemanly alacrity and took himself off. Marjorie sat down in his place, then seemed to lose steam.

"I'm glad you're feeling well enough to come down," Daisy said in an enquiring tone.

"I've been the most frightful fathead!" Marjorie's exclamation was a masterpiece of suppressed violence. "Poor Daddy, watching me make an ass of myself when he has so much else to worry him. But even worse . . . . Daisy, you're chummy with Annabel—my step-mother—aren't you?"

"Call her Annabel. She just asked Wilfred to. Yes, you could say we're chummy."

"Will you tell her I don't hold her to blame because Lord Stephen liked her better than me? I know I acted as if I thought she was trying to take him away from me, but he never really wanted anything to do with me even before he came down here. He was . . . he was rather a scaly character, wasn't he?"

"A real snake in the grass," Daisy agreed. "Won't you tell her yourself?"

158

"Oh, I couldn't!"

"Try. She's not very happy and it might cheer her up."

"She must be in a fearful huff at me."

Daisy shook her head. "I think you'll find she understands. She's not much older than you. Go on."

A few minutes later she had the satisfaction of seeing Marjorie and Annabel embrace each other. Marjorie, like Wilfred, was turning out to be not half such a blister as she had made herself out to be. The trouble was, the more her resentment had been directed at Lord Stephen rather than Annabel, the more likely that she had decided to give him a ducking.

Daisy slipped out of the room. She wanted to think about what she was going to tell Alec. It was beginning to dawn on her that, whoever was responsible for Astwick's death, the whole family was going to be dragged through the courts. Her increasing liking for Annabel made her quail at the prospect.

However, her duty as a citizen to cooperate with the police was unchanged. Besides, what they didn't learn from her they'd probably dig up anyway, perhaps with more disruption of everyone's feelings. Alec was a good detective who would leave no stone unturned. Even exhausted by lack of sleep, he had jumped on a coincidence of names leading to the recovery of a fortune in stolen gems!

Where was he? She was dying to know what Astwick's ferret-faced manservant, Payne, had to say about the burglaries.

As she reached the Great Hall, a footman came

towards her. "The detective's back, miss. I was just coming to tell you he's asking for you."

"In the Blue Salon again? Thank you." Daisy was taken by surprise by the lightening of her heart. Alec was back, and he wanted to see her—purely for professional reasons, she reminded herself.

"The Blue Salon?" Phillip had overheard as he arrived in the hall, Fenella in tow. "The Chief Inspector's here? It's belly well about time, too." He and Fenella followed Daisy to the Blue Salon, where he instructed his sister to wait outside.

Alec, flanked by Tring and Piper, glanced up and smiled as Daisy entered. He looked as if he had slept well, his eyes restored to brightness, no longer hollow beneath the fierce eyebrows.

"Good morning, Miss Dalrymple. Ah, Mr. Petrie." The eyebrows rose, giving him a sardonic air. "I understand you wish to leave us."

"Not me, my dear chap, my sister. My people want me to take her to her aunt's, near Reading. It's an infernally awkward situation, here, don't you know."

"It is indeed," said Alec gravely, but Daisy would have sworn he was hiding a smile. "I take it you're referring not only to my investigation but to Miss Petrie's broken engagement."

"How the blazes do you know about that already?" Phillip was properly impressed by this evidence of omniscience. "Hang it all, one can't keep much from you chaps. Yes, that's right. Deuced uncomfortable for the poor old thing being stuck in the same house with the blighter she's handed his papers."

"You don't feel the same discomfort?"

"What, me? By Jove, I've been in worse holes, I can tell you. You were up above it all, I see." He nodded at Alec's Flying Corps tie. "Ever meet von Richthofen?"

"I never had that honour." Alec patiently returned him to the point. "I gather you intend to return to Wentwater Court after leaving your sister with your aunt?"

"Oh yes, can't leave Daisy—Miss Dalrymple—in the lurch. Have to keep an eye on her. Dash it, I've known her since she was no higher than my knee."

"What rot, Phillip! You're only two years older than me. I was higher than your knee when I was born."

"No, you weren't, old bean. Not until you were old enough to stand up," said Phillip triumphantly.

Sergeant Tring managed to turn a guffaw into a muffled snort. Ernie Piper frankly grinned.

Alec preserved his countenance. "May I have your word on that please, Mr. Petrie?" His lips twitched at Phillip's blank stare. "No, not on the height of your knee, on your return to Wentwater."

"My hat, I believe you still suspect me!" Phillip fidgeted under Alec's suddenly piercing gaze. "Yes, confound it, you have my word."

"Thank you, Mr. Petrie. I regret to say that so far only Miss Petrie and Miss Dalrymple have been eliminated from my enquiries. Everyone else at Wentwater Court is still under suspicion of having caused Lord Stephen Astwick's death."

CHAPTER 10

With a subdued "toodle-oo," Petrie departed. Alec sent Tom Tring off to the servants' quarters to ask the questions they had discussed on the drive from Winchester, then he turned to Daisy.

"I must thank you, Miss Dalrymple, for supporting Piper this morning."

All the same, he thought, he must have been more tired than he had realized yesterday to put such trust in her, to treat her almost as another police officer under his command. Had he really called her Daisy, or was it a dream? He had been too happy to see her when she walked into the room a moment ago. He must keep reminding himself that she was the Honourable Miss Dalrymple and he was merely a middle-class copper, doing his job.

"I'm sure Phillip didn't do it," she said, her smile becoming uncertain as if she recognized his withdrawal, "but I reckoned if he walked out you'd be mad as a wet cat. Do you really still suspect him?"

"I must. The lodge-keeper's statement together with the skates Astwick was wearing virtually rule out an outside agency connected with his financial shenanigans or the jewel robberies."

"Have you found out anything more about the robberies?" she asked eagerly. "Has Payne talked? I suppose the man you picked up in the Lanchester really is Payne?"

"Chummie admitted to being Astwick's 'personal gentleman,' and that's about all we got out of him. He only admitted that much after we told him we'd found the loot, the passports, and the tickets to Rio, and had arrested his lordship."

"Arrested!"

"One of our little tricks that often works. They're so keen to put the blame on the other fellow that they spill the beans."

"I can't imagine Lord Stephen claiming his servant was the brains of the show," said Daisy. "Too, too humbling."

"Nor can Payne, apparently. He remained unmoved. Still, a few more hours behind bars and we'll see what news of Astwick's death does to his tongue. In the meantime, there are blocks on the roads around the area where he was found lurking, and half the Hampshire force combing the countryside. That business is under control. I wish I could say the same of this. Have you anything new to tell me?"

"If you know about Fenella's engagement being broken, then you know about James's outburst, which means you know about Geoffrey sloshing him. I take it Piper found out from the servants . . ."

"Yes, miss," young Ernie confirmed proudly.

". . . though I'd swear none of them was in the room at the time and I can't think how they found out."

"The footman on duty was just about to go in to make up the fire, miss, when it all happened."

"What did I say about servants and sneezes?" Alec

teased, momentarily forgetting his good resolution. "Still, I'd like to hear the story from you to make sure what I heard is accurate."

The tale she told was essentially the same as Ernie's report, and once again Alec marvelled at the servants' espionage system. One difference caught his attention.

"You say Geoffrey cast a *heartbreaking* glance at Lady Wentwater as he left the drawing-room. What exactly do you mean by that?"

She hesitated. "I wish I hadn't said that. After all, I might have imagined it. One can't draw conclusions from a passing expression."

"Not conclusions, but inferences, or my job would be impossible. Tell me."

"I'll show you," she said with a sigh, "or at least show you something which seems to confirm my inference. A photograph. It's in the darkroom." She started to rise.

"Can you describe to Piper where to find it? Good." He sent the constable off to fetch the photo. "We'll leave the subject of Geoffrey until he comes back. I understand Lady Marjorie has emerged from seclusion. Have you talked to her?"

"Yes." Again Daisy seemed reluctant to continue. "Or rather, she talked to me. She wanted me to tell Annabel she doesn't really believe Annabel tried to take Lord Stephen away from her."

"Which suggests she realizes that Astwick was the villain of the piece."

"She called him a scaly character," Daisy admitted. Clearly she recognized—and deplored—the strengthening of Lady Marjorie's motive. "I'm sure James did it," she hurried on. "If you'd heard his beastly attempt to put the blame on Annabel . . ."

"He's already tried that on me, remember, and I'll be speaking to him again. I assure you, he's high on my list."

"Good! Wilfred's turned out to be a bit of a brick, you know. Besides standing up for Geoffrey last night, he made a special effort to be friendly to Annabel this morning."

"He's low on my list." Alec smiled at her. "Didn't we decide he'd more to lose than to gain from making Astwick mad as a wet cat?"

"Yes, like Annabel," she agreed with a grateful smile. "I'm so glad Annabel is out of it. I've been talking to her a lot and I like her awfully."

Alec didn't disillusion her. True, Lady Wentwater had had nothing to gain from angering Astwick, and she knew it, but would she have considered that in a passion of desperate hate and fear? Or might she not somehow have ensured that the ducking should end in drowning?

Except that he couldn't think how.

"She didn't say anything helpful?" he asked.

"Helpful to you? No."

"To you?"

Daisy nodded, a haunting sadness crossing her face. If Lady Wentwater had said something to comfort her, Alec prayed fervently that her ladyship would not be implicated.

165

Piper returned, breathless, with a stack of photographs. Skimming through them, Daisy picked out four, discarded three, and handed Alec the fourth. "I shot it just as Annabel and Astwick came into the hall together."

"A family group, yet Lady Wentwater wasn't included?" He took out his magnifying glass.

"I'm not sure whether she was left out on purpose or by accident. I think it was a misunderstanding."

The figure in the centre of the photo, her boldly patterned dress standing out, was a young woman he recognized only as a type. Her boyish figure, marcelled bob, and sharply defined lips were the current uniform of fashion. "So that's Lady Marjorie? A bright young thing bent on grabbing the limelight."

"It's a bit thick, isn't it? I was pretty fed up when she bobbed up wearing that frock, but she's really quite sweet."

"And there's Geoffrey." He studied the large youth's face. "Good Lord, don't tell me the lad's in love with his stepmother!"

"That's what it looked like to me," Daisy agreed. "And if he loves her, he wouldn't have wanted to hurt her by getting Astwick in such a dudgeon he'd make trouble for her."

"He might not have thought so far ahead," Alec pointed out, scanning the rest of the photographed group, "or he might not even have realized Astwick was threatening Lady Wentwater with . . . Great Scott! To think I put Wentwater down as one of those stoic gen-

166

tlemen incapable of violent emotion! He's practically foaming at the mouth."

"Yet just a moment later, when I looked up, he seemed as unruffled as ever. He came to the darkroom to talk to me last night. I'd done a bunk after all the fuss and bother," she explained apologetically.

"I don't blame you. It must have been a deuced awkward situation." In her place most girls would have fled the house, like Fenella Petrie, but Daisy soldiered valiantly on, doing her best both to aid the course of justice and to protect her friends. Alec wished he had never enlisted her, dividing her loyalties. It was his job, though, to make use of anything and anyone who could help him solve the case. "What had Lord Wentwater to say to you?"

"He wanted to convince me that he trusts Annabel."

"So he has already assured me," said Alec cynically.

Daisy chuckled. "He advised me in his most earlish manner not to bother to pass it on to you as repetition wouldn't make a believer of you."

"Then why . . . ?"

"I think he came to me for Annabel's sake, in case James's beastliness had influenced me against her. He swore he hadn't realized what James was up to. I'm almost sure he also hoped to persuade me not to pass on the slander to you. When I said James had already flung the dirt, he was absolutely appalled."

"I'm not surprised. If I don't nab that young brute for manslaughter, I sincerely hope he'll get his comeuppance from his father." He held up his hand as she opened her mouth to speak. "Wait a minute, didn't you tell me Sir Hugh insisted on sending for the police? I was in a bit of a fog yesterday and I didn't catch the significance, but I assume that means the earl himself objected to calling us in."

"Only because he didn't want the Chief Constable poking his nose in. He and Colonel Wetherby are at daggers drawn, I gather. Didn't the Commissioner explain?"

"He just said to keep the local people out of it as much as possible. I didn't realize Wetherby himself was the problem. They're incredibly lucky that I was down here in Hampshire already, you know. No one from the Yard could have come without a request from the Chief Constable, or at least his consent."

"I don't think Sir Hugh can have known that. He did say something about not being sure of the protocol."

"Had it turned out to be an accident, the Commissioner might have been able to hush it up, I dare say. As it is, the only reason I haven't had to notify Wetherby yet is the connection with the case I'm already working on."

"He'll have to know eventually?"

"Oh yes, he'll get a copy of my report. It can't be kept from the press forever, either. Tring and Piper are good men and haven't breathed a word to the local chaps. Only Gillett, the Inspector knows my whereabouts or you'd have had swarms of reporters here by now."

"Too ghastly!"

"Fortunately they're quite happy at present. The conservative papers want to know when the police are going to start protecting delicately bred ladies from the scum of the earth. The left-wing rags are inveighing against the poverty that drives men to steal the purely ornamental wealth flaunted by the fashionably useless."

"You haven't told the press about recovering the gems?"

"No, partly because of the link with Astwick's death, mostly because I'd like to keep it out of the papers until we've recovered the latest haul. Too many people know, though. I give it twenty-four hours at most, and then another twenty-four before they're onto Astwick."

"Golly, forty-eight hours before ravening hordes of reporters descend on Wentwater Court?"

"At most."

"Don't tell Lord Wentwater!"

"Don't you, either," he recommended, smiling. "Well, unless you have anything more to report, I'd better go to work on Lady Marjorie to start with. Thank you, Miss Dalrymple. I'll see you later. Are your pencils sharpened, Ernie?"

Daisy left the Blue Salon with mingled disappointment and relief. Alec had no need of her shorthand today. Though she disliked being excluded after feeling herself part of his team, she was also quite glad to be spared the second interview with James. Besides, she hadn't done a stroke of work on writing her article yesterday. It was her only excuse for staying at Wentwater, and she wanted to stay until everything was cleared up.

On the way to her room, she met Geoffrey on the

stairs, togged out in riding kit. She didn't think he'd defy his father so he must have been released from confinement. He stopped three steps above her, his tall, solid-muscled frame looming over her.

She wouldn't want to make him angry, but his violence was the violence of a hot temper. Though Geoffrey would strike out in a fury, she simply couldn't imagine him coolly planning a nasty trick.

"Miss Dalrymple—Daisy—I must apologize for the dustup last night," he said, shamefaced.

"I don't blame you," Daisy told him warmly. "James was asking for it." Finding herself with a choice of craning her neck or addressing his waistline, she continued up the stairs, halting a few steps higher.

He turned to face her. "I shouldn't have started a roughhouse in the drawing-room. I didn't think, I just wanted to stop him spouting such filth. You don't believe what he said, do you?"

"Certainly not, and your method was jolly effective, if not quite the thing. Are you going riding? I don't think you should, you know. Mr. Fletcher's going to want to talk to you."

"To me?" Geoffrey blanched. "Again?"

"I shouldn't worry, I don't expect he'll have you up for assault," she said with a smile. "Why don't you ask if he can see you right away, then you can ride afterwards."

He nodded, but in the moment before his stolid mask shut down, Daisy saw that her words had not reassured him. Despite his size and strength, he was awfully young and vulnerable.

How perfectly ghastly for the poor prune to be in love with his stepmother!

When Daisy reached her room, Mabel was dusting. "I haven't touched your papers, miss," the maid assured her. "I'm that sorry I'm not done yet but things is all at sixes and sevens what with the p'leece in the house and all."

"Have you been talking to the sergeant again?"

"Not today, miss." She giggled. "He's a right caution, that Sergeant Tring. 'Smorning he just wanted to see Dilys, she's the girl did my lord's room that drownded. On about boots again, he is, but our Dilys don't know nothing about them. Mr. Payne's the one to ask, being as Albert the bootboy's thick as two planks. Is it true, miss, Mr. Payne's been nicked?"

"How on earth do you know that?" Daisy suspected Mr. Tring's questions must have given it away, but perhaps Alec had no reason to keep it quiet.

"Summun told me," said Mabel vaguely. "A nasty piece of work, Mr. Payne, that's what Cook says. He done it, for sure."

"Done . . . did what?"

"Why, done his lordship in, miss, or at least swiped them boots. That's what we all thinks, or why'd the p'leece pinch him?"

"Did Payne have a reason to want to get rid of Lord Stephen?" Daisy asked hopefully, though she was sure Tom Tring must have asked already. That was the trouble with being on the fringes of the investigation: she'd missed the sergeant's report to Alec.

"Didn't seem like it, miss. He wasn't one to talk but summun asked him what it was like working for Lord Stephen and he said his lordship was a good master and ever so generous. But he clammed up after that, and you never know, do you? A good pair of boots costs a pretty penny, after all. Well, you'll be wanting to do your writing, miss. I'll leave you be, and beg pardon for chattering on."

Shaking her head at the notion of Payne stealing a pair of boots when he must have been aware of the despatch case full of priceless gems, Daisy settled at her typewriter. If only the manservant might turn out to have killed Astwick, for reasons that had nothing to do with the Beddowe family. But she couldn't work out how he'd have managed it, and he'd have to be barmy not to have pinched the jewels.

She shrugged her shoulders and turned to her notes on the history, architecture, and furnishings of Wentwater Court. Who killed Astwick was Alec's problem not hers, thank heaven.

At that moment, Alec would have been quite happy to shrug his shoulders and turn over the problem to someone else. Lady Marjorie was proving as unhelpful as the rest of his suspects. At least, somewhat to his surprise, she hadn't brought guardians with her.

She sat opposite him, too demure to be true in a dark blue tweed skirt flecked with pink and a long, pale blue, knitted V-neck jumper over a pink silk blouse. With no more than a dusting of powder on her face, her lips their natural shape and colour, she looked much younger than in the photograph, and defenceless, as if cosmetics were her armour.

"Yes, I knew Lord Stephen in London. He didn't go to deb dances much, or afternoon teas and that sort of thing, but we were introduced at a dinner party. I used to see him at nightclubs and . . ." she hesitated.

"And?"

"And gambling-rooms," said Lady Marjorie defiantly.

Alec was careful not to react as new possibilities opened before his eyes. Had she, like her brother, owed Astwick money? Or had he introduced her to a life of vice? Could she even be a cast-off mistress, clinging to the hope of winning him back, rather than the foolish, infatuated girl everyone believed her?

"You enjoy gambling?" he asked in a casual tone.

She relaxed. "Not much. An occasional rubber of bridge and half a crown each way on the Derby and the Oaks is enough for me. But one's escorts . . . you know how it is." She regarded him with doubt. "Or perhaps you don't."

"I can imagine. How long had you known Astwick?"

"About a year. Since Aunt Jo stopped insisting on chaperoning me everywhere."

Alec waited. Silence sometimes brought more results than questions.

"You only saw him . . . dead," she said. "He was frightfully handsome and sophisticated. He made the fellows who took me out seem like silly boys playing at being grown-up. And he was always escorting older women, the really smart set, married women usually. I never thought he'd take any notice of me."

"But he did?"

"Yes, in a sort of teasing way, as if he considered me a little girl."

"When? When did he start paying attention to you?"

"It was at Henley. Ronnie—the chap I was with—was cheering on his college crew, and I was bored, and Stephen took me to get strawberries and champagne. It was ripping. All my friends were fearfully envious." She frowned in thought, then looked up at Alec with stricken eyes. "Oh gosh, I've just realized, that was the first time I'd seen him since Daddy and Annabel were married. What an awful, unmitigated, hopeless chump I've been. He was after her all the time wasn't he?"

"He may have been. You have every right to be angry for the way he made use of you."

"Well, I was pretty fed up, I must say, when Will invited him down and he actually came, and then he ignored me. In fact, if you want to know the truth, I was jolly peeved—not enough to kill him!" she added hastily, aghast.

"Just enough to want to pay him out," Alec suggested.

"Is that what you think? That someone arranged for him to fall through the ice, just to make him suffer a bit?"

Alec decided it was time to admit his suspicions. "It was no accident," he said.

"Obviously, or you wouldn't still be here. But I reckoned that meant it must be murder, and you were trying to find out if anyone had seen a tramp, or a sinister stranger, or something. It was a practical joke that went wrong?" She considered the matter, then said candidly, "Well, I might have done it, if I'd thought of it. But I didn't."

Rather than disarming Alec, her candour rang alarm bells. Misleading frankness was one of the oldest tricks in the book and immediately made him wonder whether he was facing a clever actress.

Though she claimed to have failed to see through Astwick, Lady Marjorie was clearly quite bright. Presumably she had played the innocent to her father and aunt with such success they didn't realize she was frequenting gambling dens in Astwick's company. Her hysterical reaction to Astwick's death savoured more of acting than of a natural response. And just why had she chosen not to wear her usual sophisticated make-up today, when she must have guessed she was bound to be interviewed by the police?

Alec made a mental note to consult Daisy. Not that he considered her an infallible judge of character, let alone unbiased, but her insights were definitely useful to a confused detective. With a dearth of clues and alibis, and a plethora of motives and opportunity, character might yet turn out to be the only key to this case.

In the meantime, the girl sat there in her modest skirt and jumper, her pale-faced innocence a startling contrast to the fashionable flapper in the photograph. Which was the real Lady Marjorie?

CHAPTER 11

I t wasn't me, honestly," said Lady Marjorie, earnest and uneasy.

"If it was," Alec said in his most fatherly manner, "and if you were to make a confession, I'm sure you'd get off lightly. There's nothing a jury likes better than a pretty young girl, especially with a title, who's been led astray by a rascally older man. I shouldn't be surprised if . . ."

The door opened, interrupting him. The footman stuck his head into the room. "Beg pardon, sir, it's Mr. Geoffrey wants to know, if you has to see him, can you do it soon, please, being as he's all set to go riding?"

Alec suppressed a sigh. "Tell him I'll see him next, in a few minutes." As the door closed, he turned back to Lady Marjorie. "You see, I don't believe for a moment that you meant to kill Astwick, so you'd very likely get a suspended sentence."

"But you really believe I'm the one who played the trick on him?" She shook her head violently. "I'm not! Why me?"

"I didn't say that, Lady Marjorie. You are by no means the only person I have reason to suspect. I'm just pointing out that confession inclines the courts to take a lenient view, and in the circumstances you need not fear severe consequences."

"I can't confess to something I didn't do!"

"Just bear my words in mind. Tell me . . ."

"I wish I had let someone come with me."

"We can send for someone now." He had no desire to figure as a bully. "Whom would you like? Your father? Your aunt?"

"Daddy? Oh no, nor Aunt Jo. I wouldn't want them to hear . . . Could Daisy come? She won't get upset."

"Certainly, assuming she's willing." Surprised and a little amused by her choice, he rang the bell. His efforts to detach Daisy from his enquiries appeared to be doomed to failure.

While they waited, he ventured one question. "Did anyone other than Astwick ever skate so early in the morning?"

"Heavens, no. Skating is supposed to be fun. Stephen did it as part of a fitness regimen that included cold . . . Wait a bit. Someone—Phillip Petrie, was it?—said something about trying it. It wasn't Wilfred, that's certain. I wasn't really listening, and I certainly don't know if Phillip actually went down to the lake. He would have seen Stephen fall in, wouldn't he? He could have pulled him out."

"Or fallen in himself."

"Golly, yes. How frightful if the wrong person had drowned! I mean, no one wanted Stephen to drown, but better him than Phillip. He's such a sweet old fathead."

"An amiable gentleman," Alec agreed gravely. Her answer to his query was no more helpful than he had expected.

Daisy came in, her face suitably solemn except for the sparkle in her blue eyes. Whatever her misgivings, she enjoyed being involved in the investigation, Alec realized.

She flashed him a mischievous smile as she sat down beside Lady Marjorie and said, "Is he being beastly to you?"

"Gosh no. Not really. He's just asking awkward questions, but that's his job, isn't it? I hope you don't mind my asking you to come and hold my hand."

"Not a bit. One would so much prefer one's relatives not to hear the answers to awkward questions." Daisy spoke with such heartfelt sympathy that Alec couldn't help wondering about her own relatives.

Lady Marjorie turned back to him. "Right-oh, fire away, Chief Inspector."

"Thank you. I'd like you to explain why you were prostrated with grief on learning of Astwick's death. You have recovered remarkably fast if true love was the cause of your distress."

She flushed. "You know quite well it wasn't true love. It was a stupid pash. I was flattered that he noticed me, and I liked having my friends envy me. I was already disillusioned when he . . . died."

"Then how do you account for your state prompting Dr. Fennis to prescribe a bromide?"

Her pink cheeks turned crimson and she looked wildly at Daisy.

"I can guess," Daisy said gently. "Tell him."

"I wanted everyone to believe I was frightfully upset," she said in a low voice. "I'd been making such a fuss over him, I'd have looked a fearful idiot if I'd

178

just said good riddance."

"I see." Alec nodded. "Instead, everyone is sorry for you."

"That was the idea. Of course, in fact everyone thinks I'm an idiot anyway, for loving such an absolute cad."

Again the suspicious candour. What was more, Lady Marjorie admitted to feigning hysteria well enough to deceive a medical practitioner. Yet her embarrassed flush was real.

Alec asked a few more questions, then dismissed her and said to Daisy, "I want to discuss that interview with you, Miss Dalrymple, but it had better wait. Young Geoffrey is champing at the bit."

"Yes, he wants to go riding. I told him he must speak to you first."

"So that was your doing? I might have guessed. Thank you."

"Are you going to see Annabel again? I'll find out if she wants me with her today, before I go toddling back up all those stairs to my typewriter."

"Yes, I'll see her, and everyone else, though I did manage to ask most of the necessary questions yesterday in spite of being half asleep. Now I'm wide awake, watching them tell their stories may suggest new lines of enquiry that I missed before and that aren't apparent in the written report. I don't have much hope of breaking new ground, other than with Lady Marjorie and Geoffrey, of course, and perhaps Lord Wentwater."

"Marjorie's just . . .

"Later, if you please." He smiled at her indignant

look. "Sorry, but I'm sure to have more to discuss with you by the end of the day, and if we put it all together, we're more likely to see connections."

"Oh, all right. Anyway, I absolutely *must* get some work accomplished today."

She departed and Geoffrey came in. His impassive face gave no hint of the emotion which had driven him to attack his brother in his father's drawing room. Yet the evidence said that love and fury seethed beneath the calm exterior.

"Tell me about last night," Alec invited.

The lad's jaw tightened and his hands clenched on his thighs, then loosened slightly as though he forced himself to relax. "Last night? You must have heard every detail by now," he said dully.

"I'd like your side of the story."

"James started spewing filthy lies about An . . . my stepmother. I had to stop him."

"Do you often lose your temper and resort to fisticuffs?"

"No! Good Lord, no. I box for my University, and one can't box scientifically if one's always losing one's temper. Last night, I . . . I just saw red."

"What exactly was it that infuriated you?"

Geoffrey's mouth set in a stubborn line. "I won't repeat the vile things James said."

"No, no, that's not necessary. I meant something more on the lines of: Was it just because you believed he was lying?"

"I *know* he was lying. Annabel's an angel. She'd never

do anything mean or underhanded. What got my goat was that James was deliberately trying to hurt her. To say such things in front of everyone, in front of my father!"

"You were afraid Lord Wentwater might believe his lies?"

"Yes. He doesn't. He told me so."

"I've been informed by several people that Lady Wentwater was a good deal in Astwick's company. How do you account for their apparent intimacy?"

His face, which had grown animated, closed down again. "There was nothing in it. She knew him years ago and he took advantage of old acquaintance. She was too kind to give him the boot when he kept pestering her."

"So you tried to help her."

"I interrupted their tête-à-têtes whenever I could, but he was a guest here. It was up to my father to ask him to leave."

"And when he didn't, you took matters into your own hands and decided to warn him off by giving him a ducking in the lake."

Geoffrey's expression altered not an iota. "I might have, if he had been harassing her on the bank on a summer day. It never crossed my mind to crack the ice and wait for him to fall through. Anyway, he'd have presumed it an accident so it wouldn't have served as a warning. It wouldn't have helped my stepmother."

"Unless you told him afterwards and threatened more to come," said Alec halfheartedly. Geoffrey did indeed appear far more likely to biff Astwick in public as he had his brother than to plot a delayed vengeance or make threats. Time to move on to his other suspects. "Does Lady Wentwater know you love her?"

"No!" The denial exploded from his lips as his face first paled and then suffused with blood.

For the first time, Alec was certain he was lying. He didn't blame the boy. As long as his love was secret, his situation was merely miserable. Once his stepmother knew, it became impossible, for both of them. Whatever his faults, he was a chivalrous youth and no doubt hoped a pretence of her ignorance might make matters easier for her. Only time could ease his own heartache, but, being young, he wouldn't believe that.

No wonder his eyes were filled with apprehensive wretchedness. Geoffrey Beddowe's life was in a hell of a mess. "Don't tell my father," he begged.

"I shan't, unless it should become absolutely necessary, and I don't foresee any such circumstances. Let me give you a word of advice. As much as you possibly can, stay away from Wentwater Court, and when you must be here, avoid Lady Wentwater's company."

"Yes, sir."

"And watch that temper, or your fists will land you hock-deep in the soup one of these days."

Geoffrey made a strange sound, halfway between a bitter laugh and a strangled sob, as if worse trouble than he was already in was beyond his imagining. Alec let him go.

"Whew!" breathed Piper from his window seat. "There's that song says a policeman's lot is not a happy one, but I reckon most people makes their own unhappiness, don't you, Chief?"

"As often as not, Ernie," Alec agreed. "As often as not."

He had been going to request the earl's attendance next, but, remembering that Daisy was postponing her work in case the countess wanted her, he called Lady Wentwater in next. To his professional relief and personal disappointment, she came alone. In a plain straight, turquoise woollen dress with ivory buttons down the front and an ivory sash about her hips, her figure was no less ripely inviting than in last night's silk. However, today the Madonna face was masked by cosmetics in the modern fashion.

The reverse of Lady Marjorie's transformation— why? Alec's searching gaze detected signs of pink puffiness around the dark, soulful eyes. Lady Wentwater had been weeping.

Weeping for a lost lover, a hopelessly devoted boy, or a publicly supportive husband's privately expressed doubts? Lord Wentwater must surely have suffered moments of mistrust, though Geoffrey's absolute belief in her innocence was understandable. In the way of the young, he had put her on a pedestal.

"Why did Geoffrey attack his brother last night?"

"To protect me against James's false accusations," she said quietly. "He is a gallant, unselfish, and courageous young man."

"He is in love with you."

She flushed. "What makes you say that?"

"I've been talking to him."

"He told you . . . ?" The brief colour fled from her face, leaving two patches of rouge on her high cheekbones. She clasped her slender hands to her breast. "You mustn't tell Henry! Oh, please, you won't tell Henry?"

"Not unless it becomes unavoidable, which I don't foresee." He was interested to discover that Lady Wentwater, like Geoffrey, was afraid of the earl's reaction. Lord Wentwater must be a formidable man when roused. Alec hoped against hope that he himself was not going to be the one doing the rousing.

He might at least be able to knock her ladyship off his list of suspects. He continued, "Nor do I see any need to pass on to your husband any disclosure you may make to me regarding your relationship with Astwick."

"You want to know what he was holding over me? I *cannot* see that it matters."

"Probably not, if there actually was a secret. You do realize that if in fact you were enjoying an amicable affair with him, your motive for wishing him dead would vanish?"

"I suppose it would," she said despairingly. "Since I'm caught between Scylla and Charybdis, I might as well stick with the truth. I was never his mistress. I hated him."

With that, Alec had to be satisfied. Lady Wentwater preferred to be suspected of causing Astwick's death rather than to be revealed as an unfaithful wife. He admired her for it.

He had to wait until after lunch to see her husband. Alec and Piper were provided with veal-and-ham pie, coffee, and bottled beer, and after eating Alec ventured to light his pipe. As he went over his notes of yesterday's interview with Lord Wentwater, he decided he must stop holding back in deference to the earl's social status. Certain questions needed asking. If his lordship chose to complain to the Commissioner, so be it.

Alec was knocking the dottle from his pipe into the grate when Lord Wentwater arrived. Piper hastily tossed his Woodbine into the fire and retreated to the window seat.

Once the earl was seated with the light from the window on his face, Alec spent a moment studying him. No sign of the passionate emotion of Daisy's photograph showed on those aristocratic features. Even his eyes met Alec's with calm gravity. Alec felt he'd never get anywhere unless he could shake the man's self-possession.

"I understand you and Lady Wentwater do not have separate bedrooms," he opened.

"That is neither a secret, nor unusual." Lord Wentwater seemed faintly amused.

"However, you have been known to sleep in your dressing-room. Did you do so the night before Astwick's body was found?"

"If you want an alibi, I have none." The trace of amusement was gone. "As it happens, I learned that my wife had retired early that evening, so I did not disturb her."

185

"Astwick also retired early. You claim to trust her, yet you must have wondered why she made no vigorous effort to repel his advances."

"Not at all. I am sure you are aware that my wife's life for some years was somewhat . . . Bohemian. She is still unused to the role of hostess to a house party and undoubtedly feared insulting a guest."

"And that was the only reason?"

"It was sufficient." If Lord Wentwater had had any inkling of blackmail, he didn't betray it by so much as the flicker of an eyelid.

"Are you so sure Astwick's pursuit was unwelcome? I'm not suggesting, at present, that there was any question of her permitting him to seduce her, but the most respectable of ladies may enjoy a light flirtation."

"Respectable in some eyes, perhaps," he said coldly. "It was perfectly obvious that my wife neither encouraged nor enjoyed the scoundrel's attentions."

"Then why did you not intervene to protect her?" Alec rapped out.

A faint tinge of pink coloured the earl's cheeks but his voice was still more frigid. "I suppose I am obliged to put up with your prying. However, this was a matter of some delicacy which I doubt you would understand."

Alec fought to suppress his annoyance. "I may not understand the gentlemanly code that obliges you to entertain a scoundrel," he said pointedly, "but I'm not entirely insensitive, I hope. Try me."

"I felt she might interpret any interference on my part as a lack of trust." Though his positive tone expressed belief in the rightness of his course of action, or rather inaction, his form of words suggested uncertainty.

"It's possible," Alec conceded, but he envisioned the unhappy young wife feeling herself abandoned to the unscrupulous snares of a vengeful blackmailer. If she was indeed innocent, he pitied her with all his heart. He found himself pitying the earl, too, for all his wealth and position. "You did nothing, yet you must have been distressed and angry."

The flash of anger in Lord Wentwater's eyes could have been remembered wrath or offence at Alec's suspicions. "Not so angry as to descend to playing a childish trick upon Astwick, I assure you," he said dryly.

"You knew his habit of skating at dawn."

"I did?"

"Your valet recalls mentioning it to you."

"Chief Inspector, I don't listen to, let alone remember, whatever nonsense my valet may babble when he's shaving me."

"A pity. You might have caught wind of Lord Beddowe's persistent spite towards Lady Wentwater."

And now the façade briefly cracked. For just a moment, fury, hurt, and despair chased each other across his face. Then he regained command of his features and spoke with icy calm. "My son's conduct was unforgivable. You may be sure I bitterly regret not having been aware of it."

"You give no credence to his accusation, I take it?"

"That Annabel was responsible for Astwick's

drowning? If you knew her, Mr. Fletcher, you'd not ask. My wife is the gentlest of souls. She hesitated to repulse him verbally, so how can you imagine she'd resort to violent measures to discourage him?"

"Stranger things have been known. Has it crossed your mind that Lord Beddowe might have engineered the accident in order to blame his stepmother?"

Lord Wentwater's calm shattered with a cry of aghast incredulity. "No! Oh God, no!" He dropped his head into his hands. "If I ever obtain the slightest evidence of that, you shall have it on the instant."

Which was precisely what Alec wanted. Though he regretted the effect of his question, it told him a good deal. In his experience, men who successfully hid their feelings were rarely capable of dissimulation once forced to reveal them. Lord Wentwater loved his wife; and he'd not have shown such horror at the possibility of his son's guilt had he himself caused Astwick's death.

Yet Alec could not quite write him off the list. "We're always grateful for evidence, of course," he said, "but I own I'm a bit surprised by your offer of assistance. You strongly objected to calling in the police, didn't you?"

"I did." Once again the earl quickly recovered his dignity. "I was satisfied that it was an accident. In fact, I've yet to hear of any proof to the contrary, though I presume you are convinced of deliberate intent to cause harm if not death."

"We are."

"But believing it an accident, I saw no need to have

the local constabulary prying into Astwick's business at Wentwater Court. Whatever the truth, inevitably innuendos would fly. No doubt you've heard that Wetherby, the Chief Constable, and I are not on good terms."

"'At daggers drawn,'" Alec quoted Daisy.

"Near enough," his lordship said with a wry smile. "Now if you had found Wetherby dead in the hall with Queen Elizabeth's dagger in his back . . . Naturally, when Menton persuaded me that the police were inevitable and offered to consult Scotland Yard, I accepted."

Unable to credit that anyone could think the Met less likely than a mere county force to solve a crime, Alec was inclined to believe him. On the other hand, he might have counted on being able to sway Menton's friend at the Yard, whereas Colonel Wetherby was beyond his influence. Lord Wentwater remained on the list.

James Beddowe still topped it, a matter of wishful thinking for want of evidence. Alec sent for him.

The earl's heir was by no means the cocky, vitriolic young man he had appeared yesterday. He came in with a hang-dog air, accentuated by the purplish bruise on his chin, and slumped into the seat Alec indicated.

Alec wasted no sympathy on him. "Do you wish to add to or amend your statement?" he enquired.

"Statement!" James looked distinctly rattled. "Here, I say, what I told you yesterday was pure speculation. If you're calling it a statement, I'll withdraw the whole bally thing. Tear it up."

"I'm afraid I can't do that, though I'll note that you have changed your mind since last night."

"I suppose you've heard all about last night," James said sulkily, fingering the bruise.

"I understand you more or less accused Lady Wentwater to her face, in your father's presence, of having murdered her lover. Is that correct?"

"I was kidding! If Geoffrey hadn't cut up rough, no one would've taken what I said seriously because Astwick's death obviously wasn't murder. It was an accident. People are always falling through weak ice. The silly ass should have checked it, and it's sheer folly to go skating alone, anyway."

"The ice was firm, and overnight temperatures were well below freezing."

James managed a sneer. "Ice varies in thickness, you know. Astwick hit a thin patch. Just bad luck. It was an accident."

"An 'accident' which you attempted to blame on your stepmother. An 'accident' which you caused in order to blame it on your stepmother?"

"Good gad, no! You can't believe that!"

"I have evidence that the ice was tampered with."

"Not by me! You must be mistaken. It was pure chance." Alec shook his head.

"Then how can you be sure *she* didn't do it? *I* didn't, I swear it. I had no motive for harming Astwick."

"Except to lay the blame on Lady Wentwater," Alec pointed out inexorably.

James reverted to insisting that the police had misinterpreted the evidence, that Astwick had simply struck a weak patch of ice. "It might have happened to anyone," he maintained.

"Phillip Petrie, for instance."

He grimaced at the mention of his ex-fiancée's brother. "Or me. But someone would have been there to pull us out."

So he hadn't heard Petrie's boast. Another mark against him. On the other hand, he had taken Fenella skating with him when he found the body. Was he so callous he'd subject the inoffensive girl to such an experience? His behaviour to his stepmother argued that he was.

Alec took him again through the story of the discovery of Astwick's drowned body, hoping for a slip of the tongue indicating prior knowledge. He learned nothing new.

Wilfred was next. Breezing into the Blue Salon, he said at once, "You mustn't believe what my brother's been saying about Annabel. Jolly poor show, I'm afraid. The poor old pater's pretty shattered."

Alec found himself liking the natty young man, who was unashamedly relieved by the removal of the threat Astwick had presented to him. Unless he was very devious indeed, it seemed unlikely that he had had a hand in that removal. Nonetheless, he could not be crossed off the list.

Nor could the Mentons, though a second interview with them gave no new cause for suspicion. Altogether, though the weight of Alec's suspicions had shifted somewhat, the list remained unchanged. Even a full night's sleep had shed no light on the confusion. He requested Daisy's presence.

When the footman knocked on her bedroom door, Daisy was gazing out of the window. The sky was overcast and a few drops of rain were beginning to fall. By morning, she guessed, the snow would be gone, the grim evidence of the hole in the ice a thing of the past.

She hurried down to the Blue Salon.

Greeting her with flattering pleasure, Alec said, "I'm hoping you can straighten out my thoughts, which are going round and round in circles."

"So are mine," she admitted. "I've hardly done any work on my article. Yet at the same time, I'm beginning to find it hard to believe anything really happened. How I wish it hadn't!"

"If you'd rather not . . ."

"Oh no, I'll help if I can."

"Thank you. Let's go back to Marjorie, for a start. She feigned hysteria well enough to convince the doctor, but I'd swear her embarrassment was real when she told me why. Surely it's impossible to blush deliberately?"

"Heavens no. Lucy, the friend I share a house with, can blush at will just by turning her mind to something frightfully embarrassing. She claims it's an essential part of flirting. It doesn't work for me," Daisy added mournfully.

"So even that could have been acting, which makes me think she left off her cosmetics in order to look the part of an innocent."

"She might have, but if you ask me, she just felt too wretched at the prospect of having to face everyone to bother."

"Maybe. Lady Wentwater did the opposite, trying to disguise with make-up that she'd been crying."

"That was on my advice."

"Oh. All the same, it's odd that she's so miserable when she no longer has anything to fear from Astwick."

"She's not miserable, she was crying because Lord Wentwater was so kind to her." She wrinkled her nose at Alec's sceptical face. "I don't expect kindness makes men want to cry, but I assure you . . ."

"All right! The earl was especially kind to his wife and it made her cry. Does he know Geoffrey is in love with her?"

"I can't see that that's relevant."

"Who knows? I'm at a loss and clutching at straws."

"Well, I wondered myself. He didn't see Geoffrey's look at Annabel in the drawing-room, nor the photograph. The earl could well suppose that Geoffrey attacked James just from a general sense of chivalry, towards Annabel or even towards their father. After all, James's accusations hurt him, too."

"True. Did—does—Lord Wentwater know Astwick was blackmailing his wife, or was his violent emotion in the photo caused simply by jealousy?"

"I don't know. He did say Annabel was withholding something from him, but as far as I could tell he didn't appear to guess that it might be a secret from her past. Certainly he was more sad and worried than angry with her, as if he wished she'd bring herself to confide in him."

"To trust him as much as he trusts . . . ." Alec broke off as the door opened and the footman's head appeared. "Yes? What is it?"

"A call for you on the telephone, sir. It's from Inspector Gillett in Winchester."

"Thank you, I'll come at once." Alec sprang to his feet. "Ernie, go and tell Tom I want him in the Great Hall. If this is what I think, we'll be off."

Daisy trailed after him to the hall and waited at a discreet distance to find out whether he was about to leave. He listened, spoke briefly, listened again, then hung up the receiver as his sergeant and the constable came in.

"Gillett told chummie Astwick's dead and he's ready to talk. Let's hope we can get there before he changes his mind, Tom. Ernie, you're on duty here as last night. Miss Dalrymple, thank you for your help. We'll be back."

He and Tring strode off by the back way to the garages. Daisy stepped out onto the front porch for a breath of fresh air, and a few minutes later watched the yellow Austin Seven disappear down the drive into the rainy dusk. When she returned to the hall, the disconsolate Piper was still there.

"I expect you'd like to be in on Payne's interrogation," she said.

"Yes, miss, wouldn't I just."

"You're needed more here, or Mr. Fletcher wouldn't have left you," she consoled him. "Have you worked with him before?"

"Not on an out-of-town case, miss."

"Is he sent out of town often?"

"Pretty often, miss. He's been in charge of all these jool burglaries, besides other cases where there's nobs involved. He's got a degree, see, he knows how to talk to them sorts of people."

Daisy gathered that Piper no longer numbered her among "them sorts of people." Fishing for information about Alec, she remarked casually, "It must be hard on his family, having him away from home so much."

"All coppers has irregular hours, miss," he told her, unintentionally unhelpful, "and it's worse for us detectives. My girl, she knows what she's in for."

Before Daisy had to pretend to a polite interest in his girl, the telephone bell rang and Drew appeared as if by magic to answer it. "For the Chief Inspector," he announced.

"He's left," said Daisy, dismayed.

"I'll take it," Piper said importantly, taking the apparatus from the butler, who disappeared as magically as he had appeared. "Hullo, hullo, this is Detective Constable Piper, C.I.D."

The receiver squawked at him in an irascible tone, cutting off his attempted explanation of his superior's absence. Piper felt in his pocket and produced his notebook and pencil. Daisy removed the elastic band holding it shut and opened it for him. He scribbled desperately for a few minutes.

"Yes, sir, I think I've got that but . . . Hullo, operator? Bloody hell, he's gone!" He blushed. "Beg pardon, miss."

"Oh, never mind that, who was it? What did he say?"

The constable studied his notes with an air of bemusement. "It were Dr. Renfrew, miss, the pathologist. Best I can make out, he's saying the deceased drowned not more'n two hours after he ate his dinner."

CHAPTER 12

Daisy and Detective Constable Piper stared at each other. "So Astwick died that evening?" Daisy said. "Not in the morning?"

"That's what it sounds like to me, miss. Everyone seems sure he didn't eat no breakfast, and anyway, by what I heard them doctors can tell pretty much what a body's ate recent by what's in the stomach."

"Ugh! What on earth was he doing going skating in the dark? It seems a frightfully peculiar thing to do, and I distinctly heard him say he was going to bed." She recalled wondering whether he was aiming towards his own or Annabel's bed, but Piper didn't need to know that. A sudden longing for Alec's competent presence swept over her. "Oh Lord, this does complicate matters," she exclaimed. "You'd better ring up the police station in Winchester and leave word for the Chief. He may want to come back tonight."

"Dr. Renfrew said he telephoned there first, miss, and left a message. That's why he chewed my ear off, like it were my fault he couldn't find the Chief nowhere."

"Too unfair," Daisy commiserated. "Did he tell you anything else?"

"Summat about confusions and cold water." Piper eyed his notes dubiously. "And imaging?"

Daisy racked her brains. "Contusions and haemorrhaging? Bruises and bleeding?" Not for nothing had she done a brief stint in a hospital office during the War.

"I couldn't say for sure, miss, 'cepting he's doing some tests as he'll have the results of come morning. Such long words them doctors use, you can't rightly make head nor tail of 'em."

"Right now, I can't make head nor tail of anything. Confusions is about right. I simply can't believe Astwick went down to the lake after dinner."

"If 'tweren't for them skates he had on, you'd think he'd gone to meet Payne, or one of his burglar chums. Lumme, miss, you don't think the skates were kind of like a disguise, in case someone saw him there?"

"He could just as well have said he was out for a stroll and a breath of fresh air."

"I s'pose so," Piper agreed, disappointed. "And it's true there weren't no sign I could find of anyone coming in from outside. So it was still someone here done him in. The time's narrowed down to a couple of hours, though, and some on 'em has alibis. I can't remember who, off-hand, but it'll please the Chief."

Almost everyone had been in the drawing-room for two hours after dinner. Almost everyone. Lord Wentwater had been alone in his study, and Annabel had left shortly before Astwick. Unless her maid could give her an alibi, she had to be considered a chief suspect.

"No," Daisy cried, shaking her head, "it's not so

197

simple. It gets dark so early, anyone could have made the hole before changing for dinner, expecting Astwick to fall in in the morning."

"True, miss, but it still leaves just a few hours to account for. We didn't look for alibis for before dinner, reckoning there was all night to do the job in. Some on 'em'll be in the clear. Just knocking two or three off the list'll cheer the Chief up."

At that moment, the Chief was in dire need of something to cheer him up. His pipe clenched grimly between his teeth, he peered out through the open upper part of the windscreen into the darkness. The headlights illuminated silver needles of rain slanting across the lane, and the drumming of rain on the raised roof-hood vied with the drone of the engine. The little car sloshed bravely through the slush. The surface beneath was still frozen, and every now and then Alec had to correct a skid as the narrow wheels hit a patch of ice.

Squeezed into the seat beside him, Tom Tring reported on his questioning of the servants. "Nothing new on Astwick's boots, Chief."

"Blast the boots. Payne may tell us whether there's a pair missing or not, but I can't see it's going to help us much. What else?"

"Talking of boots, Lady Wentwater's boots and other outdoor clothes didn't show no signs of having been worn for a day or two, nor Lady Josephine's, nor Mr. Wilfred's. That's according to their personal servants.

All the others, we know they was out at some point, when the body was found if not before."

"Hmm, interesting. And?"

"Ah, let's see now. The housemaid that did Astwick's bedroom, Dilys her name is, and a neat, perky little baggage as I wouldn't mind . . ."

"Spare me the rhapsodies, Tom. What did she have to say?"

"Well, as a rule she didn't have owt to do with Astwick's clothes and that, but being as Payne was gone she tidied up a bit. Snooping, if you arst me," said the sergeant tolerantly. "A good job he'd locked the despatch case. Anyways, there's two things she noticed that morning she thought was a bit fishy. It seems Astwick's dressing gown was damp. Hanging on the back of the bathroom door, it was, and she took it down to the kitchen to dry."

"Some men put on a dressing gown before they towel themselves dry," Alec pointed out. "Or perhaps he dripped on the floor when he got out of the bath, and dropped his dressing-gown in the puddle. We know he was in the habit of taking a bath before his dawn exercise. A cold bath, wasn't it?" Shivering, he braked as they reached an unsignposted fork in the road.

"Right, Chief. No, go left here," he contradicted himself as Alec turned the wheel. "I meant, you're right, a cold bath was what he took."

A flurry of cold raindrops hit Alec in the face as he swung left, narrowly missing the ditch. "Silly ass," he growled around the stem of his pipe. "Didn't know when he was well off. What else did your pretty house-maid notice?"

"Astwick's bed hadn't been slept in," said Tom bluntly. "The covers was turned back neat, the way she left them. No wrinkles in the sheets, no hollow in the pillow."

"Oh hell. It looks as if he spent the night with Lady Wentwater, then."

"Looks like it, Chief. Her ladyship's maid, Miss Barstow, was the only one as went upstairs between dinner and the chambermaid putting hot-water bottles in the beds at half ten. Lady Wentwater ordered her to draw a bath and then dismissed her for the night."

"But the earl might have walked in on them at any moment! Perhaps Astwick didn't care. He was doing a moonlight to Rio anyway, so the social consequences wouldn't bother him, and he'd have his revenge on Lady Wentwater one way or the other. I must admit, whatever it was she did that gave him a hold over her, I'm sorry for her."

"His lordship didn't walk in on them, though," Tom reminded him, "at least by his own account. And she couldn't've chopped a hole in the ice if she was having a bit of nooky with the victim, so it lets her out."

"Except that her only witness is dead. We've no proof he was with her, after all. He might have been exploring your Dilys's charms in some garret. There's a lamppost. Damn it, where the devil are we?"

The sergeant glued his nose to the bespattered side window, then let it down and stuck his head out. "Alresford," he announced. "Next right, then straight ahead.

Not *my* Dilys, Chief, not but what she'd hardly've told me about his bed if he'd been in hers."

"He could have been in any other female servant's," Alec said with a sigh, trying to find a way out for the countess. He turned right into the broad main street of the little town.

"Don't think so. Fact, I'm pretty sure not. Like Lady Josephine told you, I haven't picked up the slightest hint he was interested in the maids. Someone'd've tattled if there was owt to tattle about, I'll be bound. There's always jealousies belowstairs like you wouldn't believe, Chief. No, Astwick only fancied upper-crust ladies and at Wentwater he hadn't eyes for nowt but her ladyship."

"Nonetheless, we've no evidence he spent that night in her bed. I'm not quite ready to dismiss the possibility of his having spent it in Lady Marjorie's, if not in a maid's. We're really no further forward than before. I don't see how I'm ever going to clear up this case unless Payne comes up with something startlingly new, which seems unlikely."

"He may lead us to the loot from the Flatford job, and even if he don't, we picked up the good stuff from the other burglaries," Tring reminded him cheerfully.

"True."

"That's a feather in your cap, Chief, even if chummie's no help with the Wentwater business, if it's all in the family, like."

"As seems probable." Gloom returned. "It'll take a sheaf of peacock feathers to make up for arresting the earl, if that's what I end up having to do. Suppose he overheard Astwick and his wife making love? His dressing-room's right next door to the bedroom. He might have reckoned that setting up an accident would allow him to get his own back without ever admitting to knowing he'd been cuckolded."

At the police station in Winchester, a stout, grizzled constable who looked well past the age of retirement was nodding off on a high seat behind the front desk. His blue uniform jacket strained at the seams, as if resurrected from slenderer days.

The telephone at his elbow rang just as Alec and Tring entered the station. Startled to wakefulness, he blinked at them, then turned his head to regard the shrilling instrument with deep suspicion. Taking the receiver from its hook, he held it at arm's length and turned back to Alec.

"What can Oi be a-doin' fer 'ee, zir?" he enquired in a slow country voice, ignoring the chittering coming from the telephone.

"Deal with your 'phone call first."

"Don't 'ee moind that, zir. Truth to tell, Oi can't roightly foller what folks be zayin' on the machine," he confided. Suddenly raising the receiver to his mouth, he bellowed into it, "*Yes,* zir!" and hung up. "If it be important, they'll zend round or step by come marnin'. What can Oi be a doin' fer 'ee?"

Wondering how many messages had been lost or delayed, Alec exchanged an exasperated glance with Tom.

"I'm Chief Inspector Fletcher, Scotland Yard," he announced.

The constable lumbered down from his stool and saluted, with the genial, placid air of one doing a favour. "Constable Archer, retired, zir," he introduced himself.

He had been recalled to duty because all able-bodied men were out hunting for the stolen jewels, at Alec's request, so there was no point making a fuss about his incompetence. Alec asked for Gillett and was told that the Inspector had gone out to call off the search for the night.

"Did he leave any message for me?"

Archer pondered. "Come to think on it, he did zay to tell 'ee he'd step home fer a bite o' supper afore he come back."

"I could do with a pie and a pint meself, Chief," the sergeant rumbled behind him.

"I suppose we'd better wait for Gillett, as he was the one who nicked Payne," said Alec resignedly. "All right, Tom, we'll go and get something to eat. At this rate, we might as well have stayed to dine on the fat of the land at Wentwater."

Dinner at Wentwater Court was as delicious as ever, but Daisy paid her food the scantest attention. The postmortem discovery dismayed her. The more she considered the changed time of Astwick's death, the less she was able to imagine any reason for him to be skating at that hour. Yet how else could he have ended up drowned in the lake? It didn't make sense.

Desperate for someone to discuss the matter with, she wished Alec would return. In fact, she was rather surprised when he didn't. Surely the news was of sufficient moment to bring him back!

Payne's revelations must be of still more interest to him. Of course, the recovery of Lord Flatford's guests' jewellery would bring grateful applause, whereas the arrest of Astwick's killer, presumably a member of the earl's family, meant nothing but trouble.

One of Lord Wentwater's family was a killer. The word reverberated in Daisy's mind. The simple change of a few hours in the time of death had somehow changed everything. Now she found it difficult—nearly impossible—to believe in a prank gone wrong. What had Astwick been doing down at the lake after dinner?

Surreptitiously she glanced around the table. With Phillip and Fenella gone, she was the only non family member. Except for James, all of them were there. Not one looked like a killer. They were subdued, even Wilfred, the weight of the continued police presence in the house making itself felt. Lady Jo, never one to despise her victuals, was eating as if it were her last meal. Annabel was pale and withdrawn. She jumped visibly when Sir Hugh asked her to pass the salt.

James? He had been in the drawing-room the whole of that evening. Daisy started to build a fantasy in which he had broken up the ice before dinner and forged a note from Annabel to Astwick inviting him to meet her to skate by moonlight. Astwick would have skated about to keep warm while he waited for her—but he'd never believe she'd issue such an invitation in the first place.

Somehow James must have managed it. Daisy couldn't bear to think that any of the others were guilty.

She was glad to find Phillip in the drawing-room when they all repaired thither for coffee. He looked a bit down in the mouth, but he bucked up when he saw her. "What ho, old thing," he greeted her. "Bearing up all right?"

"I'm perfectly all right," she said crossly, annoyed by his tactlessness.

"Have you dined, Mr. Petrie?" Annabel asked.

"Yes, thanks. I stopped at a little place on the way when I realized I was going to be rather late. The roads are absolutely foul." He launched into a tale of motoring through rain and icy slush and narrow escapes from ditches. Daisy hoped Alec's continued absence wasn't due to a motoring mishap.

Coffee and its alcoholic accompaniments were served and consumed. Lady Jo invited her brother to partner her at her inevitable bridge, playing against Sir Hugh and Wilfred. Occasional dismayed exclamations of "Oh, Henry!" suggested that the earl's mind was not on his cards. Geoffrey drifted off in his unobtrusive way and Annabel and Marjorie talked quietly together by the fire.

"Fancy a game of snooker?" Phillip asked Daisy. "Lord, we haven't played together in years. Do you remember when you and I used to team up against Gervaise? He usually beat both of us." He rambled on in a sentimental vein as they made their way to the billiard-room. "Things just haven't been the same since Gervaise bought it," he concluded. "Well, my dear old thing, what about it?"

Daisy, who had been trying to remember Gervaise's instructions on choosing a cue, said absently, "What about what?"

"You and me, old girl. Teaming up. Tying the knot. Making a match of it."

"Oh, Phil, it's awfully sweet of you to ask me again, but I still think we shouldn't suit."

"Hang it all, I don't see why not."

She tried to let him down lightly. "For a start, neither of us has a bean. Setting up a household costs pots. What would we live on?"

"I'm bound to make money soon," he said, incurably optimistic. "It stands to reason, bad luck can't last forever. You have that bit from your great-aunt, haven't you? If you go back to live with your mother until we get married, you can save up enough for a rainy day."

"Phillip, I am *not* going to live with Mother. You know what she's like. She's never forgiven my cousin for inheriting Fairacres and she never stops complaining, as though poor Edgar had any choice in the matter!" She held up her hand as he opened his mouth. "And yes, Edgar and Geraldine have invited me to make my home with them at Fairacres but I'd be mad within a fortnight."

"They are rather stuffy," he admitted.

"Stuffy! They're absolutely mediaeval. Geraldine considers the tango debauchery and lipstick the sign of the devil. And I'd always be a poor relation. Thank you, I prefer to work for my independence."

"What about your sister? You always got on well with Violet. Surely she and Frobisher would take you in."

"I'd still be a poor relation, though Vi and Johnnie are dears. Even though Violet earned Mother's approval by marrying young, she supports me when Mother starts ragging me about working."

"You wouldn't have to, if you married me."

"I *like* earning my living, Phil. I like writing. I wouldn't stop just because I married. You don't understand that, and you'd hate it."

"Dash it, Daisy, I know I'm a frightful idiot, but I am deuced fond of you."

"You're an old dear, but it wouldn't work, believe me."

"You're not still mourning your conchie, are you?"

Daisy flared up. "Don't call Michael that!" With an *effort* she smothered her anger. "You see, we disagree about practically everything. Let's agree to disagree. Are you going to set up the balls, or shall I?"

"We can still be chums?" Phillip enquired anxiously, collecting the red pyramid balls within the triangular frame.

"Of course, you silly old dear. You have the white ball, you go first."

They played an amicable game, Daisy sternly holding her tongue when he let her win by a couple of points.

He'd have been hurt and baffled if she'd insisted on losing honestly.

Later, lying in bed, listening to the blown rain spatter against her window, she pondered his question. Was she still mourning Michael? She'd never forget him, never forget the breathless joy of being with him, of knowing he loved her. Yet the biting pain of her loss had dulled. Was it Annabel's sympathy, her respect for Michael's courage and dedication, that allowed Daisy to begin to let go?

Annabel, too, had loved a man disdained by society, and lost him. Daisy vowed to do all in her power to protect her new friend from the further troubles Astwick's death was certain to bring upon her.

For the moment, Daisy didn't want to think about the mystery of the drowning. If she tried to work out an answer to the latest complication in the riddle, she'd never fall asleep. Instead of speculating, she proposed to wander through memories of happy hours with Michael.

Somehow Alec's dark brows and keen grey eyes kept intruding.

After a restless night filled with agitated dreams, Daisy drifted into a sound sleep shortly before dawn. She woke later than usual. When she went down to breakfast, Detective Constable Piper was talking on the telephone in the hall.

Not so much talking as listening and frantically scribbling, Daisy saw. She lingered, just out of earshot.

At last Piper hung up the receiver. His face was taut with excitement as he stared down at his notes, oblivious of Daisy's presence. "Gorblimey," he said on a long, exhaled breath. "This'll put the cat among the pigeons, right enough."

"What is it?" Daisy demanded, her heart in her mouth. "Who were you talking to?"

Startled, he looked up. "Dr. Renfrew, miss, the pathologist." He was bursting with news. "I got him to tell me in ord'n'ry words this time. That bruising and bleeding? You was right about that. Seems the gash on Astwick's forrid and the bruise on his chin . . ."

"He had a bruise on his chin?" Daisy recalled the horribly blotched face of the drowned man.

"That's what he says, miss. Seems they didn't look right for if Astwick got dumped in icy cold water right away, so Dr. Renfrew did some more tests, like I told you last night."

"And?"

"And"—Piper paused dramatically—"he found stuff in Astwick's lungs as looks to him like soap and bath-salts."

"Soap and bath-salts!" She sank onto the nearest chair. "So he couldn't have drowned in the lake, could he?"

"Reckon not, miss."

"He drowned in the bath, and his body was carried down to the lake."

"That's the way I sees it, miss."

"To make it appear to be an accident." Daisy shuddered and, with the utmost reluctance, acknowledged, "But he can't have drowned accidentally in his bath or someone would have found him and reported it, not moved him. It must have been murder."

CHAPTER 13

I wish the Chief was here," Piper groaned.

"Oh yes!" Daisy dragged her mind from contemplation of the awful fact of murder. "Did Dr. Renfrew ring up Winchester?"

"No, miss, he said he's too busy to go telephoning all over the country leaving messages with morons."

"How rude!" She was growing quite fond of Ernie Piper and didn't care to have him insulted. Besides, she was glad of the distraction from her imaginings.

"He didn't mean me, miss. He said so. The bloke he talked to at Winchester last night was"—frowning, he consulted the notebook—"'a congenial idiot.'"

"Congenital, I expect."

"Could be. Anyways, I wish he told me yesterday. D'you think the Chief might not've got that message?"

"I've been wondering why he hadn't come back yet."

"So've I, miss. I ought to've rung up meself, I know I ought." The young detective looked ready to weep.

"Too late to worry about that now, but you'd better call up the police station at once with the latest."

Eagerly Piper turned back to the telephone. Without consulting his notebook he gave the operator the Winchester police number.

Daisy listened intently to the cryptic half of the conversation she could hear, trying to guess what was being said on the other end of the wire.

"Hullo? Hullo, give me Chief Inspector Fletcher. It's urgent . . . Detective Constable Piper here. Where did he? . . . He did? . . . You don't . . . Couldn't you send a messenger after? . . . I *can't* tell you what's so . . . No, I haven't, but . . . Yes, I know the numbers . . . Yes, I will, but if they comes back or calls up, you better be bloody sure you ask the Chief to give me a ring! Operator? Operator!"

He gave the exchange another number, and then a third, asking each time for the Chief Inspector. At last he hung up the receiver and turned back to Daisy, his face disconsolate.

"You can't find him?"

"I tried his hotel, miss, and Lord Flatford's place, on the offchance. The copper on duty at the station says Payne's come clean and the Chief and Sergeant Tring went off after them jools—Inspector Gillett, too—but he don't know zackly where. He won't send someone to find 'em acos I won't tell what's so urgent."

"Quite right," Daisy approved. "It's to be kept from the local force as long as possible."

"I'll have to go after 'em meself, miss. The Chief'll want to know right away, for sure. Will you tell him what's what if he telephones?"

"Of course."

"But don't you let on to anyone else, miss. We don't want to warn the bloke who done it and have him

211

scarper. 'Sides, it might be dangerous if he knows you know there's a murderer in the house."

Daisy discovered she had lost her appetite. As the constable went off to get the police car from the garages, she started up the stairs. She'd ask Mabel to bring her tea and a bit of buttered toast in her room, and try to get some work done.

A murderer in the house! Who was it? Bits and pieces began to come together in her racing mind.

Stephen Astwick had been drowned in his bath, not long after dinner. Why had he taken a bath in the evening, since he was accustomed to two, one cold and one hot, every morning? Was he preparing for a seduction?

He had shared a bathroom with Geoffrey. Suppose he had failed to lock the connecting door to Geoffrey's bedroom. Geoffrey had left the drawing-room shortly after Astwick and might have accidentally walked in while he was in the bath. But Daisy simply couldn't imagine Geoffrey cold-bloodedly pushing him under the water and holding him there while he struggled, blew bubbles, and finally grew limp.

In hot blood, then? Could Astwick have boasted about his intention of seducing Annabel, taunting the youth, perhaps, until Geoffrey attacked in a fit of over-whelming fury?

That was, a more likely scenario. Not unlikely, in fact, yet Daisy sought for other explanations. She liked Geoffrey and didn't want to believe he was a murderer.

Astwick might not have bothered to lock the other

doors. Perhaps someone else had entered the bathroom, through the door to the corridor or through his bedroom. Someone who knew he was there and went deliberately to confront him, if not intending to kill.

James, for instance, might have wanted to press him to reveal Annabel's secret and have been angered when he refused to speak. It seemed an inadequate motive for murder, however, even for the loathsome James. Worse, Daisy had to admit that he couldn't have done it. He'd been in the drawing-room that entire evening, playing bridge with his aunt.

Phillip and Wilfred had gone to play billiards. How much time had passed between Astwick's leaving the drawing-room and their return? Long enough for Astwick to draw a bath and get into it, and for one of them to drown him? How long did it take to drown a man? Daisy wasn't sure.

Either Wilfred or Phillip could have excused himself from their game for a few minutes without the other thinking to mention it. It hadn't been important as long as Astwick was supposed to have died in the morning. They could even have been in collusion, Phillip cheated, Wilfred blackmailed, finding a common grievance. But neither had been in the drawing-room when Astwick retired. They didn't know he'd gone upstairs.

Conceivably both or either might have gone up to his bedroom, expecting to find it empty, with some sort of mischief in mind, and seized the chance to dispose of him. Not that Daisy believed for a moment that Phillip was guilty. As for Wilfred, was he strong enough to hold down a man who prided himself on his fitness, and then to carry his body all the way to the lake?

The same argument applied to Annabel. She had motive and opportunity; though Daisy was sure she'd never voluntarily go to Astwick's bedroom, he might have forced her; but surely she hadn't the strength to carry a body all that way!

Which left Lord Wentwater: alone in his study or upstairs drowning his rival?

Without conscious volition, Daisy's footsteps had carried her past the end of the passage leading to her room. Lost in speculation, she passed the Wentwaters' suite, turned the corner, and found herself before the door to the fatal bathroom. She turned the handle.

Locked. She hadn't meant to come, but since she was here . . .

She glanced quickly around. No one in sight. The wall behind her had two doors. One, she worked out, must be to Annabel's bathroom, for use when the house was full of guests. The other was to the back stairs. A maid or footman might pop out at any moment.

Daisy ducked into Astwick's bedroom, closing the door swiftly and silently behind her. The room looked just as it had when she'd seen it before: the bed made up with a chocolate-and-cream-patterned coverlet, a gentleman's toilet articles arranged on the chest-of-drawers, a couple of chairs, the wardrobe where Piper had found passports and tickets. He and Sergeant Tring were neat, efficient searchers, or else a housemaid had tidied after their search.

There was the door to the bathroom. On tiptoe, holding her breath, Daisy made for it. A moment later she was contemplating a vast Victorian bath with brass taps in the form of the heads of a lion and a lioness. Were they the last things Astwick had seen as water filled his lungs?

Tearing her gaze from the gruesomely fascinating sight, she noted the jar of bath-salts on a low shelf above the tub. The crystals were green—pine or herbal for the gentlemen instead of flower scents. Within easy reach of a bather, a heated towel rail bore an assortment of thick, white towels, matching the bath mat that lay on the green linoleum floor. A rubber-footed and -topped stepstool stood in one corner, a cork-seated wooden chair in another.

It was just like the bathroom she had shared with Fenella, an innocent setting for a horrible crime. She turned her attention to the doors.

None of the three doors had keys in the keyholes. The one to the corridor was fastened shut with a bolt, but neither of the connecting doors to the bedrooms had a bolt. Geoffrey had easy access at any time. Things looked black for the chivalrous young man.

Daisy frowned as an overlooked snag struck her. Astwick had a jagged gash on his forehead and, according to the pathologist, a bruise on his chin. The latter had immediately reminded her of the bruise on James's chin after its unexpected encounter with his brother's fist. But a blow used to fell a standing opponent made no sense against a man in a bathtub.

She returned to the bath and stood gazing down into it, trying to picture the scene. Even if Astwick had sat up rather than reclining in the hot, scented water, his shoulders would scarcely have cleared the rim of the deep tub. Biffing him on the chin seemed a peculiar thing to do, especially for a tall chap like Geoffrey. His nose would have made a more obvious target.

Still, Daisy knew nothing about boxing. What about the laceration? She didn't see how either Geoffrey's fist or the smooth, enamelled bathtub could have caused an irregular wound. Probably the ice had done it, when Astwick's body was dropped into the hole. Dr. Renfrew had implied that it was caused before death, but she wouldn't be at all surprised if Piper had misunderstood his . . .

Click. The latch of the door behind her. The hinges gave a faint squeak as the door opened. Daisy froze.

"Miss Dalrymple!" Geoffrey's voice, startled, not threatening. Not yet.

Turning, Daisy summoned up a bright smile. "Hullo! This is your bathroom, too, is it? I just asked the way to the one Astwick used. Mr. Fletcher wanted me to . . . to check that his . . . his missing boots hadn't somehow hidden themselves in here." Of all the feeble excuses! "I expect the maid would have taken them away by now, though. I can't see them, can you?"

"No." He glanced around distractedly, his normally ruddy face pale. "His boots! I forgot . . ."

She took a step backwards.

His voice shook. "You think I killed him, don't you?"

The dangerous words escaped her against her will. "Did you?"

"I didn't mean to!" he cried, slumping against the door-post and covering his face with his hands. "I didn't mean to! It was like a nightmare I couldn't wake up from."

There was no anger in him, only despair. Daisy no longer feared him. She crossed the bathroom to lay a gentle hand on his arm. "Do you want to tell me about it?"

"The police will find out anyway, won't they?" he said drearily.

"If I can work it out, you can be sure Mr. Fletcher will."

"The boots . . . I forgot he couldn't have walked down to the lake in skates."

"It seemed unlikely." She didn't tell him that particular error had led the detectives nowhere. "But there's also new evidence, from the autopsy. Astwick died soon after dinner, and he drowned in his bath, not in the lake."

"Not in *his* bath. Not in here."

"Where else?" Daisy asked, bewildered. If Astwick hadn't drowned in this bathroom there was no reason to suspect Geoffrey more than anyone else—except that now he had practically confessed.

He stared at her in horror. "You think I just walked in here and drowned him in his bath? Without provocation? In cold blood?"

"No, I was sure he must have provoked you," she

217

assured him. "I mean, with something more immediate than his general nastiness. What happened? If it wasn't here, where was it?"

"I'll tell you. I'll explain it all, but I . . . The detective hasn't come back yet today, has he?"

"The Chief Inspector? Not yet," said Daisy warily. "He's expected at any moment."

"Let me tell *you,* before he comes. But I want Father to hear, too. Please!"

"Of course. Let's go and see if he's in his study."

Without speaking, they traversed the corridors together. Geoffrey had regained his self-control, though his face remained colourless. Daisy thought it had grown thinner since she first met him.

At the top of the stairs, he paused and said in a low, pleading voice, "Will you explain to Mr. Fletcher for me? I don't think I can bear to tell the story twice. If he already knows, he can simply ask questions."

"I will if you'd like me to, but I can't promise he won't want to hear the whole thing in your own words."

"I suppose so."

"Are you sure you wouldn't prefer to wait till he arrives?"

"No! I can't let Father find out from someone else." His gaze beseeched her. "And . . . and I'd rather you were there when I tell Father."

"I shan't desert you." Whatever he had done, now he was just an unhappy, defenceless, motherless boy. Her heart filled with pity.

They went on down the stairs and across the unoccupied Great Hall. The earl's study was empty, but for Landseer's retrievers gazing down from the wall with aristocratic indifference. No one was in the library next door. Geoffrey turned to Daisy with a lost look.

"There's no need to get any servants involved," she said firmly. "You wait here and I'll go and find Lord Wentwater."

Nodding dumb acquiescence, he crossed to the window and stood staring out at the drizzling gloom beyond the glass.

As the study door shut behind her, she hesitated. She hadn't wanted to ring the bell in the earl's private study and have a footman find herself and Geoffrey there obviously wishing to speak to his father together. Not that the servants wouldn't eventually find out every-thing—Alec had made her very much aware of that—but the later the better.

On the other hand, to hunt all over the house for Lord Wentwater would raise eyebrows and pique curiosity. No one would think twice if she enquired for him and then requested a private word. She hurried to the hall.

The footman on duty was making up the fire in the vast fireplace. He stood up as he heard her footsteps approaching. "Can I help you, miss?"

"Do you know where Lord Wentwater is?"

"In the estate office, miss." His eyes gleamed inquis-itively in his otherwise impassive face. "Can I take a message to his lordship for you?"

"Thank you, I'll go myself, if you'll be so kind as to direct me."

In her haste, the corridors seemed endless. She preferred not to leave Geoffrey in suspense any longer than necessary. Aside from his misery, he might get cold feet and decide not to confess. She had a feeling that in the end everyone would be best served if she knew the whole story before Alec returned to Wentwater Court.

She found the office at last. The door was ajar and she heard the earl's voice. When she knocked, he called, rather impatiently, "Come in!"

The small room reminded her of her father's estate office at Fairacres. Shelves contained an orderly jumble of agricultural books and magazines, prize ribbons and cups, and account books. Maps hung on the wall. On the desk lay a pile of papers and a spike of paid bills, an open ledger between them. A man she didn't know sat behind the desk. The two chairs on the near side were occupied by Lord Wentwater and his eldest son. They all rose to their feet as she entered.

James gave Daisy an uncertain smile. She ignored it. For him she felt no pity.

"Lord Wentwater, may I have a word with you?"

His grave eyes, searching her face, grew sombre. "Of course, Miss Dalrymple." He rose and accompanied her into the corridor, closing the door behind him.

What on earth was she going to say to him? Was there any way to prepare him for the frightful shock to come? Daisy's mind was a blank.

"Will you come to your study, please? Right away?"

He gasped. "Not another body?"

"No!" Filled with remorse, she touched his hand.

"No, nothing like that. But I think you'd better come."

"Very well." He returned momentarily to the office to tell his heir and his agent to carry on without him. Then, in silence, he and Daisy made their way back to the hall and on to the study.

Geoffrey still stood by the window, a drooping figure, his forehead now resting wearily against the glass pane. He swung round, straightening, as his father followed Daisy into the room.

"Sir, I . . ." His voice wavered. "I have something to tell you."

"My dear boy!" Forgetting Daisy, the earl strode past her, his hands held out to his youngest child in a gesture almost of entreaty.

They clasped hands, two proper English gentlemen incapable of giving each other the embrace both needed. Then Lord Wentwater led Geoffrey to the maroon-leather wing chairs by the fire, made him sit down, and poured him a glass of brandy from the tantalus on a corner table. He took the other chair. Daisy retreated to a ladder-back chair by the desk. Turned away from her, the earl seemed unaware of her continued presence, but Geoffrey's eyes sought her out before he took a swallow from his glass.

He squared his shoulders, ready to confess to his misdeeds and take his punishment like a man, as he had been taught. "Father, I must explain . . ."

"Wait!" Annabel appeared in the doorway.

Geoffrey started to his feet. "No! You have nothing to do with this!"

With swift steps she crossed the room to stand beside her husband, face to face with her stepson. "My dear boy," she said passionately, "you *cannot* imagine I shall let you shoulder all the blame."

CHAPTER 14

I went up to bed early that night," Annabel began in a low voice, staring down at her clasped hands. Geoffrey had seated her in his chair, with an ardent solicitude that made Daisy blink hard.

In turn, Lord Wentwater had set a straight chair for Geoffrey between them and made him sit. As he fetched it from the desk, his gaze had passed over Daisy unseeingly, his mind on his wife and son and the disclosures he must fear were about to bring his world tumbling in ruins about his ears. He listened with bowed head. Daisy saw only his aristocratic profile and one thin but strong white hand, resting in tense stillness on the maroon arm of his chair.

"I was tired," Annabel continued, "and I had a slight headache."

Geoffrey interrupted her. "It was that horrible song of James's that drove you away! The one about . . ."

"That's enough, Geoffrey," she said sharply, raising her head with a protective glance at her husband. Her eyes met Daisy's. Daisy tried hard to convey sympathy and encouragement, and hoped she was right in thinking Annabel looked a little comforted. "No matter why, I went upstairs and had Barstow draw me a bath, then I dismissed her. All I wanted was peace and quiet.

"I stayed in the bath for ages. The warmth and the rose scent of the bath-crystals were so soothing, just what I needed. Then the water began to cool. You know how you feel after lying in a hot bath, relaxed and languorous and indolent. It was quite an effort to get out and I was glad of the little stool. I was stepping down from it to the floor and reaching for my towel when I heard behind me the click of a latch.

"I flung the towel around me and turned. The door to the corridor was opening. That man"—Annabel's voice cracked—"Lord Stephen swaggered in.

"He held the key dangling from the tip of his finger in front of him, like a sort of Open Sesame talisman. He boasted that he'd stolen it. That door was always kept locked and I hadn't noticed the key was missing. He pushed the door to behind him and came towards me.

"He was wearing his dressing-gown, a frightful crimson velvet thing embroidered with gold dragons, with a gold-tasselled cord. As he came he untied it. Underneath, he was nude. I cried out, 'Go away,' and clutched the towel tighter around me, and retreated backwards. He smiled. Oh, it was a cold, evil smile! It made me cringe. He said, 'Oh no, my dear. Not when at last we have our chance.'

" 'Go away,' I cried out again. I couldn't move any farther back. The edge of the bath pressed into the back of my thighs. I told him I'd scream if he came a single step closer. 'Someone will hear!' I threatened, praying I was right. 'Someone will come!'

"He laughed. He said that would suit him almost as well, though he'd be sorry . . . to miss the seduction scene. It was revenge he wanted, you see, as much as he wanted m-me, revenge because I refused him years and years ago.

"That was when he touched me. He stroked my shoulder and I hit his hand away. Then he told me he was leaving the country very soon anyway, so scandal could not touch him. He didn't care if he was caught with me, not that he'd ever paid much attention to the gabbling of envious geese, he said.

"He tore the towel from my grasp," Annabel continued with a dry sob. "He tossed it on the floor and reached for me. I did scream then. I was terrified. But at that moment the door crashed open and Geoffrey rushed in."

"I heard her," Geoffrey said simply. "I heard his laugh. I'd been suspicious when he left the drawing-room so soon after she did. I followed him upstairs and saw him go into his room. I went to mine, but I left the door open just a crack and kept an eye on the corridor.

"The trouble was, my door hinges on the wrong side. I couldn't see towards Astwick's room without sticking my head out. I didn't think it mattered because I assumed he'd have to go past my room and round the corner to the boudoir or bedroom door. I didn't see him sneaking across the corridor to the bathroom. I heard a door close, though, and voices. I went to listen at his bedroom door. That was when he laughed and she screamed.

"Oh, God, I was so afraid the bathroom door would be locked. I'd have knocked it down, but it would have wasted time. But it wasn't even properly latched. It slammed open with a crash and he swung round, still gripping her by the arm. As I charged at him, she wrenched free and escaped.

"I hit him." Geoffrey couldn't keep a vestige of pride out of his voice. "It was a ripping left uppercut to the chin. Of course, I did catch him unawares. Anyway, he lost his balance, tangled his feet in the bath mat, and tripped over the stool. I didn't wait to see any more than that. I grabbed a towel from the rail and her dressing-gown from the chair and dashed into the boudoir after her.

"I didn't want her to take a chill," he explained earnestly to his father. "I wanted to comfort her, and to promise I'd never let that beast go near her again. I didn't look, I swear it. Besides, I had to watch the door in case he came after us."

"He kept his back turned to me," Annabel confirmed shakily, "until I had dried myself and put on my dressing gown, and a cardigan over it. I was cold, so very cold. Henry?" The word held a desperate plea.

Lord Wentwater leaned forward and clasped her out-stretched hands. "My dear, no blame can attach to you for that blackguard's actions, nor are you responsible for my son's gallantry. If I am silent it's because I don't wish to interrupt what I know to be a painful narration."

Reassured, she took up the tale. "We talked for a few minutes, not long. There was no sign of Lord Stephen, no sound, so Geoffrey returned to the bathroom to make sure he had left."

"He was still there all right," Geoffrey said harshly, pressing the heels of his hands to his eyes as if to shut out the memory. "He was bent double over the edge of the tub, his head and shoulders underwater. I hauled him out but there was no heartbeat, no pulse, no breath. He was dead."

In the tense, almost palpable hush that filled the study, a coal falling in the grate made Daisy jump.

"Geoffrey didn't come back," said Annabel, "and I heard such odd noises. I was frightened. I peeked into the bathroom and saw him crouching by the body. Lord Stephen lay sprawled on the linoleum in a spreading pool of water, with blood oozing in droplets from a gash in his forehead. I thought I was going to be sick.

"Geoffrey's face was stark white, horror-stricken, anguished. He cried out that he hadn't meant to kill him. I knew it, and I pulled myself together enough to reassure him. He stood up and glanced at the bathtub. I saw that the water was stained pink. There was blood on one of the taps.

"The taps in my bathroom are cockatoos," she said in a monotone. "When Lord Stephen tripped and lost his balance, he must have somehow spun round, falling, and hit his head on a cockatoo's crest. Between that and Geoffrey's blow, he must have been unconscious, or at least too dazed to pull himself out when he fell head down in the water. And perhaps before he recovered he was weakened by loss of blood.

"Geoffrey wanted to go to you, Henry. I stopped him. Maybe I was wrong. Maybe I should have let him go. But I couldn't bear to bring any more trouble upon you! You should never have married me!"

In an instant the earl was out of his chair and bending over her. "Never say that, my love." He took her face tenderly between his hands and kissed her forehead. She clutched his sleeve, tears trembling on her dark lashes.

Daisy hurriedly looked away. Geoffrey, scarlet to the tips of his ears, was staring with intense concentration at the window. His chin quivered pitiably.

After a moment, he gasped out in a strangled voice, "I promised. I promised not to tell you, sir, but when Miss Dalrymple guessed . . ."

Lord Wentwater threw a vague glance over his shoulder at Daisy before turning to Geoffrey and laying a hand on his shoulder. "You saved the woman I love from rape. How can I thank you? What more can I ask of you?"

"I love her too," said Geoffrey, almost inaudibly.

As though struck by a physical blow, Lord Wentwater sank back into his chair. "I see." He sounded old and very tired.

"She loves *you,* Father!"

Before the words had left Geoffrey's mouth, Annabel was kneeling at her husband's side, pressing his hand to her cheek. "Oh, my love, my love, don't look like that. There is no one in my world but you. Geoffrey knows it. He has my affection as your son, and my eternal gratitude for what he has done for me, but you are all I want or need."

And Geoffrey, to Daisy's silent applause and admiration, moved his chair close to his father's for her. She sat down, her hand in the earl's, and Geoffrey retreated to lonely exile on the far side of the fireplace.

With an obvious effort, he returned to his story. "We couldn't leave Astwick lying there for the maid to find in the morning. Lord knows what sort of scandal that would have led to. We had to get him out of there. I thought it would be best just to move him into my bathroom, the one I shared with him."

"I couldn't let him do that," his stepmother said. "If anyone had guessed more was involved in Lord Stephen's death than a simple accident, Geoffrey would inevitably have been implicated. We had to make it appear obvious that Lord Stephen had been alone, that the accident was entirely his own fault, but we weren't even sure whether he had bled to death or drowned.

"I suppose I was beginning to recover from the shock, because I began to notice things I'd overlooked. There was a strong smell of roses and I discovered the entire jar of bath-salts had dropped into the bath and broken. He must have knocked it with a flailing arm when he fell. The salts were bright pink, so presumably part of the tinge of the bathwater was from that. Then I saw the red rivulets trickling from his dressing-gown—it was sodden from the waist up—into the pool on the floor. The dye was running, and must have started to run when it was in the bath, colouring the water.

"So I realized he had not necessarily lost a great deal of blood. It seemed more likely he had drowned. We needed to stage a drowning accident and the lake was the obvious place."

"I didn't want her involved in the gruesome business, Father. I said I'd do it myself. She insisted on helping."

"While I dressed, Geoffrey went to change into outdoor clothes and to fetch Lord Stephen's skating clothes. I put them on the body." Annabel shuddered. "It was ghastly. My stomach heaved the whole time."

"And in the meantime," Geoffrey explained, "I sneaked down the backstairs and out to the woodshed. I found an axe. The moon was rising, which made it quite easy to move about outside and not to stray from the trodden path. A beautiful night! If I'd been seen I could have concealed the axe and said I was just out for a stroll.

"Once I got down there I was pretty safe in the black moon-shadow of the bridge. I hacked a hole in the ice, took the axe back to its place, and went back up to the bathroom.

"She was struggling to force Astwick's limp feet into the skating boots. I helped her, and we laced them up tightly." He looked across at Daisy. "It never crossed my mind that he would have worn ordinary boots to walk down to the lake. That was what aroused the detectives' suspicions, wasn't it? That one stupid mistake was what made them guess it wasn't an accident."

"As a matter of fact, no. Later they wondered about the missing boots, but no one could remember whether they'd been under the bench when we went down or not. The gardeners cleared everything up afterwards, so anything might have happened to them."

"Then what was it?"

"A silly little thing. There were axe-marks in the ice around the hole. If I hadn't taken those photographs, they'd probably have passed for the marks of skates, but they showed up distinctly different on my pictures. I pointed them out to Mr. Fletcher. How I wish I hadn't!"

All three rushed to reassure her.

"It was your civic duty," the earl reminded her with stern kindliness.

"You mustn't blame yourself, Daisy," Annabel cried. "You didn't know—how could you?—where it would lead."

"It's all my fault," Geoffrey said desolately. "If I hadn't lost my temper, I could have stopped him without hitting him. None of this would have happened. The whole thing's like a bad dream. The worst was carrying him down the back stairs, then down the hill. A nightmare! His feet kept knocking against the walls."

"I went first down the stairs," Annabel said, "to make sure the coast was clear, but I didn't go out. I went back up to clean up the bathroom. I wrung out the wet dressing-gown and draped it over the towel rail to dry, cleaned the bloody tap, and mopped the floor. I left the broken glass in the tub and in the morning I told Barstow I'd knocked it off the shelf reaching for it to add more to my bath. Would you believe it, she was very relieved that I hadn't cut myself!"

"Meanwhile Geoffrey was struggling down the hill with that ghastly burden on his back."

"He weighed me down, upset my balance. I kept slipping and sliding on the packed snow and I was terrified of letting him fall, leaving an inexplicable hollow in the untrodden snow to either side of the path.

"I got him down to the bank, though he seemed to grow heavier and heavier. I had to lay him down to take a breather, and I thought I'd never be able to lift him up again. The moon was high by then, reflecting brightly off the snow. I felt as conspicuous as a beetle on a sheet of white paper. If anyone had looked out . . .

"I picked up the body in my arms, heaved myself to my feet, and set out across the frozen lake. Beneath the double weight the ice creaked and groaned, and I kept thinking how ironic it would be if *two* drowned bodies were found in the morning.

"I didn't dare go right to the edge of the hole. I knelt down and rolled him towards it. I couldn't believe everyone for miles didn't hear the splash when he fell in." Geoffrey faltered. "He sank, and I thought he'd stay down, but that leather jacket of his—with the belt and tight cuffs and fastened up to the chin—it trapped air like a balloon. I nearly fainted when he bobbed to the surface. Thank God he was facedown. Thank God!

"Somehow I made it back up to the house, through the side door, and up the back stairs. By then her bathroom door was locked. I went to bed and tossed and turned for hours before I fell asleep. Yet when I woke in the morning, I didn't remember any of that horror until

I went into my bathroom and saw Astwick's crimson dressing-gown hanging on the back of the door.

"All I wanted was to get away from the house. I went riding—and when I came back, the police were here."

"We didn't talk about it," Annabel said. "Not even once. It was too risky, and I suppose I wanted to pretend it hadn't happened. Besides, there really wasn't anything to say. We had done all we could to keep scandal from your family, Henry. It wasn't enough." She hid her face in her hands. "Now we'll all be dragged through the courts. The whole world will be convinced of your wife's . . ."

"No!" cried Geoffrey. "You need not come into it at all. We'll make up a story. We'll tell them I quarrelled with Astwick over money or something, and he drowned in his own bath, not yours."

"The police know Astwick was pursuing Annabel," said Lord Wentwater, passing a weary hand over his face. "They know you attacked James to defend her, Geoffrey."

"They know he's in love with me," whispered Annabel.

The earl groaned. "I still cannot bring myself to believe that my son is in love with his stepmother. I'm not sure which appalls me more, that, or his killing a man, a guest in my house."

Huddled in the wing chair, Geoffrey seemed to shrink. "Remember, Henry, he did it for me!" Annabel reproached her husband.

"And not on purpose," Daisy reminded him, "and Astwick was a villain."

"Yes. Yes, of course. I'm sorry, my boy, I'm having difficulty trying to take it all in. Of course, it was unintentional, and Astwick richly deserved punishment, if not to meet his end."

"Will I have to go to prison, Father?" Geoffrey asked fearfully.

"I don't know. It can't be called murder, surely, but manslaughter . . . ? I don't know the penalties. Criminal law has never been one of my interests. I'll stand behind you all the way, you may be sure. You shall have the best lawyers in the country. We'll ask Hugh's advice. He will know who's best, what we ought to do first, whom to approach." Lord Wentwater stood up and moved towards the bellpull, cheered by the prospect of a practical course of action.

Not murder, Daisy thought, but would the police believe it? Would a jury believe it?

Even if Geoffrey was found innocent, or convicted of manslaughter, would sensation-hungry journalists believe the verdict and persuade their readers of its truth? There would always be those who were certain that the earl had used the influence of his title to save his son from the gallows. Mud always stuck.

Not only to Geoffrey. Suppose some reporter, not satisfied with scandal easily acquired, dug up the secret from Annabel's past that had allowed Astwick to blackmail her. Annabel would be ruined, her marriage and her life destroyed.

Overwhelmed with guilt, Daisy couldn't bear the possibility that she might be responsible for so much misery. If only she had more time to think up some way to prevent it! Once Alec came back and arrested Geoffrey it would be too late.

CHAPTER 15

I have it!" To Daisy, her plan appeared gloriously inevitable in its simplicity, the solution to every problem—as long as Alec didn't come back too soon.

Lord Wentwater's hand hesitated on the bellpull.

"Listen!" Daisy jumped up from her chair. Three faces harrowed by emotion turned to her. "Listen! I have the most utterly spiffing idea you've ever heard. Do go ahead and send to ask Sir Hugh to join us, please, Lord Wentwater. We shall need him, and we must hurry."

"Hurry?" asked the earl with a frown, ringing the bell. "I fear a hasty and ill-conceived scheme can only lead to further disaster."

"At least let Daisy tell us her idea, Henry," Annabel proposed, a light dawning in her dark eyes.

"I can't see how things could possibly be any worse," said Geoffrey dully.

"Let me explain," Daisy begged.

"Of course, Miss Dalrymple." Lord Wentwater's habitual courtliness prevailed over his mistrust. "I beg your pardon if I seemed to reject your assistance. We are in need of any help anyone can offer."

"Everything comes together so neatly it must be Fate," said Daisy. "Geoffrey must . . ."

She was interrupted by the arrival of Drew himself. The butler's outward stateliness was unimpaired by the troubled times the household was passing through. Yet Daisy sensed a certain commiseration in the swift glance that swept over the gathering in the study.

Nothing but deference was apparent in his tone. "Your lordship rang?"

"Please tell Sir Hugh I should be glad of a word with him in here." The earl looked at Daisy and shrugged slightly. "At his earliest convenience. And, Drew, bring glasses."

"At once, my lord." Bowing, the butler withdrew.

Reminded of the brandy his father had poured him, Geoffrey reached for the glass and finished it at a gulp. A tinge of colour crept into his pallid cheeks. "What must I do, Miss Dalrymple?"

"Go abroad. I suppose you have a passport?" she asked anxiously as the others gasped.

"Yes, I went climbing in Austria last summer." He stared at her, hope restoring the vitality and resolution to his youthful features. "But . . ."

"You would have my son running from justice?" said Lord Wentwater harshly, hauteur in every inch of his tall, stiff-necked figure. "He will stay and take his punishment like a gentleman."

"Henry, no!" Annabel protested. "He didn't mean to kill Stephen, and it was all for my sake, for *your* sake."

"It's not only Geoffrey," Daisy reminded him. "Can you stand aside and let your private life be made public? Let James's conduct become common knowledge?"

"James!" he groaned.

Inexorable, she continued, "Let Annabel be pilloried in the papers?" She was rather pleased with her rhetoric.

His shoulders sagging in defeat, he returned to his chair, took Annabel's hand, and said remorsefully, "Forgive me, my love."

"Never mind that," she soothed him. "Let's just think of how to send Geoffrey abroad in a hurry."

"I'll do whatever you say, Father," Geoffrey promised.

"I'd say go, but it's impossible. However fast we move, the police will have plenty of time to close the Channel ports, and I believe the French police work closely with ours these days. If you somehow escaped the net here, you would simply be arrested in France."

"Not France," said Daisy, impatient with his pessimism. "Not the Channel. Not *Europe*." She stopped with a frustrated sigh as Drew came in again.

"I sent a footman to request Sir Hugh's presence, my lord." He set a tray of glasses, bottles, and decanters on the desk. "Shall I pour the drinks, my lord?"

"No, thank you, Drew."

"Does your lordship desire anything further?"

"No!" the earl snapped impatiently, then retrieved his calm courtesy with an effort. "No, thank you, that will be all for now."

"Very good, my lord." A hint of reproach in his bow, the butler once again departed with his ponderous tread.

As the door clicked shut, three eager faces swung

towards Daisy. "Where?" they demanded as one.

"Brazil." Daisy savoured their astonishment. "It just so happens that I know the S.S. *Orinoco* sails from Southampton this afternoon, for Rio, and there will be at least two empty berths aboard."

"This afternoon?" Lord Wentwater pulled a gold hunter from his fob pocket.

"At three."

Annabel and Geoffrey turned to look at the clock on the mantelpiece. Though Daisy felt as if a century or so had passed since she stepped out of bed, it was not yet noon.

"Southampton's only about thirty-five miles," said Geoffrey, and added wonderingly, "Brazil! But what shall I do when I get there?"

"That's the beauty of my plan," said Daisy with pride. "Sir Hugh owns vast plantations of rubber and coffee in Brazil. I'm sure he'll be able to give you a job."

"I will, will I?" said Sir Hugh's dry voice behind her. He entered the study, followed, to everyone's dismay, by Lady Josephine.

"What's going on, Henry?" she asked plaintively, her plump face alarmed.

"It's all right, Jo," said her brother as he and Geoffrey rose to their feet. "Nothing that need concern you. I'll tell you about it later."

"You needn't think you can hoodwink me." Not to be fobbed off, she settled in Lord Wentwater's chair in a determined way and patted Annabel's hand. "Maybe I can help."

While they argued, Daisy whispered to Geoffrey, "There's no time to waste. You'd better go and find your passport and pack a few things."

Nodding assent, he whispered back, "Is it all right if I say good-bye to Marjie and Will?"

She frowned. "I suppose so. Yes, of course you must, but for heaven's sake try not to tell them anything. Don't let them ask you questions."

"Right-oh." He slipped out, oddly enough no less unobtrusive for being the centre of the present storm.

Lady Josephine had won the argument simply by refusing to budge. "So you might as well just tell me what's going on," she reiterated.

Lord Wentwater sighed. "Miss Dalrymple, will you be so good?" Abandoning the floor to her, he moved to the desk to pour drinks.

Daisy turned to Sir Hugh. The baronet had watched with mild amusement his wife's quarrel with her brother. "Yes, do please explain, Miss Dalrymple," he invited, his tone affable but with an authoritative note.

"First, Sir Hugh, let me ask if I'm right in thinking you can employ Geoffrey in one of your South American concerns. Because if not, there's no need to trouble you further."

"It's possible," he said cautiously.

"Of course you can, Hugh," Lady Josephine insisted. "Only a few months ago you found a position for Mr. Barnstaple's cousin, and Geoffrey is your own nephew. Or mine, which comes to the same thing."

"Very true, my love, but young Barnstaple was not

fleeing the law, which, unless I'm greatly mistaken, is young Geoffrey's problem."

Lady Josephine's round, pink face crumpled. "Oh, Daisy, is that what it is?"

Daisy decided candour was the best policy, though she had no intention of revealing the full story. If Annabel and Lord Wentwater wanted the Mentons to know all, they could tell them at a later date.

"I'm afraid so, Lady Jo. He was responsible for Lord Stephen's death, though it was entirely unintentional. He was just trying to protect Annabel."

"The dear boy! Breaking up the ice was a simply marvellous scheme. If only the rotten bounder hadn't drowned, he'd certainly have left Wentwater with his tail between his legs after falling into the lake. Too too mortifying, like a careless schoolboy!"

Daisy didn't disillusion her. The fewer people who knew that Astwick had drowned in the bath, the better. "So, you see, if Geoffrey doesn't go away, there will be a trial and the newspapers will make up the most frightful stories."

"As sure as night follows day," Lady Josephine agreed with a shudder.

"And if he does go away . . ." Sir Hugh began in an ominous voice.

"I'm sure the police will decide to let the matter drop, to treat it as an accident," Daisy hastily interrupted, her fingers crossed behind her back and a prayer winging its way heavenward. So far she'd been too busy putting her plan into action to dwell on possible consequences.

"But he must be gone before Chief Inspector Fletcher returns, which he may at any moment. Luckily there's a ship sailing from Southampton at three."

Everyone turned to consult the clock. The hands stood at a quarter past twelve.

"It could be done," said the baronet reluctantly.

"It *will* be done," Lady Josephine declared. "Don't be difficult, Hugh dear. Astwick was an absolute wretch and the world should be grateful to Geoffrey."

"Very well." His decision made, Sir Hugh was all business. "I'll take the boy to Southampton in my motor. Henry, would you send a message to Hammond to bring the Hispano-Suiza round at once, please? I must telephone my agent in Southampton to arrange passage, and write a letter of credit for Geoffrey. He'd better carry a recommendation to my Rio agent with him, too, though I'll send full instructions by wireless later. May I use your desk?" He was already moving towards it, taking his fountain pen from his pocket.

"There's notepaper in the second drawer on the left." Lord Wentwater had rung the bell. Now he cleared the desk of the tray of drinks and stood holding it, looking rather helpless. "Miss Dalrymple, where did Geoffrey go?"

"I thought he ought to go and pack." She took the tray from him and in turn deposited it in the hands of the butler as he entered. "Please get rid of this, Drew."

"Yes, miss."

She glanced back. The earl had turned away to listen anxiously as his brother-in-law asked the telephone operator to look up his agent's number and connect him.

"And, Drew," Daisy continued, "tell Sir Hugh's chauffeur to bring the Hispano-Suiza to the front door. At once."

"At once, miss."

"There's no sign of the Chief Inspector, is there?"

"No, miss."

"Thank heaven."

The imperturbable butler's eyebrows twitched. "Will there be anything else, miss?"

"No, thank you. But tell Hammond to *hurry*."

As Annabel and Lady Jo were talking quietly together, Daisy followed Drew out of the study and sped off upstairs to find Geoffrey.

She knocked on his bedroom door and entered in response to his subdued invitation. The room was sparsely furnished, its most notable feature a shelf displaying gymkhana trophies: blue, red, and white rosettes and engraved silver cups. A Stubbs horse and groom hung on the wall opposite the bed, and several lesser paintings, drawings, and photographs of equine beauties completed the decor.

Geoffrey had retrieved two large, brass-studded, leather portmanteaux from the boxroom. They lay open on the bed, half filled with coats and trousers. Tactfully ignoring his reddened eyes, Daisy helped him stow away the contents of his chest-of-drawers.

"You needn't worry about when you arrive in Rio. Sir Hugh is writing a letter to his agent, and he'll wireless him, too. You'll have a job to go to."

In a strangled voice, Geoffrey blurted out the

thought that tormented him. "I'll never see her again."

"No." She had no comfort to offer.

"I'd almost rather go to prison, if it weren't for dragging her through the courts."

"You couldn't do that," said Daisy urgently. "You absolutely must go."

"Yes, I know." He blinked hard. "It's best, really, that we don't meet again, isn't it? I put her in an impossible situation."

Her throat tight, Daisy nodded. She had been no older than Geoffrey when she fell in love with Michael, not much older when the telegram came announcing his death. Though he now existed only in her memory, the memories still hurt. How would Geoffrey ever begin to heal when the woman he worshipped still lived, so far away? She couldn't dismiss his pain as a youthful infatuation he'd soon get over.

In silence they continued the hasty packing. Daisy had just folded a warm pullover—he'd need it on board if not in Brazil—when she heard a sound.

"Listen!"

Footsteps in the distance rapidly approached along the corridor. Just outside the bedroom door they halted. Geoffrey froze, his hands full of balled socks, and Daisy sank onto the bed, her heart in her mouth. Too late! The police had come back.

The bedroom door edged open. Marjorie's face peeked around it. In her relief, Daisy felt positively light-headed—and increasingly aware of a sense of desperate urgency.

CHAPTER 16

Marjorie came into the bedroom. "Geoff! It's true, then. You're leaving?"

Wilfred was close behind her. "So it was you who bumped him off, old fellow. A spilling piece of work. Congratulations!"

Marjorie tearfully hugged her brother and Wilfred shook his hand with a vigour astonishing in so languid a young man. Daisy regarded them with exasperated resignation.

"I hope you two can keep your mouths closed," she said crossly, dumping a last load of shirts into one of the portmanteaux and closing it. "Come on, quick, we must get these down to your uncle's car."

Geoffrey fastened the other and effortlessly set both on the floor.

"I'll carry one," offered Wilfred, and attempted to lift the smaller of the two. With an effort, he raised it an inch or so. "Too many late nights," he said with an uneasy laugh. "Well, boxing's not for me but perhaps I'll take up riding."

"Take care of Galahad for me," said Geoffrey abruptly, his head down as he picked up the portmanteaux and made for the door.

"I will, old man, I will." Wilfred's eyes were suspiciously bright. "I expect I'll be spending more time down here, don't you know. Town palls on one after a while."

"Now I know Annabel better," said Marjorie, "I'll come home more often, too."

Daisy followed Geoffrey and Marjorie out into the corridor. Behind her, Wilfred drew in a sharp breath and groaned. "Oh Lord, what now!"

He was looking ahead down the corridor. Daisy peered past Geoffrey's bulk. James stood in the doorway of his bedroom, watching them, his heavy jaw set, his face stony.

Coming abreast of him, Geoffrey hesitated. Then he put down a portmanteaux and offered his hand. James simply stared for a moment before, with obvious reluctance, he gave his brother's hand a brief shake. Without further ado, he stepped back into his room and closed the door.

However unsatisfactory, Daisy was glad for Geoffrey's sake that he had made the gesture of reconciliation. Among the regrets that would haunt him, he'd not have to remember parting from James in anger.

"I'll jolly well have to spend more time at Wentwater," said Wilfred quietly as they turned into the cross-passage. Thoughtful and rather pale, he looked daunted by the prospect of trying to compensate his father for the loss of two sons.

"Lord Wentwater told me he believes you are not without redeeming traits," Daisy informed him. She knew what it was like to be compared with a sibling and found inadequate.

"High praise," he snorted, but he seemed relieved.

As they descended the stairs to the Great Hall, a

footman rushed to relieve Geoffrey of the portmanteaux. "The motor's out front, Mr. Geoffrey. Mr. Drew just went to tell his lordship." With a quick glance behind him, he leaned forward and hissed, "Us in the servants' hall all wants to wish you Godspeed, sir." Straightening, his nose in the air in proper footmanly fashion, he lugged the portmanteaux across to the front door.

The Wentwaters and the Mentons came into the hall from the east wing. With a cry of distress, Lady Jo swooped on her erring nephew and enveloped him in her substantial embrace, to his uneasy embarrassment. Daisy moved back, out of the way of the family's farewells. She had intruded enough—more than enough—on their troubles.

Kissing Geoffrey's cheek, Lady Josephine allowed her husband to tear her away. Geoffrey turned to Annabel.

"I'm sorry," he muttered, head hanging.

She took his hand in both hers and whispered something in his ear that made him raise his chin and stand tall and proud as he faced his father.

"I'm sorry, sir."

"My dear boy, if you hadn't . . ." Lord Wentwater left his sentence unfinished. He shook his son's hand with the grave propriety of a gentleman parting from an acquaintance he expects to meet again at no distant date. But then he turned away from the others and Daisy caught a glimpse of the deep sorrow he couldn't quite conceal.

Geoffrey distracted her, coming up to thank her heartily for her help.

"I do hope all goes simply swimmingly from now on," she said, reassured that her interference was valued. He was not yet out of the woods, though. "You really must buzz off before it's too late," she urged.

Behind him, she saw Hammond in his chauffeur's uniform, peaked cap in hand, consulting with Sir Hugh. A sudden alarm sent her hurrying to join them.

"We are ready to leave, Miss Dalrymple," said the baronet dryly. "Have you any further instructions for carrying out your enterprise?"

"Yes," she said, unabashed. "For heaven's sake avoid the Winchester road." Not wanting to explain before the chauffeur, she was relieved when Sir Hugh nodded his understanding, with a wry smile.

It would be altogether too frightful if, on their way to Southampton, they met Alec on his way back to Wentwater.

Everyone went out to the front steps to wave good-bye. Sir Hugh and Geoffrey stepped into the long, sleek, midnight blue Hispano-Suiza with the silver crane in flight on its bonnet. Hammond took the wheel. Smoothly swift, the motor-car swept down the drive, over the bridge across the lake, and away.

He was gone. Daisy breathed a deep sigh as the silent group returned into the house. She had got him safely away and his fate was out of her hands now. Thank heaven Alec had not come back too soon!

But now she had all too much leisure to wonder how

on earth she was going to face Alec after thwarting him of his prey. However justified she felt herself, he was bound to be absolutely livid. The whole scheme had been hers; she couldn't leave it to someone else to tell him that Geoffrey was well on his way to Brazil.

Dreading Alec's arrival, nonetheless she was beginning to worry about his continued absence. Constable Piper had left hours ago to find him. Surely the arrest of a presumed murderer must take precedence over the recovery of even the most valuable loot? He ought to be here by now. Suppose he had caught up with the burglars, and they turned out to be a gang of violent ruffians, and he had been hurt?

Ghastly images flitted through Daisy's mind as she dropped onto a chair by the hall fire, drained of energy.

Phillip wandered in, disconsolate. He brightened when he saw her. "What's going on, old bean?" he asked. "Hang it all, where has everyone disappeared to?"

"As a matter of fact," said Daisy, "Geoffrey has disappeared to Brazil, but keep it under your hat, won't you?"

"You're ragging me," he said without resentment.

"No, Phil, I'm far too fagged to rag you."

"Brazil, eh? Plenty of good opportunities out there."

"I hope so, though that's not quite why he's gone."

"Oh, I see. I think. The poor prune left in a bit of a hurry, what? The busy's not back yet?"

"If you mean Detective Chief Inspector Fletcher," she said reprovingly, "no, he's not. I can't help wondering whether something dreadful has happened to him."

"Not to worry, old dear. Coppers have nine lives, like cats. I just hope he doesn't turn up to bring a hornet's nest about our ears until after lunch."

"Lunch!" Daisy sat up straight. "Of course, that's what's wrong with me! I didn't have any breakfast. I'm starving."

Fortunately she didn't have to wait long before Drew came in to ring the gong for lunch. Despite her hunger, before dashing to the dining-room she remembered to entreat the butler, "I know it's not correct, but *please* let me know the *moment* Chief Inspector Fletcher arrives. Before you tell his lordship or anyone else. I know what to say to him."

"Very good, miss," Drew promised, with what almost might have been an approving look.

Throughout lunch, Phillip, Lady Josephine, Wilfred, and Marjorie kept up a flow of social chitchat, though now and then one of the latter pair would fall silent for a few abstracted minutes. Both Annabel and the earl were conspicuous by their absence.

So was Alec when coffee in the drawing-room brought the meal to a conclusion. Daisy's concern for him warred with the hope that he wouldn't turn up until after the *Orinoco* had safely put out to sea. She was prepared to employ delaying tactics, but she'd much prefer not to have to try to mislead him. Remembering his piercing gaze, she wasn't at all sure she'd succeed.

Four of the five in the drawing-room kept glancing surreptitiously at the clock. When Daisy caught herself at it for the third time (five past two), she decided to go and see Annabel. However, when she left the room she met in the passage a footman sent by Lord Wentwater with a request for a few minutes of her time. She entered the study with some trepidation, afraid that he might have changed his mind and decided his son must face the music, regardless of the consequences to his wife.

He was seated at the desk, writing. When he looked up, she was shocked by the deep lines in his drawn face. His hair and moustache seemed to have grown much greyer, aging him by ten years since she first met him just three days ago. He rose to his feet with a visible effort.

"Miss Dalrymple, I just wanted a few words with you. I hope I haven't interrupted your work."

"I haven't even tried to work today. I'd never be able to concentrate. Actually, I was on my way to see Annabel."

Whatever he had intended to say was forgotten. He leaned heavily on the desk with both hands, staring down at the papers he had been writing on, though Daisy was sure he didn't see them. "Annabel needs your friendship more than ever," he said painfully. "She still doesn't trust me. There is still something she won't confide to me."

"Do you want me to talk to her about it? I will, if you will come up and wait in your dressing-room. I can't promise anything, but if she chooses to make a clean breast of it, I'll fetch you."

They went upstairs together. Lord Wentwater retreated into his dressing-room and Daisy went on to Annabel's boudoir. She found her pacing the floor, white-faced and distraught.

"Daisy, I don't know what to do. Perhaps I should go away. I've brought Henry nothing but disaster and I can't bear it, waiting for the next blow."

Daisy drew her to the chaise-longue by the fire and sat down beside her, an arm about her waist. "Henry loves you, and Astwick's gone for good. There won't be a next blow."

"There might be." Tears trickled down Annabel's face. "That's the awful thing. Other people know what he knew, and any one of them could take it into his head to tell Henry."

"Then why don't you tell him? Your fear of confiding in him hurts him far more than anything you did in the past possibly could."

"Do you think so?"

"I'm certain. He's waiting in his dressing-room. Will you let me bring him to you?"

Annabel clutched Daisy's hand. "You'll stay? You won't desert me?"

"If that's truly what you want," she demurred though by now she was dying of curiosity.

"It is, oh, it is."

She went to fetch the earl. His face brightened as she said, "Annabel has agreed to speak to you."

"Miss Dalrymple, how can I ever thank you?" He was already past her and into the corridor.

She scurried to keep up with his long strides. "She wants me to be there with her."

"Anything!"

"She's more afraid of giving you pain than anything else, but I think she's also afraid you might cast her off."

"Never!" He burst into the boudoir and went straight to sit down beside Annabel, pulling her to him with a possessive arm about her.

Daisy retreated to a chair by the window as Annabel clung to her husband, sobbing into his shoulder. "Oh, Henry, it's all my fault, all this misery . . ."

"What utter nonsense. Haven't I already said that you're in no way to blame for Astwick's villainy and its consequences?"

"But I am! If I'd been brave enough to tell you, then he couldn't have blackmailed me . . ."

"Blackmail!" thundered Lord Wentwater. "The devil was blackmailing you? If I'd known, I'd have cut his throat with the Queen Elizabeth dagger, without a qualm."

She raised an adoring face to him. "Then thank heaven you didn't know. But if I'd never done anything to be ashamed of . . ."

"My darling, I doubt there are any in this world can truly say they have never done anything they regret. And I think I can guess . . . What a fool I've been!"

"You can't have guessed, Henry." Annabel once more buried her face in his shoulder. Daisy barely caught her words. "I wasn't a widow when you met me. You see, Rupert and I were never married."

Daisy suppressed a gasp of shock. In all her wildest imaginings about Annabel's secret, it had never crossed her mind that she and Rupert might have lived together for years without being husband and wife. Few misdeeds could have been calculated to offend more deeply against Lord Wentwater's Victorian view of morality.

But he was saying tenderly, "I know. I've known from the first, or very soon at least. As soon as I began to court you, some expatriate busybody made it her business to reveal the worst."

"You never said!"

"And how I wish I had. I didn't want to cause you any discomfort, but if I'd spoken, Astwick would have had no hold over you. Can you ever forgive me?"

"Oh, Henry." Annabel sighed.

Unnoticed, Daisy crept from the room.

On her way down the stairs, she considered what Annabel had told her about Rupert. He had sounded likeable but far from practical. Add his poor health and the difficulty of finding a Protestant minister in southern Italy—

Daisy could picture time drifting by without a wedding until it was too late.

Reprehensible, of course, but after all, artists were expected to lead a Bohemian life, as she and Lucy had discovered when they moved to Chelsea. Lord Wentwater had known, and had married Annabel anyway. He wasn't as frightfully old-fashioned as Daisy had feared.

Her thoughts elsewhere, she was stunned when, just as she reached the foot of the stairs, the front door opened and Alec walked in. And she'd forgotten to powder her nose in all the excitement!

Her eyes flew to the grandfather clock. Ten to three.

Alec's grim face was decorated with a square of sticking plaster on the forehead. Behind him, Tring limped slightly and Piper's arm was in a sling. Crossing the hall to meet them, Daisy saw that all three had damp overcoats and filthy turnups to their trousers.

"I've been so worried about you," she exclaimed. "What happened? Did the burglars attack you?"

"Nothing so dramatic," Alec grunted sourly. "The lanes are knee-deep in mud. I skidded into a ditch and Ernie, who was following me, tried to dodge and went through a hedge."

"Thank heaven none of you was badly hurt."

"And both cars still running," Tom Tring informed her genially. "A couple of cart-horses put us back on the road."

"That's good, but you look as if you got pretty wet in the meantime. Take off those coats and come and sit by the fire. Have you lunched? Yes? I'll order something hot to drink, at least."

Alec shook his head, winced, and raised his hand to feel the plaster on his brow. "Not now." He watched the footman bear away their coats before he continued, "This has turned out to be a case of murder, as you know. I've a fair idea of what happened but it's just guesswork so far. We'll have to do a bit of investigating before I can make an arrest. Stay out of it, Daisy. I don't expect things to get dangerous but I can't be sure." He started towards the stairs.

She caught his sleeve. "Wait, Chief. I simply *must* talk to you first. I can tell you exactly what happened."

He gave her a hard stare, then sighed wearily. "All right, Five minutes."

"Come to the Blue Salon, where we shan't be disturbed." Leading the way, she asked, "Did you find the jewellery?"

"Yes, we nabbed the lot," he said, cheering up, "and the two chummies who did the job. What's more, Payne gave us leads on the previous burglaries. Astwick had him find local housebreakers in each case, as a way to vary the *modus operandi* and so that no one had a chance to learn too much about him. It was a clever racket. I suspect he'd be safely on his way to Rio if he hadn't ended up dead."

"No, you'd have caught him once Sergeant Tring picked up the clue of the grey Lanchester." She glanced back to smile at Tom Tring and he winked at her.

Daisy's nerves caught up with her as she reached the Blue Salon. How on earth was she going to persuade Alec that Geoffrey had deserved the chance to make good in a distant country instead of going to prison? He was not going to be pleased.

Her knees felt wobbly. She sat down on one of the blue-and-white brocade chairs, leaving places nearer the fireplace for the men. But Tring and Piper took straight chairs at a distance and Alec stood with his back to the fire, looking alarmingly formidable. He frowned down at her.

"It was Geoffrey, wasn't it? He left the drawing-room early; Tom says he shared a bathroom with Astwick; and he may well be the only one strong enough to have carried the body down to the lake."

"Yes," she admitted, "only . . ." She paused as somewhere in the distance a clock chimed three. Within her a tense spring began to uncoil.

"I was afraid of it," Alec said. "I liked the boy. I can't picture him murdering even that blackguard in cold blood. There was immediate provocation?"

"Plenty. Only it didn't happen in his bathroom. Astwick assaulted Annabel in *her* bathroom and Geoffrey heard her cries for help."

"Good Lord, provocation indeed. I'll be sorry to take him in." He groaned. "And no doubt Lady Wentwater helped him dispose of the evidence."

"You can't arrest him," said Daisy with more trepidation than triumph. "It's too late. You see, I remembered that the S.S. *Orinoco* was leaving for Rio today, and Sir Hugh has plantations in Brazil where Geoffrey can work. He sailed from Southampton at three."

Alec stared at her with an expression of utter disbelief. "He *what?* And you . . ." His quiet voice was somehow more terrifying than any shout. "You little idiot, don't you understand? That makes you an accessory to murder."

CHAPTER 17

How the blazes was he going to save her from the consequences of her folly? As Alec glared down into Daisy's face, frightened yet defiant, he realized that he was not about to play the part of a stern police officer with a misbehaving citizen. He was going to have a blazing row.

Young Piper was gaping at him with fascinated dismay, while Tom's eyes twinkled with sly amusement in an otherwise stolid mask.

"You two," Alec snapped, "go and find yourselves a hot drink." He waited in grim silence until the door closed behind them, then turned on Daisy. "I must have been raving mad to trust you!"

Guiltily she protested, "But I . . ."

"Or have *you* gone raving mad, to try to help a murderer go scot-free?"

"He's not going scot-free. Besides he's . . ."

"You're damn right he's not. I'll wireless the ship before it reaches the three-mile limit and have him put ashore." His wits, scattered by outrage, returned to him. "In fact, the sooner the better." He started forward.

"Wait!" Aghast, she jumped up and put out her hand. "Let me . . ."

"I'll be back in a minute."

"For pity's sake, will you stop interrupting and listen to me?" she demanded angrily. "Geoffrey's not a murderer. Just let me explain what happened!"

"All right." With a weary sigh he subsided into the nearest chair. His head ached where he had bashed it as the Austin slid into the ditch. "The *Orinoco*'s a British ship. I can always have her ordered to turn back."

Daisy sat down rather suddenly. "Can you really? I thought he'd be safe once the ship had sailed."

"We don't let killers go unpunished so easily."

"He won't be unpunished. He's going into exile, leaving his family and friends and the woman he loves. And he's not going to the French Riviera for a rest cure. He's going to Brazil, which is full of beastly snakes and natives with poisoned blowpipes and those frightful fish that reduce you to a skeleton in less than a minute."

"I'm surprised he didn't opt for Dartmoor," said Alec sardonically, "if, as you claim, he's not a murderer in danger of hanging."

"He almost did, but a trial would have exposed Annabel to the worst excesses of the scandal sheets."

"His absence wouldn't prevent a trial, you know. Lady Wentwater's guilt as an accessory after the fact, if not before, is even clearer than yours."

"Oh, it all seemed so simple!" she wailed.

"Far from it. I'm surprised a canny old bird like Sir Hugh went along with your wild scheme."

"Is he an accessory too? He still believes Geoffrey only mucked about with the ice. We never told him the rest."

"It's time you told me. How did you find out, by the way?"

"When Constable Piper left . . . You won't blame him for telling me what the pathologist said?"

257

"How can I, when he was only following my example?"

"Good. It seemed as obvious to me as it did to you that Astwick had been drowned in his own bath. Though it seemed all too likely that Geoffrey had done it, I couldn't be sure. I went up to the bathroom to try to work out if someone else could have got in."

Alec's heart skipped a beat. "My dear girl, have you no common sense at all? Didn't it occur to you that you were putting yourself in deadly danger?"

"I was just a bit scared when Geoffrey came in," she confessed, "but there wasn't really the least chance of his hurting me. He was really quite keen to get it off his chest."

"And you believed every word," he said sceptically.

"I might not have, I suppose, if it had been only Geoffrey's word, but he and Annabel told the story together without the least disagreement. I refuse to believe they conspired to invent such a perfectly dreadful business."

"They conspired to dispose of the body."

"Just listen, will you? Astwick pinched the key from the corridor door to Annabel's bathroom. It's right opposite his bedroom door, you know. He went in and assaulted her as she stepped out of her bath. Geoffrey heard her cry out. He rushed in and biffed Astwick one on the chin, just as he did to James. Then he followed Annabel into her boudoir to promise her his protection. When he went back into the bathroom he found Astwick doubled over the edge of the bath with his head underwater, drowned. They decided he'd tripped when

Geoffrey hit him, bashed his head on the taps, and been too dazed to help himself. So, you see," she said earnestly, "his death was completely unintentional."

"That's the whole story?"

"Apart from how they tried to make it look like a skating accident. I gave you the bare bones, not all the beastly details I'd rather forget."

He couldn't resist. "'Corroborative detail intended to add verisimilitude to an otherwise bald and unconvincing narrative'?"

She spread her hands in a gesture of helplessness. "I can't force you to believe it wasn't murder."

"I was teasing you. At an inappropriate moment, I admit. On the whole, I'm inclined to credit their account. However, manslaughter is still a felony, with serious penalties. The law is the law."

"Do you believe the law always serves justice?" Her blue eyes demanded honesty.

"Perhaps not always," Alec said cautiously, "but without law there would be no justice, only the strong preying on the weak. And I serve the law."

"Do you never make exceptions? When you were on the beat—were you on the beat?"

"Yes, all detectives have to spend some time on the beat. No exceptions."

"Did you never let anyone off with a warning? Under extenuating circumstances, or if you were pretty certain they'd never do it again?"

"Now and then," he conceded with a wry grimace. She was doing her best to back him into a corner. "But

259

a kid lifting a bar of chocolate is hardly on a par with a killing."

"Unintentional. To save Annabel from a fate worse than death. Hasn't she suffered enough?"

"Have you discovered what misdeed Astwick was using to blackmail her?"

"Yes, though I see absolutely no reason to tell you. It wasn't so dreadful. In fact, Lord Wentwater knew all along and married her anyway, so she suffered for nothing."

Alec recalled the sorrowing Madonna, the moon pale from weariness. Yes, Lady Wentwater had suffered. And Geoffrey had gone into exile, a chivalrous knight protecting his fair lady.

And his victim had been an out-and-out rotter.

"I can't just ignore the whole thing," he said pettishly. His head hurt.

"Can't you simply say you were mistaken in thinking he didn't just fall through the ice by accident? Geoffrey, Annabel, and Lord Wentwater are the only ones who know about the axe-marks and that Astwick didn't drown in the lake. Besides Sergeant Tring and Constable Piper and the pathologist, of course, unless you told anyone else?"

"No, no one. Tring and Piper will do as I say. Dr. Renfrew never expresses any interest in a case once he's finished cutting up the body."

Daisy wrinkled her nose in disgust but said cheerfully, "Then you can easily claim it was a skating accident after all."

"Easily!" he exploded. He sprang to his feet, wincing as the bump on his brow sent an arrow of pain shooting through his skull. "I'm a police officer. I have a duty to uphold the law. I'm going to send a wireless ordering the *Orinoco*'s captain to turn back to port."

"Alec, wait!" She looked at him with concern. "Is your head aching? Do sit down for just one more minute. There's one thing you haven't considered. If the *Orinoco* has to turn back so that you can arrest Geoffrey, you're going to have the shipping line and all the passengers after your blood, not to mention Lord Wentwater, Sir Hugh, and very likely your own Commissioner, who, you may recall, is a friend . . ."

He groaned as her voice trailed off. "True, but my duty must come first."

"That's it! Telephone your Commissioner, tell him everything, and ask him what to do. He's your superior. If he orders you to drop the case, you will have done your duty, won't you?"

"And if not?"

"Well, I suppose I'll have to stop trying to persuade you," she said, disconsolate. "At least you can make him wireless the ship, so that no one blames you."

Gazing down at her upturned face with its scattering of freckles and the tiny, bewitching mole, he did not doubt that she was genuinely concerned for him. All her efforts to talk him out of chasing down Geoffrey were due to concern for her friends, not herself. She had already forgotten that she was an accessory to the crime. He'd keep her out of this, he vowed, whatever the Commissioner decided.

"Not a bad idea," he admitted.

"I expect you can use the telephone in Lord Went-water's study. The last I saw of him, he looked as if he'd be busy upstairs for some time."

She saw him settled in the study and tactfully disappeared. Alec had less difficulty being put through to the Commissioner than he had expected, because of Sir Hugh Menton's involvement, no doubt. In guarded terms, avoiding names where possible, he explained the situation.

He had nearly finished when Daisy reappeared, bearing a tray with a pot of tea and a plate of biscuits. He smiled at her and continued, avoiding all mention of the fact that Geoffrey's departure was her idea.

"So you see, sir, we can have the *Orinoco* turn back, or wait till he reaches Tenerife or even Rio and have him extradited."

"No need for that, Chief Inspector," the Commissioner's voice boomed down the wire. "Send the Coast Guard out and have him taken off."

"Yes, sir. I hadn't considered that possibility."

"All sounds to me like a vast waste of public monies. The boy was protecting a certain lady from rape, wasn't he?"

"Yes, sir. I'm willing to accept their story, based on what I've learned of Geoffrey's and Astwick's characters."

"Hmm. Whole thing was an unfortunate accident. Astwick's family likely to give us any grief?"

"I doubt it, sir. Lord Brinbury seems to have been anxious only to hear that his brother was underground."

The Commissioner's bellow of laughter rocked his head. "What about the coroner. Reasonable man?"

"I'd say he knows his duty, sir—and which side his bread is buttered. He is Lord Wentwater's solicitor. If you and his lordship were both to advise his directing the jury to find accidental death . . ."

"Done, Chief Inspector. Accidental death it is. I'll have a word with Lord Wentwater later but my secretary is pulling faces at me now. Good job. Good-bye."

Alec also pulled a face. At least Daisy was safe but . . . Good job? Well, he had been chosen for his discretion. He hung up the receiver and gulped the tea Daisy had poured for him. "It's all settled," he said as she refilled his cup. "Wealth and rank win again. It leaves a sour taste in my mouth."

She regarded him uncertainly. "When I came up with the plan I was thinking mostly of Annabel, but I hoped I was solving a problem for you, too. I must say I expected you to be delighted not to have to arrest the son of an earl."

"Delighted!"

"Well, relieved, at least."

She was right, to his chagrin. He was relieved to have avoided running foul of Lord Wentwater and Sir Hugh. Despising himself as a craven toady, he was irritated with her for guessing.

"Are you sure you weren't simply trying to shield your own kind, people of your own class, Miss Dalrymple?"

"No," she said, hurt. "Why should I champion a class that includes James and Lord Stephen? I wanted to protect Annabel because she's become a dear friend and hadn't done anything really wrong. All the same, I wouldn't have intervened to prevent a trial if I hadn't considered Geoffrey's actions justified."

"It's quite possible he would have got off with a warning anyway," Alec admitted reluctantly. Her eyes brightened and she beamed at him. She was too pleased with herself, too satisfied with the success of her scheme to outwit the law. He couldn't let her get away with it so easily, or the Lord alone knew what she'd be up to next. "Nonetheless," he continued in his most severe official voice, "that decision was for police, coroner, judge, and jury to make, not you. You could have been in extremely serious trouble."

Her face fell. "I know. Thank you for not telling the Commissioner it was my idea."

"The fewer people who know, the better. And now, if you will excuse me, I must speak to Lord Wentwater, prepare a statement for the press, and write my reports." Three reports, he thought with a mental groan, one on the Flat ford affair and two for this Astwick mess: one for the records, and the eyes of the Chief Constable of Hampshire; and one for his own superior, the Assistant Commissioner for Crime, who had to know the whole thing, even Daisy's part in it.

Filled with regret, he watched her trail despondently from the study. He had dished his chances of seeing her again. Not that there had ever been a future for a friendship between the Honourable Daisy Dalrymple and a common-or-garden police detective.

Daisy turned towards the drawing-room. Alec had every right to be furious, she thought mournfully. Though everything had worked out for the best, that didn't make up for her letting him down. She couldn't blame him for dismissing her so coldly, stern policeman to erring citizen.

Her reception in the drawing-room bucked her up a bit. Wilfred rushed to meet her, his usual nonchalance abandoned. "We heard the police are back," he said. "What's up?"

"Everything's all right," she assured him, joining Marjorie, Lady Jo, and Phillip by the tea trolley. She'd been too upset to share Alec's tea. "Mr. Fletcher was going to have the *Orinoco* called back but instead he telephoned the Commissioner at Scotland Yard and persuaded him that Lord Stephen's death was an accident."

"Oh, good egg!" Wilfred exclaimed.

"I knew he'd come through," said Marjorie dreamily. "He's really rather scrumptious, don't you think, Daisy?"

Her aunt regarded her with considerable misgiving. "A most worthy officer," she said repressively. "This is good news, Daisy. Now dear Geoffrey will be able to come home again."

"He might as well stay in Brazil once he gets there," said Phillip. "All sorts of opportunities for the right sort of fellow, what?"

"I daresay he will," Daisy agreed. "He always

seemed to me the sort to go off to bring civilisation to some benighted tropical country." If he had any sense he'd stay, for Annabel's sake.

"I say, Daisy, does this mean we're free to leave?" Phillip asked. "The detective chappie doesn't want to see us again, does he? I've already outstayed my welcome."

"It's nearly dark. You mustn't leave until the morning," said Lady Josephine, and Marjorie and Wilfred assured him that he was more than welcome at Wentwater.

"Very kind and all that, but after the fuss and botheration with m'sister, I'd better toddle off, don't you know. It's stopped raining and the old bus buzzes along quite happily in the dark. Daisy, old girl, can I give you a lift back to town?"

She was tempted. Driving up to London in his nippy little Swift two-seater, even at night, would be much more fun than going by train. But she wasn't certain whether she had enough material for her article, and besides, she wanted to make sure Annabel didn't need her anymore. "Thanks, Phil, but my work here has been rather interrupted and I still have quite a bit to do."

"Work!" he grumbled. "Oh well, right-oh."

He went off to pack and to make his farewells to his host and hostess. Daisy went up to her room to try to reacquaint herself with her article before dinner. Seated at the little desk by the window, she read over her notes and the pages she'd already written. Phillip, in his motoring coat, found her there.

"I say, I haven't got your new address. You won't mind if I drop round? I haven't given up hope, you know, old dear."

"I shan't marry you, Phillip, but I'll always be happy to see you."

Writing down the address for him, she wished it was Alec who was asking. She wondered whether he had already left Wentwater. She wanted to apologize to him, though she was not sorry for what she had accomplished—but one didn't apologize to a policeman for breaking the law, did one? To do so would imply that she regarded him as a friend. Which she did, but there wasn't much chance he reciprocated the feeling after she'd aided his quarry's escape.

Gazing glumly out of the window into the deepening dusk, she saw his Austin Seven proceeding down the drive, the police car close behind. They crossed the bridge over the fateful lake and their red taillights disappeared into the woods at the top of the opposite slope. A fat chance she had of ever seeing Alec again.

Not long after, Phillip's jaunty two-seater followed them. Apart from Daisy, only a diminished family remained at Wentwater Court. She'd better leave tomorrow, she decided. Her presence would be a constant reminder of the frightful events of the past few days. She drew the curtains and turned back to her work.

Dinner was more cheerful than any of Daisy's previous meals at Wentwater. The departure of the police had raised everyone else's spirits. Marjorie, Wilfred, and Lady Josephine were all buoyant, James's disgrace forgotten for the moment. Sir Hugh, back from Southampton, was relieved to hear his friend the Commissioner had come to the rescue. He vowed to write a commendation of the Chief Inspector's common sense and discretion.

Lord Wentwater looked nearer forty than fifty. His habitual gravity had given way to an air of contentment punctuated by fond smiles, and Annabel positively glowed. To Daisy, their happiness made everything worthwhile.

They were all embarrassingly grateful to her. She was quite glad to claim pressure of neglected work and retreat to her room after dinner.

In the morning, a windy day with the sun coming and going between clouds, she went down to breakfast quite early. Only Sir Hugh was before her, ensconced as usual behind his *Financial Times*. Emerging, he folded the paper to show her a modest headline: FINANCIER DEAD. Underneath, in smaller letters, it said: "Astwick dies in skating mishap. Company expected to fail, say experts."

"There's a paragraph or two about Flatford's burglary, too," said Sir Hugh, "but you'll find more about it in the other papers."

Daisy dashed out to the hall. A selection of daily newspapers was spread on the table by the front door. Alec had made the front page of most of them, under headlines such as: YARD MAN RECOVERS LOOT. Two or three had photographs of him, recognizable only by his dark, thick eyebrows.

The demise of Lord Stephen Astwick, City mogul and *bon viveur,* in an unfortunate skating accident was relegated to the inside pages.

Taking all the newspapers to the breakfast-room, Daisy read every word as she consumed Cook's homemade sausages, toast, and tea. Though Lord Stephen's connection with the burglaries must surely come out at Payne's trial, for the moment the reporters were apparently unaware of the makings of a spectacular story. Alec being discreet again, Daisy thought. He was the hero of the hour, the articles full of gushing quotations from grateful ladies whose diamonds, pearls, and emeralds were to be returned to them.

Daisy wondered whether he enjoyed being a celebrity. She rather thought it would bring out his sardonic side.

With a sigh, she went off to the darkroom to sort out her pictures.

By three o'clock that afternoon, having shot a few more photographs and filled in a few gaps in her information about the house, she was ready to leave. She had sent a wire to Lucy to say she'd be home for dinner. The dark green Rolls stood gleaming at the front door with her luggage already stowed away. In the Great Hall, she took her leave of the family. As they pressed her to visit again soon, she found it hard to believe she had been at Wentwater Court for less than a week.

They all came out to the front steps to wave good-bye. Jones handed her into the backseat and took his place at the wheel. The Silver Ghost rolled smoothly on its way.

When Daisy glanced back for a final look as they started down the hill, the Mentons, Marjorie, and Wilfred had gone in. Annabel and the earl still stood on the step, locked in a loving embrace.

A pang of envy stabbed at Daisy's heart. With a wistful sniff, she settled back in the seat.

The sodden countryside was dun and depressing. When they reached the station, Jones and the one-legged porter carried her luggage onto the up-platform. As the Rolls drove off, she waited beside the pile of stuff, gazing down the track towards Winchester, hugging her coat around her. Though the wind had dropped and it was much warmer than the bitter day of her arrival, she felt chilled.

She heard another car pull up in the station yard but she didn't turn until a voice behind her called, "Miss Dalrymple!"

Alec! His neck swathed in an orange-and-green-striped scarf, he was leaning on the fence where the crow had huddled. A curl of smoke rose from his pipe, hiding his expression.

She went across to him, a spring in her step. "I thought you'd have gone back to London by now," she said.

"One or two bits and bobs to clear up."

"I didn't know you smoked a pipe."

"Not when I'm on duty, except in my own office."

270

"I suppose you don't wear that natty scarf when you're on duty, either."

He smiled around the stem of the pipe. "Do you like it? My daughter, Belinda, knitted it."

"Your daughter?" Her heart sank. "What a clever child. How old is she?"

"Nine. Not bad, eh? Listen, will you trust your life to my driving? I know a nice little place in Guildford where we could stop for tea. I telephoned my mother and she's not expecting me home till after six."

"Your mother?"

"She lives with Belinda and me, takes care of us. Here comes the train," he said as an approaching whistle sounded. "Can I give you a lift?"

"A lift? Tea in Guildford? Yes, *Chief!*"

"Oh no, not Chief!" He shook his head determinedly. "Never again. If our acquaintance is to continue, it will be on a strictly nonprofessional basis."

"Right-oh, Alec," said Daisy.

Center Point Publishing

600 Brooks Road ● PO Box 1
Thorndike ME 04986-0001 USA

(207) 568-3717

US & Canada:
1 800 929-9108
www.centerpointlargeprint.com